CARDIFF DEAD

signed

£4 PB
18/6

BY THE SAME AUTHOR

CARDIFF DEAD

JOHN WILLIAMS

BLOOMSBURY

First published 2000

Copyright © 2000 by John Williams

The moral right of the author has been asserted

Bloomsbury Publishing Plc, 38 Soho Square, London W1V 5DF

A CIP catalogue record for this book
is available from the British Library

ISBN 0 7475 4997 4

10 9 8 7 6 5 4 3 2 1

Typeset by Hewer Text Ltd, Edinburgh
Printed in Great Britain by Clays Limited, St Ives plc

ACKNOWLEDGEMENTS

Thanks to Abner Stein for help, advice and lunch well above and beyond. Thanks to Matthew Hamilton for his faith and editorial perception. Thanks to Sarah-Jane Forder for fine copy-editing. I would also like to gratefully acknowledge the financial assistance offered by a Writing Bursary from the Arts Council of Wales. Thanks to Phil John, Mike Parker, Mary Bruton, Rosemarie Buckman, Pete Ayrton, Carlton B. Morgan and Richard Thomas, and to a mystery Australian surfer for the dead dog. Thanks finally to Charlotte, as ever.

For my sister, Sophie Athanasiadis

I'm Cardiff born and Cardiff bred
And when I dies I'll be Cardiff dead

Frank Hennessey

I

THE CUSTOM HOUSE

1999

Mazz was riding the ghost train. The 125 from Paddington to Cardiff. Ghosts everywhere. Ghosts behind him in London. Susie the night before – this must be the last time. Ghosts of Camden Town this morning, walking through the market. Thirty-nine years old and feeling like his time was done and gone, walking through a sea of teenage Goths. Ghosts ahead of him in Wales. His family, what was left of it, up in the valleys, his mam long gone and passed away, his dad a ghost for years, haunting every pub that'd have him from Newbridge to Newport. Ghosts in Cardiff. Ghosts he didn't even want to think about. And Charlie. A ghost now for sure, Charlie dead and gone.

He was standing in the bar drinking cans of Stella with a couple of squaddies from out Ammanford way and, as the train pulled out of Bristol Parkway, he started telling them about Charlie.

'You boys ever hear of Charlie Unger?' Mazz asked, getting the answer he expected: a couple of shaken heads.

'Not into the boxing, then?'

This time one of the squaddies, a big lad named Bren, said he used to box a bit himself, in the army, like, and his mate's mate was a mate of Joe Calzaghe's, or some such regulation bullshit.

'Joe Calzaghe?' said Mazz. 'Charlie would have taken him one-handed. What's Calzaghe – QVC champion of the world? WBX? Christ, when

Charlie was fighting, back in the fifties, he was just plain world champion; there weren't half a dozen of them all swanning about exclusively on Sky Sports.'

'Yeah?' said Bren. 'What weight was he then?'

'Lightweight, least that's what he was when he was champion. Later on he went up to middle.'

'Lightweight.' Bren scratched his head a bit and squinted. 'Yeah,' he said again after a little while, 'no one remembers a lightweight. Comes to boxing, it's heavyweight or nothing really, isnit?'

Mazz shook his head. It was true. No one remembers a lightweight. No one remembered the Wurriyas either, the ska band that had brought Mazz and Charlie Unger together, twenty years ago when Charlie was already on the long slide down and Mazz was on the way up. The way up to this. Mazz Marshall, guitar player for hire. Heavyweight or nothing. Never a truer word.

Suddenly Mazz couldn't stand the squaddies any more. Didn't want to talk about rugby or where they were planning to go on their big night out in Cardiff. The train went into the Severn Tunnel and Mazz said he needed a fag and headed for the smoking carriage.

Other side of the tunnel, back in Wales, Mazz stubbed out his fag and looked out left at the Llanwern steelworks. One of the last hold-outs of Welsh heavy industry. He wondered if his cousin Gav was still working there. Probably, you didn't give up a job like that lightly these days. Man's work. Not a lot of it about.

Course it had seemed like there was plenty of it about when he was growing up, mind; man's work. Been the main reason he'd got the hell out of the valleys soon as he could.

Train was coming into Newport now. Newport. A couple of years ago some idiot rock writer called it the new Seattle. Just cause it had one decent rock club, TJ's, and a couple of bands looked briefly like they might be the new Oasis. He'd played TJ's a year or two back, done a tour with these bad-tempered Scottish brothers, indie legends for about ten minutes back in the eighties. Last time he'd seen his dad too, over in the Engineers just by the railway line.

Newport: when he was a kid it had seemed like some place, capital of the Gwent Valleys; now it looked like the town time left behind. And suddenly he had a fierce pang of nostalgia and before he knew what he was doing he was picking up his bag and getting off the train.

And as quickly as it had come the impulse passed and he was left looking at the departing train thinking, Newport, what the hell am I going to do in Newport? The answer was obvious – do what you always did in Newport. Go for a drink.

Same time Mazz was in Le Pub, cursing the jukebox, getting nowhere with the barmaid, Tyra Unger was down the gym. She had an hour there every day before picking the kids up from school. This had been her New Year's resolution. Stop going round her mates for a coffee and a smoke, start getting into shape. Thirty-six you had to start working at things. And right now, in the days after her dad's death, she was damn grateful for every routine she had.

And she liked it. Hadn't been looking forward to it beforehand. The place would be full of teenage bodybuilders, that's what her friend Linz had said, but the time of day Tyra went it was fine. Guy did the inductions, Mark, seen him round over the years, he was nice, took her through the machines properly, didn't try to feel her up, another thing Linz said. Sad, really, but the fact was she was a little bit disappointed. Not like she was interested or anything, but way she saw it you spent half your life complaining about blokes trying it on, and the rest of it complaining 'cause they didn't, too busy giving the eye to some little sister hasn't even screwed up her GCSEs yet.

Anyway, it was a nice little routine she had there. Saw the same faces most days. This dread Col she'd known for ever, been in the band together even, he was there pretty much every time. Col worked with Kenny Ibadulla now and again but she didn't hold it against him. Col brought his ghetto-blaster down too, played the music she liked – old seventies and eighties funk, bit of reggae. Nothing she liked better in this life just at the moment than pumping some iron, SOS band kicking into 'Just Be Good to Me'; you could just feel the chemicals get busy inside your body, endorphins or whatever. Course now and again some kid would come in with his own sound system, start blasting out this garage stuff they liked these days. Look from Col was usually enough. Carried a bit of respect with him, Col.

Been a good three or four months now she'd been seeing Col in there every day more or less, so God knows why it was today she said it but there it was.

'You fancy taking a girl out for a drink later on?' she said.

Bit pushy maybe, but at thirty-six you can't waste time waiting for blokes to ask you out and her mum could have the kids easy enough and frankly all this working out was great but it didn't make you forget there were other ways to work out, in fact it got you right up for it. Course that wasn't what she was suggesting. Col was a mate, they saw each other every day. No reason she couldn't have a drink with him. Not like he was married either. His baby mother was a lesbian now, and a hustler what Tyra heard. As for Tyra, her kids' father had fucked off to God knows where right after he came out of prison the last time, so there wasn't no armchair keeping warm round her place. Length of time Col took to answer, she had space to think all these things.

'Yeah, girl,' he said, 'see you down the Baltimore. Nine o'clock.'

And that was that. Col picked up his bag and went off to shower. Tyra worked on her pecs for a bit, pushing her chest out hard as she could. And then stopped suddenly, laughing at herself. Got a date.

'You reckon? You reckon that's a good fucking band? Mazz was on his fourth or fifth by now, been in Le Pub all the time but now he was sat at a corner table with a couple of little indie girls. 'Sounds like bloody Queen to me. And what's the bloke on about anyway? Paranoid android? It's just shit, what's that mean to anyone? Only two kinds of songs in this world, you know.' He looked at the girls expectantly.

'Oh, yeah, what are they then?' said the Asian one.

'Love songs and novelty songs. If it's not a love song, it's just some piece of shit made up to make students feel like they're on to something. You two students?'

'Art college,' said the dyed-blonde one, Emma she'd said. Anita he thought the other girl had said. Was that an Asian name? Fuck knows.

'What, here in Newport?'

'Yeah.'

For a moment Mazz was lost in reverie. Art college in Newport. A vision of a life path not taken. A memory of his art teacher back in Cross Keys Tertiary, when he was pissing about pretending to do A levels. Mr Hughes thought he was good, Mazz doing all these cut-up collage things, stuff he'd read about in the *NME*, told him he should go to art college, Newport. Bloke was hip enough, as it goes. Told him Joe Strummer had been there, like that would be the clincher for Mazz. Nearly was too, but playing guitar was the only thing he'd given a shit about then. Well, that and getting his leg over. And at the time the two seemed to go hand in hand.

Now, well he frankly didn't know if he'd care if he never picked up a guitar again, all the good it had done him over the years. He was still keen enough on the other thing, though, idly figuring out which of the two girls in front of him was the better prospect, but still he couldn't help wondering how things might have worked out, if he'd gone to art school. Mate of his worked in animation, he was doing all right. He'd known a few designers over the years; mostly the work was bollocks – designing fucking brochures for electronics companies and shit – but the money was there all right. Not like for some people.

Mazz had five hundred quid in his pocket, less the train fare and the drinks. More money than he'd had in one go for a while, but he'd practically had to beg to get it out of the fat American junkie and his evil Jap wife who'd been his last employers. Backing them up on a totally shit tour of Italy, the pair of them fighting every second they weren't sticking needles in each other and only unanimous on one thing: let's not pay Mazz what we told him we'd pay him. Fuckers had made him beg. Made him meet them in the departure lounge at Heathrow to get the money. But at least he had it now. Wouldn't last long, though, even in Cardiff. But still, beneath it all, Mazz wasn't worried; he'd survived too long to worry. Something usually turned up. Usually a girl, as it went.

'So,' he said, winking extravagantly, 'you two fancy a little toot?'

Back at the house making the kids' tea, Tyra figured it was the routines got you through a time like this. Her dad dying. Her dad was dead. Charlie was

5

dead. Weird, when he was alive she called him Charlie like everyone else did. After all, at his best he was just like some uncle came round and brought you sweets. Wasn't like he ever lived with them. Uncle Charlie would have been about right, but he wasn't. He was her dad. Later on, when she grew up, he'd been better. Well, better and worse. She'd seen him for what he was and she'd loved him, she supposed. Everyone loved Charlie Unger. Least they did till the drinking and the gambling took him down. And she hadn't been much better than the rest. Hardly saw him at all the last couple of years. Charlie was just another man, just another loser to her by then, and she'd had it with all of them. But he shouldn't have died like that. Left there for a week before anyone noticed. Her dad.

Thing that made her sick, though, was the way everyone was getting all pious about it. Now Charlie was dead everybody cared like hell about him. The funeral was going to be a circus. It made her feel ill really, and guilty too.

At least the gym had been good and now, taking the peanut butter sandwiches into the front room where Jermaine and Emily were watching *Nickelodeon*, she felt like her kids were the only things anchoring her to the planet. Worst thing – well, not the worst thing but the oddest thing – was she felt so horny. It was embarrassing really. Got any worse she'd be rubbing herself up against the furniture.

'Mum,' said Jermaine, 'more peanut butter.'

She took his proffered plate automatically, not even bothering to tell him to say please.

Mazz woke up feeling like shit. Which was nothing new and wasn't it Tony Curtis who said that the worst thing about being teetotal must be waking up in the morning knowing that's the best you're going to feel all day? Sounded like it ought to be Dean Martin or one of those big-name boozers but Mazz was pretty sure it was Tony Curtis. Anyway, whatever, time to survey the situation.

He was in a strange bedroom in an unknown building; he was by himself lying under an opened-out sleeping bag and a blanket. There was a bookshelf near his head which contained what looked like a bunch of student textbooks and an ashtray complete with the butt ends of several joints, smoked right down to the roach. By the side of the bed there was a pile of clothes – his – and a couple of CDs, the Manics and something else – not his. He raised his head and looked around the bed and floor a little more carefully, sniffing as he did so. No sign of any vomit. Always a plus. On the wall there was a poster advertising a Howard Marks gig. He'd obviously landed up in some kind of student lair. What was it with students and dope these days?

Mazz wasn't really bothered about dope either way: if someone was smoking a joint he'd smoke some too, just to be friendly, like, but it'd never occur to him to go out and buy some. These days, though, far as he could see, it had turned into an interest in itself. People made records about smoking dope, read books about smoking dope and even went to gigs where they sat down on the floor smoking dope listening to some old reprobate talk about how he used to be a dope smuggler. People funny, boy.

Next question was what the hell had happened. First off, had he scored? He ran his brain through the faulty memory program marked 'last night', not once but repeatedly, and still there was absolutely nothing of a carnal nature in there. Bollocks, the rest of it was starting to come back. The hours in Le Pub, the coke in the toilets with the indie girls, the movement on to some other pub, the quick visit to the takeaway, the walk to a third pub, and – bollocks again – the arrival of the indie girls' boyfriends. Actually – it really was starting to get clearer now – he hadn't minded that much. It had already been feeling like more effort than he was up to, going through the final ritual-seduction part of the night, and the blokes had been all right, as it went. Some more drinking then someone saying you want to crash at ours then, mate, and that must have been what happened.

Try as he did, he still couldn't conjure up any memory of the walk back from the pub or club or whatever, or the cup of tea and the joint that must have been passed round, or the undressing and getting into bed that had evidently taken place, but still he reckoned he had the measure of it now and it wasn't too bad. Nothing broken.

'All right, mate.' He was out of the bedroom now and standing in the living-room. The person who'd spoken was a bloke sitting at a table drinking a cup of tea and leafing through a Richer Sounds catalogue. He looked vaguely familiar, presumably one of the boyfriends.

'All right,' said Mazz and kept on going, heading for the door that looked most likely to offer a route to the outside world. Mazz was getting too old for small talk this time of the morning.

'You want a cup of tea?' said the bloke, his eyes not moving from the catalogue.

'No, ta,' said Mazz, 'better get going.'

'All right,' said the bloke.

'All right,' said Mazz, 'and thanks, yeah.'

Out on the street he still didn't have much of a clue where he was. Looked left and saw what seemed like a bigger street and headed that way. On the bigger street the sight of a bus going the other way with the word Caerleon on the front helped him figure out he was on the Caerleon road over the river from the station. A bus came but he ignored it. Walk would do him good, he reckoned.

He'd just made it over the bridge and was skirting the town centre when he walked into his dad. It was pitiful really, his dad stood outside the boozer waiting for opening time. A can of Special in his hand already, wearing the same ancient camel-coloured coat he'd been wearing two years ago, last time Mazz saw him.

Mazz shook his head in the vain hope the apparition might go away. When he was younger he'd have laughed, seen his dad's steady plunge into the drinking pro-leagues as a laugh. These days it looked a lot too close for comfort. Mazz's old man had been a miner once, and was happy enough to remind you of the fact. That was a while back now, though. He hadn't worked since 1971, if Mazz remembered it right. Not 'cause of the pit closures or the strikes – he'd been gone before all that got going, he'd been on the permanent sick. Black lung Mazz had always thought it was when he was a kid, the way his dad would point at his lungs and cough theatrically if anyone asked why he wasn't working. Most of his childhood Mazz was waiting for him to keel over dead at any minute. He'd been in his twenties before his mam told him the truth. It was his nerves, that was all she'd said even then. Claustrophobia or sheer bloody terror; Mazz didn't know and couldn't blame him anyway. One thing he'd known from as far back as he could remember, he wasn't going down no big hole in the ground to work. Course that nice Mrs Thatcher had made sure there was no question of that.

It took a moment for the old man to focus on him but, as soon as he did, to be fair he did his best, stuck the hand with the can in it behind his back, gave Mazz a smile of genuine pleasure.

'Fuckin' hell, butt. It's been a while.'

'Yeah,' said Mazz.

'Where you been then? Travelling the world?'

'Yeah, well,' said Mazz. Oh yes, the rock'n'roll lifestyle; after a while it was like a cross between being a long-distance lorry driver and an itinerant brickie. No fate more glamorous than to trek round Italy in the back of a minibus with a fat American singer passed out across the back seats, his evil Jap wife bitching about Mazz smoking, and bloody Massive Attack playing for the eight zillionth time on the stereo.

'Lot of girls, eh?'

Christ, thought Mazz, the old feller must be well gone. 'Yeah,' he repeated, 'lot of girls.'

And it was true, of course. Particularly this last tour, to be honest. One thing to be said for the fat American, he pulled a lot of nice little Italian Goth girls to his gigs. They'd all show up expecting him to look like the skinny dude with the cheekbones he'd been on his first album cover. Then they'd discover him to be a fat asshole with a scary wife and more than a few would have the good sense to turn their attention to Mazz, whose cheekbones were at least still visible.

That seemed to have exhausted the old man's conversational gambits so they just stood there for a moment staring at each other until the welcome sound of the pub door being unlocked broke the silence.

'Fancy a quick one, then?' said Mazz's dad.

Tyra woke up crying. Six in the morning, Emily and Jermaine in the bed with her. Every morning they came in and God knows she loved to see them there. Course one of these mornings there'd be someone else there with her and God knows what they'd make of that. Fact was she'd been half thinking it might have been this morning, thought it would have been all right, Col being there. Would have been better than this anyway, them seeing her blubbing her eyes out 'cause she'd dreamed about Charlie again.

'What's the matter, Mum?' said Jermaine, doing his eight-year-old man-of-the-house bit.

'Nothing, love,' she said, pulling him close. 'I'm just sad about Granddad dying, that's all.'

'Don't worry, Mum,' he said, 'you're not dying.' She smiled and patted his head and soon the two kids had drifted back off to sleep.

The night before hadn't turned out the way she planned – the absence of Col in her bed was clear enough evidence of that – but still, lying there in the early-morning light, Tyra found herself smiling at the memory of it. They'd been sat downstairs in the Balti for a while, her and Col, both being awkward as anything. Tyra couldn't work out whether it was he didn't fancy her or whether he thought maybe she was only after a shoulder to cry on and he made a move she'd freak. So they just sat there chatting about this and that and what a great bloke Charlie had been, which he had been, you weren't his daughter. The pub was dead as anything downstairs, just a couple of old-timers watching the Sky news, and she'd almost been feeling like saying sod it and going home when Col said why didn't they pop upstairs, got the karaoke up there, might be a laugh.

And it was. First off there were a bunch of gay guys sat round a table at the front, all doing the maddest songs you could imagine – Shirley Bassey and Blur and all sorts – before this little guy with a dodgy peroxide job did 'The Greatest Love of All' and Tyra couldn't help it, found herself tearing up.

Col started looking at her, all concerned like, and she was on the point of saying she had to go when the trainee barman, some teenage fat boy from Ely, came out from behind the bar, walked up to the tiny stage and launched into 'Bat Out of Hell'. And you'd have had to have had your whole family massacred before your eyes in the previous half hour not to have laughed. It wasn't that he was crap at it; quite the reverse, the kid was brilliant, bellowing out the lyrics like old Meat himself, dropping to one knee with the passion of it all. The whole mood of the room switched in an instant – the old fellas with their long slow pints started to perk up, the gay guys started whooping and hollering – and by the second time the bloke launched into the chorus Tyra was shaking with laughter.

The guy, Lee his name was they found out later, got the whole place stamping and clapping when he finished, so he did another one, 'Tainted Love', had everyone shouting out the chorus. Things calmed down a bit then as a couple of young girls made a bit of a mess of the All Saints thing, 'Never Ever', and Gary the doorman did his usual balls-up of 'Satisfaction'. Every week he did it, and every week he screwed the timing up at the exact same place, but what could you do? Gary wasn't exactly the kind of fella welcomed constructive criticism.

Still Tyra's mood stayed with her; she nudged Col's leg under the table as Gary did his thing and Col nudged back. The end of the song Tyra marched straight up the front, had a little word in the DJ's ear. He nodded, rooted around a little in his collection of tunes and came out with the one he was looking for. He slipped it in the karaoke machine and drew Tyra's attention to the video screen where the words came up. Tyra just shook her head, smiled, walked a couple of steps forward and closed her eyes, letting the first few chords of the song wash over her, then the backing vocals. If you don't know me by now, they refrained, and then Tyra came in with the first line. 'We've all got our own funny moves/You've got yours and I've got mine,' she sang and opened her eyes to stare straight at Col.

And Col, bless him, was up to it. He smiled back, let her finish the first verse and get straight into the chorus, and then he was there beside her, took the second verse himself, and if he wasn't much of a singer, his piano-player's phrasing carried the day. Then they did the big chorus together and Tyra wasn't the only one there reckoned something was happening.

The end of the song, though, they walked back to the table and Col let her have it.

'Sweetheart,' he said, 'you and me, we known each other for ever, right?'
Tyra nodded.
'We been in school together, right?'
Tyra nodded again.
'We been in the band together, right?'
Tyra carried on nodding.

'Had the hit single and stayed in plenty of hotels together, right?'

'Yeah.'

'We been living round the corner from each other all the time since. You knows my kid, I knows your kids. I knows your Tony fucked off. To Spain from what I hear. You knows my Maria and you got the good grace not to talk to me about what's happened to her.'

Tyra nodded one last time, suddenly aware of where all this was leading.

'Well that's how it is: you knows me and I knows you and I loves you like a sister, you know what I'm saying? But something else was going to happen it would have happened long time ago. What's happening now you need a friend and you got one here, sister. So let's have a good time, yeah, little drink, little smoke and who knows, maybe we'll both get lucky before too long. You cool?'

Tyra smiled weakly, trying to ignore an errant tear forcing its way down her cheek. 'I'm cool,' she said.

And funny thing was a little while later it was true. She was cool. Did a couple more numbers, old Motown things, yelling out 'Heatwave' at the top of her voice, flashing back on the Wurriyas, the craziest year of her life. Playing bass and shouting out the backing vocals. Col to one side playing keyboards, her dad on the right playing his congas, and Bobby and Mazz in front. Mazz. Damn, the memories you keep buried inside you, the things that seem like they happened to someone else, they have so little to do with the way you live now.

Mazz was proud of himself. He'd got out of the pub after having just the one. Bought his dad a next drink and then scarpered, saying he had a train to catch. It was an achievement really. There's something so seductive about a pub in the late morning. There are no illusions left. You're not a successful young professional popping in for a quick one on the way to the theatre; everyone's hardcore at eleven-thirty in the morning. And in a good mood too. You've got twelve hours' drinking time ahead of you, a pint on the bar ready for you, a little sunlight poking in through a window, and the barman watching *Richard and Judy* on the TV. It's a time to savour life and your lack of a part in it. And leaving that behind, walking out of there at twelve, that first pint of Guinness still warming its way around your body, makes you feel pretentious, absurd, like you think the world cares what you do.

And if that wasn't a triumph, maintaining that he did have a purpose in the face of overwhelming worldly indifference, Mazz didn't know what was. His sense of purpose carried him easily through the fifteen-minute wait at Newport Station, through the ten-minute journey to Cardiff, and the five-minute walk past the monument and under the Bute Street bridge. It dissipated the moment he walked through the door of the Custom House, went up to the bar and ordered what he suspected would still be the only safe thing to drink in the place: a can of Breaker. It was twelve-forty-five.

'Bobby around?' he asked the barmaid, a new one to him, motherly type from up the Rhondda somewhere, he reckoned.

She looked at him closely. 'Not yet,' she said and glanced at the clock. 'Won't be long, though, I expect.'

Mazz smiled his thanks, sat back on his barstool and surveyed his surroundings.

The Custom House was a dump. Actually, it was somewhere way beyond being a dump. In fact it was a legendary dump. It had been the prostitutes' pub since time immemorial. And for some reason neither the brewery nor the landlord ever seemed to reckon that the girls needed horse brasses or carpet or shelves of fake books or ciabatta rolls or stripped-wood floors, or even a new coat of paint more than once a century. Instead what you had was as basic a boozer as ever existed: a bar along one wall, a handful of scarred tables and matching slashed plastic seats, a pool table near the door and a raucous jukebox stocked exclusively with the kind of tunes only ever listened to by very drunk people. Of which there was never any shortage in the Custom House. 'Cause just as the real football fans one hears so much about are mostly one and the same as the football-hooligan element one also hears so much about, so too are the kind of drinkers you get down the Custom House the real drinkers.

Troubling thing for Mazz was he seemed to be fitting in perfectly. Sitting there on his stool, he wasn't attracting as much as a flicker of interest. Didn't know who they thought he was. Not police, not a pimp either; way he heard it hardly none of the girls ever dealt with white guys. White girls, yeah, most of them were lesbians in their private life and Mazz couldn't exactly argue with that – he wouldn't want to listen to the kind of music he played for a living either. Course they might think he was a punter, but then he'd expect the odd look. The way he was being ignored, it was plain the girls had him marked down as one more lost soul, come home to roost.

He watched the action on the pool table: an Italian-looking girl with hard sharp features was playing a younger girl with acne and a feather cut dyed blonde on the top. The blonde girl was winning, least she had more balls down, but then she missed an easyish cut into the centre pocket and Mazz knew from the way the Italian girl smiled it was over. And so it was, four straight reds and the black arrogantly doubled into the corner.

Mazz got off his stool and walked over to the table, fifty-pence piece held between thumb and forefinger.

'Game?' he said to the Italian girl, nodding at the table.

'No, mate' said the Italian girl. 'Got to wait your turn.'

Mazz looked around, scanning first the table for a row of coins, then the blackboard for a list of names, then the room for a sign of anyone else acting like they were waiting for a game of pool.

The Italian girl just watched him then laughed dismissively in his face.

'Me and her, see,' she said, 'we're having a little tournament, like. Best of nineteen. Like the snooker. Two nil to me, now. You want to watch?' She rolled her eyes theatrically at the blonde as she delivered this last line and her mate obliged by laughing derisively.

'Yeah, mate,' she chipped in, her voice already slurring at lunchtime, 'you like watching, do you?'

Mazz just shook his head, refusing to be intimidated by a couple of pissed girls, and walked over to the jukebox, determined to find something they'd really hate.

Moments later he sat back at the bar listening to the opening strains of the Furey Brothers' 'When I Was Sweet Sixteen', and smiled inwardly as the two pool players looked at each other aghast. For a moment he thought the Italian girl was actually going to come over and get in his face when the door opened and in walked Bobby Ranger.

'All right, Treez,' she said to the Italian girl. 'How's it going, beauty?' she said to the blonde girl. And then she noticed Mazz.

'Good Christ,' she said, standing stock still for a second. Then she came over and hugged him hard. 'Christ,' she said again after a moment. 'You've come for Charlie, haven't you?'

'Yeah,' said Mazz, his voice, much to his surprise, choking slightly, 'I've come for Charlie.'

'Nice,' said Bobby. 'Charlie would have appreciated it. You met my girls then?' She pointed at the Italian and the blonde.

Mazz smiled and said, 'Well, we haven't been introduced, like.'

'Hey,' she said. 'You girls remember I told you 'bout that record I made? Well this is the fella I done it with. Mazz.'

The girls just looked totally unimpressed, mumbled a couple of quick hiyas and went back to their game.

'Drink?' she said to Mazz. He nodded and pointed to the can of Breaker in his hand. She ordered two more off Dianne and led Mazz over to a table in the far corner.

'Welcome to the office,' she said and he smiled again. 'So what's happening? How's the music business?'

She could see him gearing up to bullshit her about how great it all was, but then he caught her looking at him and shook his head. 'Shit, Bobby,' he said. 'Be honest with you, it's pure fucking shit.'

Bobby didn't say anything. What was she supposed to be? Sorry for him? They sat back in silence, Bobby watching Mazz kill off his drink with two huge swallows. Then he dug in his pocket for a packet of Camels.

'Fag, Bob?' he said, holding them towards her. She shook her head and he lit himself one.

'You see any of the others, Bob?'

'Others?'

'Out of the group.'

The group, the Wurriyas. The one shot they'd all had of getting out of Cardiff.

'Col,' she said. 'I sees him now and again. He does a little bit of business. You likes a little draw still?'

Mazz shrugged.

'Well, you want some, Col'll sort you out. Charlie you knows about.'

Mazz nodded.

'And Emyr I 'spect you know more about than I do.'

Mazz shook his head.

'But I 'spect you don't care much about any of the rest of us. It's Tyra you wants to know about, isn't it?'

Mazz couldn't help the blush coming to his face.

'Not just Charlie you've come back for, eh?'

Mazz wanted to deny it, didn't know if he could.

2

GRASSROOTS

1980

First time Mazz clapped eyes on Tyra, be honest, he didn't think anything of it. Tall skinny girl came down to a rehearsal with her dad. Had his mind on other things then. Had the world at his feet. Hard to recapture, to even imagine now, the excitement of that first year in Cardiff.

Mazz came down to Cardiff in the summer of '79, nineteen years old. The second he arrived, moved into a room in a mate's flat in Riverside, he wondered why the hell he'd waited so long. He should have come at sixteen, instead of spending two years pissing around in Cross Keys Tertiary screwing up his A levels and then another year pissing around 'cause he didn't want to leave Gaynor behind. Gaynor he'd have dumped in a day if he'd known the girls he'd find in Cardiff.

Only things Mazz brought with him were a bag of clothes and a Fender Telecaster. He came down in his cousin Stevo's van on a Thursday morning and he played his first gig, jamming with some hard-rock boys from Merthyr down the New Moon, on the Saturday night. Wasn't his scene, the New Moon back then, all bikers and beer on the floor. Took him a few days to find where the punk rockers hung out, down Grassroots.

Grassroots was his base for a while; you could hang out there all day and no one hassled you. Free rehearsal space too, so you got to meet all the bands. Used to have meetings there every Tuesday night with some boys from Splott who were trying to put out a Cardiff compilation album of all the local

17

bands. Got to meet girls too, least you did if you were Mazz. First one he ever went out with in Cardiff was a sixteen-year-old Italian girl from Rumney who always wore a jacket with a big picture of Siouxsie Sioux on the back. First time he ever saw her without it was the first time they went to bed together, middle of the afternoon back in Riverside. She was wild, Maria, used to like doing it in the bath – which was going it some when you lived in a house full of bedsits, communal bathroom down the hall – but what the fuck, Mazz had never suffered much from modesty.

It was around the same time, two three weeks into living in Cardiff, he joined his first band proper. First time he met Jason Flaherty and all. It was a Friday afternoon, pissing down outside. Mazz was sitting in Grassroots reading a copy of the *NME* someone left lying around, waiting for Maria to finish school and get down there. In walked this huge bloke.

Jason Flaherty can only have been a year or two older than Mazz but the size of him always made the age gap seem greater. That and the fact you were scared of him. Size he was some of it had to be fat but enough of it was pure blood muscle you didn't ever cross him you had a choice about it. Anyway, Jason Flaherty walked into Grassroots wearing this giant Crombie, looked around, had a word with Linda behind the counter and went over to Mazz.

'You play guitar,' he'd said to Mazz, and Mazz had agreed and Jason had taken him off in his Triumph Stag, looked like it would collapse under his weight, round to a house off Richmond Road just by the railway line where this band were waiting. They were called Venomous and they were basically just a rock band who speeded up their songs enough to pretend to be a punk band. The singer had green hair which was still a bit of a novelty then but you could see he was a good five years too old for it. All of them were. Took Mazz a while to figure it out because at first he was impressed – these guys were serious, they rehearsed hard, they had gigs lined up; he didn't know the signs of desperation back then, the old lags tarting themselves up one more time to try and make it on the latest bandwagon.

Best thing about Venomous – at least at the time he'd thought it was the best thing – was they introduced him to speed. Mazz had this idea that everyone had a drug that was theirs – one that worked utterly for them – and with him it was speed. He loved it, loved everything about it – the unmistakable taste in the back of your mouth, the minutes when you think it's not working and suddenly realise you're talking like a machine gun, the way you could keep going all night – yeah, with whatever. First time him and Maria took some speed together, Christ, they nearly tore his room apart.

Venomous didn't last long, though. One single paid for by Jason, got a bunch of snotty reviews from the music papers – 'warmed-over speeded-up brain-dead pub rock' was what the man from *Sounds* said. A bunch of support gigs with the Lurkers and then Jason pulled the plug, told them they were a bunch of losers and kicked them out of the house in Roath.

Mazz wasn't bothered; he was a quick study and it hadn't taken him long to figure the emptiness of the band. Hadn't been pushed, he would have left anyway. Next couple of months he just went back to hanging in Grassroots, played with a student band trying to do some arty Talking Heads kind of thing, spent more time worrying about getting their slide show right than rehearsing the songs, but still it got Mazz launched on his student phase – Kate, Michelle, Bethan. He loved them. Specially 'cause they didn't have psycho brothers living round the corner like Maria had. They came after Mazz one time with a bicycle chain cause Maria heard what Mazz had been up to on tour with Venomous. After that they wouldn't let Maria anywhere near Mazz which frankly was fine by him in the circs.

It was with Kate he found out about the ska thing. They were up in London for the weekend, staying with Kate's brother who was a student up there. Ended up going to see the Specials. Place was going utterly wild and the audience was different. Loads of young kids, loads of girls and a lot more black kids than Mazz had ever seen at a gig before. Black guys in the band too – couple of older guys looked like they'd been in reggae bands for years and had hooked up with this bunch of punky white boys – doing old Prince Buster tunes, mixed in with their own stuff. Straight away, and for the only time in his life, Mazz could see that this was a new scene, one that was going to be big, and if he jumped in now he could be a part of it.

Back in Cardiff, Mazz got to work. Went down Kelly's secondhand stall in the market, picked up all the old ska stuff he could find, which wasn't much. But it gave him something to start with. Days on end Mazz sat in the flat completely rethinking his guitar playing – just working on getting those chicken-scratch rhythm chords together, letting the syncopation enter his soul. He started checking all the groups in Grassroots carefully, looking for musicians to steal. Only possibility was a kid called Emyr, an angel-faced skinhead looked about twelve and played the drums like a whirlwind in a band called Smegma, the absolute worst bunch of punk-rock losers you could imagine. It was pure racket but underneath Mazz could feel Emyr's time was faultless.

A Wednesday morning walking back from town after signing on, Mazz went into the junkshop at the end of his road, Frankie Johnson's place. There were a couple of cardboard boxes of records balanced on top of a three-piece suite and Mazz headed for them, pulled along by the sight of an album cover with a picture of a black girl wrapped in a snake. He picked it up – *Tighten Up* it was called – and, as Mazz suspected, it was a collection of early rocksteady tunes. He delved further into the box. And discovered he'd found a regular gold mine: three albums by Lee Perry's Upsetters, a couple of Prince Buster singles on the old Blue Beat label, *Guns of Navarone* by the Skatalites, a couple more things by people he'd never heard of but sounded like they were probably the right stuff. Mazz dug in his pockets, figured he could spend a couple of quid, and gathered together ten likely-looking singles and one of the Lee Perry albums, *The Return of Django*.

The black guy who ran the place looked at him with mild surprise. 'You like this old stuff, son?'

'Yeah,' said Mazz. 'You got any more, like?'

'Maybe,' said the guy. 'I knows the feller brought this lot in, I'll ask him he's got any more.'

Mazz said ta and thought no more about it. The records were great, though, so when his next dole cheque showed up on the Friday he headed back down the shop. This time he was hardly in the door when the guy called him over. 'Hey, Prince Buster! Over here, man.'

The guy was sat at a little table at the back of the shop playing cards with another feller, a wiry middle-aged black man. 'Hey,' said the shop guy, 'Charlie, this is who bought all your records.'

And that was how Mazz came to meet Charlie Unger. Ten minutes later Charlie had Mazz spending some more of his dole cheque on pints of

Guinness over the Four Ways. Hour or so after that Mazz was telling Charlie about the band he was planning and Charlie said he played percussion, bongos, congas, that kind of thing, and he knew a load of docks boys played and all. Mazz smiled and said yeah, that would be cool and left Charlie in the company of a couple of old geezers wanted to talk boxing and thought little more of it.

Couple of days later, though, he was walking past the secondhand store again, carrying his guitar, on the way over to Grassroots, and the cry went out, 'Hey, boss,' and Mazz turned and there was Charlie emerging from the gloom wearing a neat sixties suit, porkpie hat perched on his head.

A couple of weeks later and things were starting to move; the first rehearsal was set up at Grassroots. Mazz got there early. Emyr the drummer arrived more or less on time and Charlie showed up, with a young dread called Col who played keyboards, a full hour and a half late, which wasn't too bad as by then Mazz had got Emyr more or less familiar with the basic rhythms. Charlie kept up a constant patter, stories from his boxing days – which was the first Mazz had heard that Charlie used to be the lightweight champion – interspersed with little riffs aimed at any girls who stopped in front of the stage for more than two seconds.

After three or four hours of hard work they'd figured out the rudiments of two Prince Buster songs and 'The Return of Django' and then Charlie called a time out and they all trooped out the back door into the deserted building site for a quick spliff. 'So two things we need,' said Charlie, 'a singer and a bass player. You know any bass players?'

Mazz and Emyr looked at each other then shook their heads. 'None worth speaking of, like,' said Mazz.

Charlie thought for a little while then smiled. 'Well,' he said, 'maybe I've got an idea 'bout that. Now, either of you boys sing?'

Mazz and Emyr looked at each other once again. Mazz shook his head firmly; Emyr shrugged and said, 'A bit, like, but if I'm playing the drums . . .'

'Fair enough,' said Charlie. 'You and me can do the backing vocals, then, but we need a singer. Best thing you put an advert out there, son,' he said, looking at Mazz. Mazz wondered what was happening to the chain of command here but shrugged again and said yeah, he'd get on to it.

What Mazz did was put up a poster in Grassroots asking anyone interested in singing in a new ska band to show up the next Wednesday at six.

Once again he and Emyr were the first ones there and it was Mazz who had to deal with the unlikely gaggle of misfits interested in being the singer. Emyr wanted to wait for Col and Charlie to arrive but Mazz decided to get on with it so Emyr got behind his kit and Mazz asked bloke number one, some kid with green hair called Frog hung around a lot, what he wanted to sing. Frog said he wanted to sing something by Crass, Mazz told him to fuck off so the bloke said how about something by the Pistols then and Mazz powered into 'God Save the Queen' and Emyr started hammering at the kit and Frog started yelling his head off and it was quite all right for about half a minute at which point it quickly became clear that Frog couldn't sing a note.

The next bloke was even worse – some student type with a bit of an attitude. Demanded they played 'Honky Tonk Woman' and started bunny-hopping round the stage in the worst Mick Jagger impersonation you could conceive of. Half a minute of that and Mazz waved to Emyr to stop and told the bloke to fuck off and die.

This had the side effect of causing the other two blokes hanging round to disappear as well and Mazz was starting to feel a bit of an idiot when this little mixed-race skinhead girl came up and said was it all right she had a go.

Mazz said OK and the girl hopped on stage and asked if they knew that Specials song that was in the charts, like – 'Gangsters' – and Mazz and Emyr cranked it out as it was basically just the old rhythm from Prince Buster's 'Al Capone', and the girl – you could see she was nervous as hell but at the same time she had an energy there – gave it a go. It wasn't great or anything, but compared to the idiots they'd just tried out she looked like a godsend.

'What's your name?' Mazz said after the song stumbled to halt. 'I've seen you round, haven't I?'

'Yeah,' said the girl, 'I'm Bobby. They calls you Mazz, don't they?'

'Yeah,' agreed Mazz and right then Col and Charlie walked in accompanied by a tall light-skinned black girl, around Mazz's age, a long serious face, maybe a little Somali in there, and her hair up in very short locks. All three of the newcomers were carrying musical equipment.

'How's it going, boss?' said Charlie to Mazz. 'Meet my daughter, Tyra; she plays the bass.'

'Hiya,' said Mazz, not needing to adjust his line of vision up or down to look her in the eye.

'Hiya,' said Tyra back, holding Mazz's look but not giving it anything. Just then another figure appeared, a black guy with glasses and an Afro, bit on the overweight side.

'And this is Delroy,' said Charlie, 'my little girl's boyfriend and bass teacher, like. Delroy plays with Radical Roots, yeah.'

Mazz nodded. Radical Roots were like *the* Cardiff reggae band, which wasn't saying much. He felt pissed off really; why hadn't Charlie talked this guy into playing in the band instead of his daughter probably on lesson two? He shook Delroy's hand quickly and then said, 'Right, let's get on with it.' Col and Charlie got on the stage and started setting up, Delroy and Tyra went into a corner and Mazz's heart sank as he saw Delroy tune the bass for her. Then he fetched Bobby from over by the coffee bar and introduced her to the rest of the crew. Col and Charlie both gave her looks that were a little short of enthusiastic, Mazz couldn't help noticing.

And that was how it all started, really. The rehearsal wasn't great; Tyra was obviously not that good, fluffed her parts a few times but her time was OK which is the crucial thing with a bass player and Emyr seemed happy enough to play with her. On the upside, too, Bobby came on with leaps and bounds. After a little while she was bouncing around the stage belting out the old Desmond Dekker thing, '007', which was the one song they all seemed to know well enough. She didn't have much range but she had a big strong tone and that love for the limelight that Mazz had realised was the main requirement for pop success.

Fast-forward a couple of months and the band was ready for the first gig. They now had a name – the Wurriyas – from a Somali greeting 'Hey, wurriya', meant brother as far as Mazz knew. Hanging out with Charlie in Butetown he'd heard people use it and it kind of stuck in his head. Wurriya – halfway between worrier and warrior – suited Mazz down to the ground. They had a dozen numbers – ten ska classics and a couple of Mazz's own songs, one of them with a few changes made by Bobby – made it more of a girl's song, like.

Couple of days before the first gig, a semi-private kind of thing in Grassroots, Mazz went on a demo. What happened was, the night before, Saturday night, he'd got off with Kate again. Hadn't seen her for a couple of months, and then he'd been at this party and she'd been at this party and all of a sudden they were in some bedroom with a bottle of wine, locked the door, chucked the big pile of coats on the floor and got to it. People kept banging on the door trying to come in and get their coats while Kate and Mazz just laughed and laughed. Eventually they emerged, nicked a couple more bottles of wine and went back to hers.

Next morning Mazz was all for staying in bed all day. But around twelve Kate started getting up and told Mazz he had to go on this demo. Some Irish thing, this IRA guy called Bobby Sands was on hunger strike about something or other and it was their duty to go and support him. 'Imagine, Mazz,' she said, 'this guy's been living in this cell covered in his own shit and not eaten for thirty days. Have you ever heard of anything so heroic?'

Be honest, Mazz thought he'd heard all the heroic stories he needed to growing up in the valleys, living through the miners' strike. But it was one of the things he was getting used to, student politics. Freaked him out first time he'd heard someone going on about supporting the IRA; now he knew the form, knew the words to mouth; anti-imperialist struggle, not about religion about civil rights, the Birmingham pub bombings were carried out by MI5 and what about Bloody Sunday, eh?

And of course as a Welsh nationalist it was just the comradely thing to do, lend one's support to our Celtic brothers across the sea. Not of course that Mazz had ever thought about Welsh nationalism for two consecutive seconds before he came to Cardiff. Not beyond the sporting chauvinism level anyway. Course since then he'd met all these nice student girls from Canterbury and Leamington Spa, who had all learned about three words of Welsh and were well into it, and who was Mazz to play down his Celtic roots? So fine, he'd said, and pulled on last night's jeans and last night's wine-stained white shirt.

In the end, though, they'd had another quick one before they made it out of the door and the demo was just about moving off when they arrived at the rallying point in Splott Park. Kate immediately joined her student mates in the WRP, all gathered around their trophy member, some tough old girl from Ely they'd discovered on a housing protest. Mazz nipped into the newsagent's and by the time he came out the march was fifty yards up the road and he had to jog forward to catch up.

Suddenly he realised he was standing next to Tyra. She was walking along with a couple of other girls: a serious-looking Indian and a beefy white girl carrying a placard. Mazz quickly scanned the placard to find out what brand of revolutionary Tyra was hanging out with and nodded to himself when he saw it was the SWP. Girl had obviously been recruited at one of their Rock Against Racism things.

Just then Tyra turned her head and noticed him there. 'Oh,' she said. 'Hiya.'

'Hiya,' said Mazz. 'Didn't know you were into politics, like.'

Tyra blushed. He was sure of it. It hadn't really occurred to him that black people could blush — be honest, black people had hardly occurred to him at all, growing up in Newbridge — and he felt oddly touched.

'Well,' she said, 'I don't really know much, but Leila' — she inclined her head towards the Asian girl — 'got me to come along.'

'Yeah, well same with me really,' said Mazz, stopping short of mentioning Kate. 'Some mates of mine in the WRP got me to come. Don't think they get on with your lot.' He nodded at the SWP banner up ahead.

Tyra quickly glanced around to check no one was paying attention the looked at Mazz and rolled her eyes. 'Mad, isn't it?'

Mazz smiled back. 'Hey,' he said, 'how are you enjoying the music, like?'

'Great,' said Tyra.

'Must be a bit weird being in the band with your dad.'

She frowned. 'No. It's all right. Charlie's never been . . . Well he never lived with us, like, so he's . . . I dunno. Being in the band with him . . . it's like if I was a boy he'd have taken me out fishing with him or taken me boxing like he did. Now playing music's something we can share. Get to know each other, like.'

'Right,' said Mazz, not really sure what she was saying, but again oddly touched by the way she was talking to him. Just straight ahead. 'Looking forward to the gig?'

'Terrified, to be honest with you,' she said and smiled again, this time a real teeth-and-all grin.

'Your first time is it?'

'Yeah . . . no . . . well, I've done a few things in school. In the orchestra.'

'Oh,' said Mazz, 'right.' And they walked on for a little while, then Tyra's friend Leila started talking to her and Mazz decided it was time he moved forward a bit and found Kate.

Later on Mazz and Kate had a bit of a row. After the demo had finished over City Hall with the usual speeches and a little bit of excitement when a couple of dozen NF types made a half-hearted attempt to get at the marchers, Mazz had gone back with Kate and her WRP mates to their local guru's house. His name was Tony, some kind of lecturer as far as Mazz could gather, and frankly the whole scene was positively creepy. All these little student girls were coming up to Tony telling him how many newspapers they'd sold that week and he would nod approvingly or give them this saddened look of reproach.

And all the time these people were being terribly nice to Mazz. Took him a little while to figure out why. Eventually some girl – Helen, he thought her name was – came over and told him he must meet Tony. Tony was really keen to meet him. Telling him this like Mazz was really honoured. So Mazz shrugged and followed her over to Tony who was stood with a couple of little girls, and he shooed them all away and gave Mazz a serious look and then let the cat out of the bag straight away.

'So good to have some working-class comrades getting involved.' Course it was Mazz's accent had this lot wetting their knickers – hey, look, we've got a genuine prole here.

So this Tony gave Mazz the whole spiel. Up the miners, down with Maggie. Irish struggle is our struggle, troops out, Trots in. Wasn't a bad pitch, as it went; guy had probably made a great timeshare salesman in later life, but he'd read Mazz wrong. Had enough of that up-the-miners shit from his dad. Didn't want to hear it down in Cardiff from some smooth fucker like Tony.

'Yeah, mate, right on,' he said, the first moment Tony paused for air, and wandered off in search of a drink.

Kate was furious with him.

'How could you do that to me?' she yelled, the minute they got back to her place.

'What?' said Mazz.

'Humiliate me like that.'

'What?' said Mazz again, genuinely baffled.

'Talking to Tony like that. Don't you know who he is?'

'Yeah, he's . . .' Mazz paused. Even drunk as he by now was, he could figure that if he uttered the words 'a boring cunt' his chances of getting anywhere with Kate that night were fucked so he bit his lip and said, 'He's your leader, like, in the Party.'

'He's not a leader, Mazz, he's our most prominent intellectual theorist.' Like she was reading off the back of a book. 'He's written two books and he's met all these revolutionaries round the world and I can't believe you could act like that.'

'Like what?'

'Like such a wanker, after all he's done for you people.'

Fuck, thought Mazz, as those last two words just hung there. *You people.* To be fair, Kate realised what she'd said and did her best to apologise, but like with most apologies only made it worse. Sober, Mazz might have let her get away with it – just one of the hazards of screwing students, getting patronised once in a while – but on this night, drunk, he wouldn't have it. He came back at her with a ferocity that surprised him, all the frustrations of his year in Cardiff pouring out, then left her there crying.

Walking back across town to Riverside, Mazz realised he still had a copy of the paper stuck in his jacket pocket. He was about to chuck it in the nearest bin, when for want of anything better to do he started reading the cover story.

It was all about this Bobby Sands feller. And cynical as Mazz was, he couldn't help but be impressed by the guts of the man, this IRA activist who was well on the way to starving himself to death if the government didn't give in to his demand to be treated as a political prisoner. Seemed obvious enough to Mazz. If it wasn't political what the IRA did, what the hell was it? You didn't have to agree with their politics to see that.

The rest of the paper was all bollocks, though, and it found its way into a bin on the corner of Queen Street. Somewhere between the castle and the bridge, a distance of a hundred yards or so, a song popped into his head, fully formed. First the chorus then the first verse. Nothing to do with Bobby Sands, or arguing with your girlfriend – well, maybe a bit more the latter – but basically it was just a nonsense pop song with a ska beat. The chorus mostly consisted of repeating the words 'lick her down' over and over. It would be variously lauded as a joyous piece of sexual liberation and damned as a hymn to male violence and it was to be the Wurriyas' one and only hit.

Mazz brought it along to the rehearsal the next day. Embarrassed as hell actually. Songwriting wasn't his thing, and particularly those rare songs that just came out of nowhere – you were never sure if they were great or whether it was just something you'd heard on the radio when you weren't paying attention and your subconscious had just rehashed it. No problem this time, though. The arrangement came together as easily as the song and, once Bobby had taken the thirty seconds necessary to learn the words, the sight of her singing, 'Lick her down, lick her down, you better lick her down,' with her tongue rolling lasciviously out of her mouth was frankly hysterical.

It was also the moment Mazz realised Bobby was a lesbian. Obvious now but back then, be honest, lesbians were a bit of a novelty. You kind of knew they existed but it was mostly something blokes shouted at girls who wouldn't go out with them, not something anyone Mazz knew actually did.

The gig went well. Not that that meant too much. First gigs tended to go well in Mazz's experience. All your mates would come down and say it was great even if it was shit. Then again, playing ska you couldn't go too far wrong, not this year anyway. Long as you got the beat halfway right, there were a load of kids out there, happy to have their first local ska band on the scene . . .

Afterwards, eleven o'clock, the gear all packed away, Mazz was cursing the licensing laws, meant it was too late to get a celebratory drink.

'Don't worry about that, man,' said Charlie. 'We'll go to a little blues thing, down the docks.'

Mazz looked at the others. Col and Emyr, the sinsemilla twins, gave their customary stoned nods of acceptance.

Bobby shook her head. 'Kenny's place? Nah. Well, maybe later. I got someone to see first.'

Bobby winked at Mazz and he nearly laughed out loud. 'How about you, Tyra?' he said then. 'You and Delroy coming?'

Delroy, who was as ever sitting in the corner with Tyra, frowned. 'No, man, we got things to do.'

'No we haven't.' That was Tyra and Mazz took an involuntary step backwards. First time he'd heard Tyra argue with anything Delroy said.

Delroy took Tyra by the arm and they walked over to the far end of the room, by the coffee bar. A conversation followed, conducted in angry whispers and culminating in a bout of finger pointing. Then Delroy walked back fast past the members of the band and out the back door. Tyra came slowly over towards them, giving them a don't-you-dare-mention-any-of-that look.

Half an hour later, Mazz, Charlie, Tyra, Emyr and Col were getting out of a cab in West Bute Street by the Dowlais. Charlie led the way down the alley by the side of the pub and stopped at an unmarked door on the left. He rang on the bell and almost immediately a hugely built young man with short dreads opened the door.

'All right, Charlie,' he said. 'Tyra. Col. Who are these boys then?' Angling his head towards Mazz and Emyr.

'Boys from the ska band I been telling you about. Mazz, Emyr, this is Kenny.'

Mazz stuck his hand out and felt like an idiot when the fella called Kenny just turned his back and led the way up two flights of stairs into what looked like a fair-sized living-room with a little bar stuck in one corner and a DJ system in another.

The DJ, a rasta with waist-length locks and dark glasses on in what was already a pretty dark room, was playing some lovers' rock, all big dirty basslines with South London schoolgirls warbling off-key over the top. Charlie nodded to the guy who nodded fractionally back and then Charlie went over to the bar.

Little while later on, Charlie was off talking to Kenny, Emyr and Col were in the corner spliffing up, for a change, like, which left Mazz and Tyra standing by the bar. Mazz was drinking from a bottle of pale ale; Tyra had a glass of an unlikely mixture of Guinness and orange juice. Conversation had come to a halt when Charlie moved off, so Mazz had a go at reigniting it.

'You were good tonight,' he said.

'Yeah, thanks,' said Tyra, distracted.

'No, really. You and Emyr, you got the groove there.'

'Mmm.'

'You got trouble with your boyfriend, then? You want to talk about it?'

Tyra looked at him then, forced a smile on to her face. 'Not really.'

They fell silent again after that, Tyra sipping her drink, Mazz scanning the room for likely talent. He was just sizing up a blonde piece standing over by the DJ when a scary-looking guy with a couple of gold teeth, and a scar on his left cheek serious enough to be visible even in this light from across the room, walked over and casually put his arm round the blonde. Mazz figured it was probably best to wait a little, check out the runnings, before making a move in a place like this. So he was just drifting off, moving unconsciously to the music which was now some upbeat Dennis Brown thing, when he was jolted out of his reverie by Tyra pulling on his sleeve.

'You want to dance?'

Mazz shrugged, smiled, stuck his pale ale on the bar next to Tyra's murky concoction, and moved on to the floor.

Blame what happened next on the beat. There probably is a way to dance to reggae that isn't blatantly sexual but Mazz hadn't come across it, nor had any of the other people in the room. Nor Tyra. She was winding up her waist with the best of them and as Mazz danced with her he was struck with surprise as he realised first that she was interested, and second that he was too.

Mazz, for once, was disconcerted, blindsided, a little unnerved by knowing this girl already. Usually that didn't happen; the sex thing came first or not at all. Which made it easy. There is a thing girls say – which like a lot of things girls say sounds nice but is essentially shit – about how they want to be friends, how they want to get to know a boy before they can really fancy them. Bollocks, only reason people really fancy each other, way Mazz saw it, was 'cause they didn't know each other. Getting to know people took the shine off matters fast as anything. You didn't want to find out all that same old shit: bloke lives in a pigsty, girl has fluffy animals on her bed. You wanted to get down to doing the in-bed on-the-floor in-the-bath stuff a.s.a.p.

Now this – Mazz realised in those first seconds of dancing together, catching Tyra's eyes shining as she looked at him – was going to be harder. Already he knew more than he cared to know about a girl. He knew her old boyfriend and her dad. Her dad, for Christ's sake. And of course ticking in the back of his brain he supposed there was always the other thing. The black thing.

But, for the moment, in that moment in Kenny's blues, there was just music and dancing and two young people, neither of them yet twenty years old, looking at each other and laughing and leaving the dance floor together, on a shared smile, to get a drink at the bar.

'Hot,' she said after a minute, rolling her drink across her forehead to cool down.

'Hot,' Mazz agreed. 'You want to get some air?'

Tyra looked at Mazz hard, like she was searching for something in his face, then she smiled. 'Yeah,' she said, 'come with me.'

Tyra led the way back across the room. Charlie was engrossed in conversation with some tattooed white guy, looked like another ex-boxer, and Mazz was relieved not to catch his eye. On their way out the door, Mazz heard a hiss from behind him. He turned and saw a couple of hard young black guys, looking less than impressed by the sight of Mazz and Tyra leaving together. Mazz was about to move towards them when Tyra tugged on his shirt and pulled him after her out on to the landing.

Mazz started down the stairs but quickly realised Tyra wasn't behind him. Instead she inclined her head upwards, and Mazz followed her up two more flights of stairs to a semi-derelict attic floor. Tyra opened a door and suddenly they were out on the roof, looking up at a three-quarter moon.

Mazz closed the deal right away. Lot of blokes would have blown a situation like this, started jabbering away about what a nice night it was, all that bollocks, making themselves nervous, making the girl nervous too. Mazz didn't say a word, just leaned his back against the wall and pulled Tyra to him. And his lips were on her lips, his hands up the back of her shirt before she had time to think let alone speak.

And it was nice, she was nice, gave the kiss back hard. He liked her basketball muscles, her big eyes, laughed at the way she pulled his hand forward to rub her tits, but slapped that same hand away when it wandered near her carefully arranged hair.

A little while later they were lying on the ground on top of Mazz's coat, getting seriously intimate with each other, when Tyra said the first semi-coherent words either of them had uttered since they got on to the roof.

'You got any . . . you know?'

'No,' said Mazz. 'You taking . . .'

Tyra shook her head and Mazz said the words men tend to say in those particular situations: 'It'll be all right.' And kept on moving his fingers just where he'd been moving them for the last minute or two, and Tyra sighed and spread herself for him.

And it was good. Course it was. Nothing to beat it. Could have gone on a bit longer, Mazz had to admit, but that was the first time for you. And afterwards, be honest, she seemed a little down, but that was another thing Mazz had noticed, lot of girls went funny after sex. Guilt kicking in, he reckoned. Still, it was a bit of a chicken-and-egg thing far as he could see: it was the guilt that got you right up for it in the first place, and it was the guilt made you sad after, rough with the smooth, like.

And Mazz was a gent, he took Tyra back to her place after. Sneaking past the blues which was still going, making sure Charlie didn't spot them. Tyra lived on Angelina Street, at the town end of Butetown, so Mazz walked her there through the empty streets, kissed her on the street corner, quickly 'cause he could tell she was nervous about being spotted, and said he'd see her at rehearsal tomorrow. He walked back along the embankment to Riverside, whistling most of the way.

3

THE ROYAL OAK

1999

Tyra had an appointment. Twelve-thirty round the police station. Copper there Jimmy Fairfax, who she knew from school as it happened, wanted to see her. Something about her dad. Returning some effects of his. Walking over there she realised she'd not paid much attention to the details. She'd just felt so guilty when she'd heard. Charlie, her dad, dead in his flat, been there a week and nobody noticed. She'd just felt so like shit she hadn't even asked what happened. Suspected heart attack they'd said and that had sounded about right. Amount Charlie had smoked and drank, and all those years of boxing couldn't have helped. Now, though, she thought she'd better ask this Jimmy Fairfax, who she hoped to God had changed from the little hooligan he'd been in school, what exactly the state of play was.

Thing was he didn't seem to know too much either.

Fact was, and it was kind of funny really, he spent most of the time she was in the station just looking at her. Yeah, yeah, that look, the 'I want to get next to you' look, not the 'Oh I'm sorry about your dear old dad' look. And the awful thing was, though she was starting to get used to it now, she felt like saying, 'All right, let's get down to it right here in this little interview cubicle.' She didn't, of course, even though to be fair Jimmy Fairfax looked a whole lot better than she remembered from school, worked out a bit obviously and wearing a decent-looking suit. Bit embarrassed about it he was in fact, said he'd just been in court, but she liked to see a man in a nice suit.

'Nothing else to do then is there?' she said after Jimmy had handed her a bag containing the things they'd found in Charlie's pockets. His wallet, his lighter, couple of betting slips. She didn't look at the wallet – knew there'd be a picture of her in there and the second she saw it the waterworks would start and she didn't want that, not there in that room.

'Not as far as we're concerned, love,' he said. 'There'll be the inquest tomorrow. No need for you to come; it's just a formality, like. I mean, it's not like anyone would have murdered him, is it?'

'Nah,' said Tyra, though fleetingly the absurd fantasy came into her head that one of the betting slips might have been a big winner or maybe a lottery ticket . . . Nah, hardly, her dad never had that kind of luck.

Tyra just stared at the little plastic bag full of her dad's relics and for a moment Jimmy just sat there too. Then after a little while he stood up, moved over to her and with surprising gentleness put his hand on her shoulder, sending another shaft of unwanted electricity right through her.

'You all right?' he said. 'Yourself, like?'

'Yes,' she said, 'I'm fine, uh, Jimmy,' she said, finding it odd the sound of his name on her lips. If she'd ever spoken to him before it was probably just a 'Fuck off, Fairfax' in the playground. She stood up quickly, losing his hand in the process.

'Thanks,' she said, 'thanks for asking, though.'

He showed her out on to James Street and, as she was just walking off, called after her. 'When's the funeral then?'

'Friday,' she said. 'St Cuthbert's. Twelve o'clock.'

'Right,' he said, 'I'll see you there then, like, pay my respects to the old man.'

She turned then to face him. 'You knew Charlie?'

'Oh yeah,' he said, 'everyone knew your dad,' and he smiled and suddenly she had the sense that he was holding something back, but before she could follow up he had said goodbye and was back into the station, leaving her standing on James Street, frowning.

Mazz didn't stay much longer in the Custom House. Had a game of pool with Bobby for old times' sake and got beaten with contemptuous ease, so he said he'd see her around and headed out on to Bute Street. As the fresh air hit him he realised the first thing he had to do was find somewhere to stay. He stopped for a moment to think. He had enough money to stay in a guest house somewhere he supposed, but he'd sooner not. God knows how long the five hundred pounds was going to have to last him. And, anyway, guest houses just evoked the depression of those endless bloody tours, playing in bands who were always on the way up or the way down, never at the bloody top. No, best thing was to find someone to crash with. He dug into his shoulder bag and pulled out an ancient black notebook. Then he headed back under the bridge and into the Golden Cross to make a few calls.

Leafing through the address book in the corner of the bar, he had a sudden awful sense of just how much time had gone by since he'd lived in this place. Almost twenty years and yet here they still were, all these phone numbers from yesteryear. Michelle, Emma, Kate. Three students all lived in the same house; he'd got off with Michelle and Kate, never got anywhere with Emma. Likelihood they'd all stayed living in the same bedsits for the next two decades? Less than zero. More girls' numbers: Lucy, Gail, Bethan. Bethan? She'd lived with her parents; maybe they'd still be in the same place, and . . . And what? Hey, remember me? I'm Mazz, we had a one-night stand back in 1980. You were really keen but I never bothered to call you again. How about I come and stay with you and your husband and your three teenage kids up in Radyr? Yeah, that'd work. Christ, he started to wonder as he went through the ancient pencil-marked numbers, had he had any male friends at all, or just spent his whole time chasing girls? Then he found one: Lawrence.

Lawrence with an ancient biro address and then over the top of it a felt-tipped phone number 'cause he'd run into him up in London a couple of years back.

Lawrence had been the coolest person Mazz had ever met back when he first came to Cardiff. He was the DJ in the club they always went to, Mel's down in the docks. Tall thin guy with locks, though he was never really a rasta far as Mazz knew. Been Lawrence who'd introduced Mazz to reggae, and helped him find the old stuff: the Prince Buster tunes and that that had been the basis of the Wurriyas. Mazz found himself grinning at the memory, then he recalled the last time he'd seen Lawrence up in London, still charming but frayed around the edges, and he was put in mind that it was Lawrence who'd introduced him to a lot of other stuff too. Drugs and that.

Whatever, thought Mazz, he wasn't overburdened with options, so he reached for the phone on the edge of the bar and rang Lawrence's number.

The phone was picked up on the first ring. 'Danny,' said the voice at the other end of the line.

'No,' said Mazz. 'It's Mazz here. Is that you, Lawrence?'

'Oh,' said the voice, then there was a pause as Mazz could sense a hand being placed over the receiver and then heard a voice – Lawrence he was sure – shouting, 'No, it's not him, it's just some guy.' Then Lawrence came back on the line. 'Hey, Mazz, whassup, bra?'

'I'm down in Cardiff. I was thinking of coming to see you.'

Another pause, then, 'Great, yeah. Listen, where are you now, man?'

'Town.'

'Tell you what, I've got a little bit of business to sort out. Give us a couple of hours, and come round. You know the place?'

'No, just got your number.'

'All right, 110 Constellation Street, over Adamsdown. Later then, man,' and with that Lawrence hung up, leaving Mazz standing there at the bar with the receiver in his hand and foreboding in his heart, wearily sure what the scene would be round Lawrence's place.

Suddenly tired of drinking, Mazz left his half-finished pint on the bar and headed out into the late-afternoon sunshine. He walked past the ice rink into town, pausing briefly to mourn the passing of the Salutation, his regular drinker in the old days, now part of the foundations of Toys 'R' us. He kept moving into the Hayes, went into Spillers Records simply because it was a surviving landmark, not 'cause he had the remotest intention of buying anything. Like most of the musicians he knew, Mazz didn't even possess a CD player and had hardly bought any music since the early eighties. Only time he ever heard anything new was the stuff whatever woman he was with would play, and most of the time that would be some hideous indie dance bullshit that simply confirmed him in his prejudice. Still, it would be even worse if he was one of those sad bastard ponytails who ran around trying to be part of fucking Britpop.

Back on the street he kept walking for another hundred yards then stopped at the open-air snack bar, once again more out of familiarity than necessity, though once he'd sat down with a cup of tea and a tuna sandwich he realised he was starving and ended up eating three more sandwiches.

A quick shufti round the shops and a leisurely stroll eastwards past the prison and he made it over to Adamsdown almost exactly two hours after he'd phoned Lawrence.

The scene in Constellation Street was precisely as expected. A spectral redhead opened the door and ushered Mazz into the front room, which contained an old sofa, three bean bags, a TV showing *Hollyoaks* and precious little else.

'He's upstairs,' she said. 'I'll just go and get him for you.'

An hour passed; the phone rang three times. Mazz dozed off briefly, woke up towards the end of the Channel Four news. Still no sign of Lawrence or the redhead. He stood up, went into the kitchen, checked the fridge for beer and found it wanting, wrote a note in felt tip saying, 'Back later, maybe,' and walked back out into Adamsdown.

He kept on walking away from town, past Clifton Street with its despairing discount furniture stores and great Italian caff. No more Patrice's Grill, though: the place you used to be able to drink all night long as you ordered a portion of chips had finally bitten the dust. He carried on along Broadway, past the snooker hall and the studio the band went into once, and finally arrived at the Royal Oak.

The Oak was one of the last reminders of the old Cardiff. Three bars plus a snug and a skittle alley. One bar for the hippies, one bar for the R&B bands, and the big public bar full of boxing mementoes for anyone and everyone. There was a boxing gym upstairs where they all used to train – Peerless Jim Driscoll, Joey Erskine, Randolph Turpin, Charlie Unger – and their pictures and yellowed cuttings were everywhere downstairs.

Mazz walked into the public bar; five years at least since he'd last set foot in there but no one seemed to have moved a muscle since he first went in there twenty years ago. Same old geezers in the corner with their personal mugs drinking the SA from the wood that you couldn't get in any other pub in the known world; same old parties of three generations of raucous girls whooping it up beneath the TV screen – that was new, to be fair, the big Sky Sports apparatus, but the same phone was next to it and he was sure, he looked careful at the piece of wood next to the phone he'd find the numbers he'd scribbled down there: Michelle, Kate, Tyra . . .

No Charlie Unger, though. It hadn't been Charlie's regular, the Oak – too far from where he lived – but he loved to come down here once in a while, get a little respect, a little affirmation of who he used to be.

Mazz stood at the bar, drinking a pint of dark. After a while he saw the bloke standing along the bar from him – tall old hippy with a grey ponytail – had finished with his *Echo* so Mazz begged it off him. When he handed it back ten minutes later, he looked at the bloke closely and the bloke looked at him. Then the bloke smiled and said, 'Hey, how you doing, butt?'

Mazz was still none the wiser. 'Good,' he said. 'Good to be back in here, anyway. I've been away, like,' he trailed off and the bloke nodded sympathetically. 'How about you?' he added in the hope that the answer might shake loose some recognition.

'Yeah, you know, the usual, like,' said the bloke completely unhelpfully, then burst out laughing. 'You don't have a fucking clue who I am, butt, do you?'

'No, sorry, mate,' said Mazz, raising his glass and smiling too.

'The Colonel,' said the bloke, 'that's me. You remembering now, or you swallowed too many mushrooms since last time?'

'Christ,' said Mazz, scanning frantically through the memory banks and then striking gold, 'the Colonel. You were the bloke on *Mastermind*. Years ago, answered questions on Bruce Springsteen and the Civil War or something.'

'Yeah,' said the Colonel, 'that was me.'

'They had a little party for you in here and we played in the back room.'

'That's right, mate,' said the Colonel, 'and I came up and asked you if you could play "Born to Run" and I'd sing and you told me to fuck off.'

'And you nearly broke my fucking nose, you bastard,' said Mazz, finishing off the story.

'Yeah, well, I was wondering when you'd remember that bit,' said the Colonel. 'Have another drink, butt, least I can do for you.'

Mazz raised his near-empty pint of dark, signalling his readiness for another one.

Couple of hours down the line, Mazz and the Colonel were getting on like a house on fire. They were just standing out in the back yard of the pub, near the toilets, sharing a spliff when the Colonel said, 'Fancy a game of pool?' And Mazz said why not and next thing they were in the back of a cab and another ten minutes or so they were getting out outside what had to be the dodgiest-looking pub in Penarth – the faded Edwardian resort across the far side of Cardiff Bay, and a place longer on nursing homes than dodgy pubs. This one, though, was called The Royal and it was smack opposite the only middle-rise council blocks in town, on top of the hill looking back over the bay.

Inside it was unnervingly brightly lit and populated by a mixture of old geezers, a few lads and a bunch of long-bearded old hippies congregated next to the bar. Mazz and the Colonel were at home from the off.

The Colonel walked up to the bar, ordered up a couple of pints of something called Bullmastiff, then led the way round to the back room which sported a great big gaudy mural of the sort more usually found in youth clubs, depicting what Mazz took to be the pub's regulars, and a pool table.

The Colonel stuck fifty pence in the slot and racked up the balls.

'Break?' he said to Mazz, who nodded, walked round to the end of the table and just smashed the cue ball as hard as he could. Two reds and a yellow went down, and Mazz could see he was in luck; three more reds had ended up around the centre pockets and Mazz picked them off easily. A tricky long red into the corner pocket followed and then a bit of luck as the cue ball just kept on rolling, casually sorting out the little cluster of balls around the back as it did so, and leaving a nice easy angle on the last red back into the centre. Just the black left; another nice straight shot into the corner. Mazz found himself breaking into a smile as he lined the shot up. Only once or twice he'd ever done that – run all the balls in straight from the break. He stopped himself in mid-shot, looked over at the Colonel and winked. The Colonel winked back and Mazz returned to his shot. He rolled the black nicely into the pocket and watched disbelievingly as the cue ball seemed once again to suddenly gather momentum, and dropped straight after the black into the same pocket.

'Hard luck, mate,' said the Colonel straight-faced, and Mazz looked at him aghast. Then the Colonel burst out laughing and Mazz did the same.

'Luck like that, butt, I shouldn't show my face out of doors.'

Mazz shrugged and laughed again, but would have sworn he was cursed the way things went over the next four games of pool. Every time he seemed to have the frame in his pocket and every time something screwed up absurdly. Then, thankfully, the last orders bell rang and they returned to the bar, two more pints with double whisky chasers, and it was only when the Colonel suggested heading round the corner to some late-night drinker that Mazz realised he didn't have anywhere else to go.

Walking round to the drinker, a half-baked nightclub above a shoe shop in the high street, Mazz brought the subject up.

'There any hotels round here?' He asked.

'What,' said the Colonel, 'you need somewhere to stay? Don't worry about that, mate, stay at mine. Plenty of room.'

So that was that settled. The dodgy nightclub had two floors, one playing horrible eighties music. The other one was OK, though; just a bar, basically, with a karaoke machine on the go, anyone was interested. The Colonel got the drinks in then went over to the bloke operating the machine, and even as he walked over the bloke was digging in his CD box looking for something. Moments later the karaoke machine was blasting out the opening bars to Bruce Springsteen's 'Born to Run' and then the Colonel was giving it some welly. Total sincerity and completely out of tune, it was riveting in a disconcerting kind of way. The whole place gave the Colonel a round of applause when he finished. The Colonel walked over to Mazz and said, 'Well, they expect me to do it, like. You going to have a go, butt?'

Mazz was momentarily tempted. One of the more surreal incidents in his life had occurred in a pub up in far North London, somewhere where they were having an eighties-themed karaoke night, and on came Mazz's hit as played by some bunch of session men and then this secretary type can hardly have been born when it came out stepped out and started singing it. Weirder than hell. And drunk and exhausted as he was, there seemed something appealingly grim about going up to the DJ and asking if he had a copy of his own record so he could sing it to a bunch of uninterested pissheads. Momentary was all it was, though.

'No, mate,' he said to the Colonel. 'Be honest, I'm starting to feel totally knackered.'

'C'mon then,' said the Colonel, downing most of a pint of cider in one go, 'let's get out of here.'

Back on the street Mazz started across the road, instinctively surmising that the Colonel lived in one of the little terraces running up the hill: few bits of fabric across the windows for curtains and an old dog for company. Sofa in the front room for Mazz, no doubt – comfortable enough if you didn't let your mind focus on the stains. How many years had Mazz spent crashing in places like this?

'Hang on, butt,' said the Colonel and Mazz aborted his road-crossing. Instead he followed the Colonel down towards the seafront and then left just before the steep incline down, into a very classy-looking street of detached Tudor-Gothic piles. To Mazz's considerable amazement, the Colonel strolled to one of these, halfway along on the right, inserted his key in the lock and, as he entered the porch, started taking his shoes off and motioned for Mazz to do the same.

'Christ,' said Mazz, surveying the immaculate interior of the place, 'you win the lottery?'

'Yeah,' said the Colonel, 'well, in a manner of speaking anyway.' Then he gave Mazz a nod and a wink and changed the subject. 'You hungry, butt?' he asked.

'Yeah,' said Mazz, suddenly ravenous. 'If you've got anything lying around, like.'

'See what we can do,' said the Colonel and led the way into the kitchen. 'Here, butt,' he said, 'you sit here,' pointing Mazz at the breakfast bar, 'and I'll see what I can find. Just hang on a sec while I see if Nat's still about. Drinks in the fridge, you want one.'

Mazz sat down, his head spinning from tiredness, drunkenness and surprise. Hell was the Colonel doing in a place like this? Couple of minutes later, when the Colonel still hadn't come back, he got off his stool, went prospecting in the fridge. Looked inside and it was like peering into Tesco's gourmet-selection cabinet, box of little French beers at the bottom. Mazz pulled one out, twisted the top off and was halfway through drinking it when the Colonel reappeared, behind him a woman wearing overalls and holding a chisel.

'Mazz,' said the Colonel, 'this is Nat.'

'Hiya, love,' said Mazz, suddenly feeling energised. 'Bit late for the old DIY, isn't it?'

'I'm a sculptor,' she replied frostily before turning her head to the Colonel and rolling her eyes in a Christ-who-is-this-drunken-arsehole-you've-brought-back kind of way. Which was when Mazz started to think he recognised her. Nat, Natalie. He was sure he remembered a Natalie some-where along the line. At the end, maybe, after Tyra . . .

Shit, he was paralysed for a moment by a wave of total shame and self-loathing. The things you do, the cruelty you're capable of, when you're young. Yes, he was sure it had been a Natalie that night. Awful thing was he couldn't say for the life of him whether it was this Natalie standing in front of him now. He had this frisson of familiarity but nothing specific, and she wasn't exactly giving him the fond-remembrance look. Not that she would be even if she was the same Natalie. In fact last thing she'd be giving him probably. Or maybe she'd forgotten him too. Either way, there didn't seem a lot of mileage in asking her so he decided to play it straight.

'Yeah, sorry,' he said, giving his accent a bit more valleys; your artist types liked a nice working-class boy. 'Only joking, like.'

'You're a musician,' she said, fixing him with a distinctly inscrutable look, which he held, allowing him to check her out. No make-up, black hair with a dramatic streak of grey all scraped back and tied up in an impromptu ponytail, little bit of weakness round the mouth. Could be a real artist, could be just another flake pushing forty looking for something to do with her life in between aromatherapy sessions. Interesting, though. Christ, there he went again. One thing Mazz knew: he was a bloke and he met Mazz he wouldn't introduce him to his girlfriend. Mazz was sorry about it, but there it was. He didn't have any way of pulling back from it.

'Yeah,' he said, 'well, it's what I do, anyway.'

'Ronnie says you were in a band here a long time ago, said you had a hit.'

For a moment Mazz was totally flummoxed – who the hell was Ronnie? – before logic told him it had to be the Colonel. Ronnie, eh?

'Yeah,' he said, 'that's right,' then picked up his beer and drained it off.

'So what were you called?'

'The Wurriyas,' he said, smiling, figuring she must be the Natalie he half-remembered, joking with him now, flirting a little maybe.

But she didn't respond, just looked blankly at him for a moment then said, 'Oh right, well, nice to meet you, I'm sure Ronnie will show you the guest room.' And with that she was gone.

It was midnight and Tyra knew she should be going to bed. Long day coming up and all that, funeral to sort out. But here she was sitting in the front room drinking – nearly got through the whole bottle of white wine – and listening to records, things she hadn't heard in years.

She'd been going through the stuff in the cupboards, looking for anything of her dad's. Instead she'd found this box of records and tapes, all the stuff she used to listen to: Michael Jackson, Stevie Wonder, Elton John, *Supremes Greatest Hits*, *Rumours*, David Essex – yeah, well, she couldn't have been more than twelve when she bought that one. Awful thing was he'd been in panto in town just last Christmas, lot of the girls she was in school with had gone to see him. Tragic, apparently – same old hairstyle except thinning like mad and a little old man underneath it. Never a good idea to see people you used to fancy.

Last hour or so she'd been listening to all the real girly stuff. Joan Armatrading singing 'Love and Affection'. Tyra remembered seeing her on telly, *Magpie*, the show with the white bloke with the Afro you were meant to fancy, Mick something. Anyway, there she was, this little black girl with a proper Afro, looking terrified and singing this lovely song, just sounded so grown-up. Followed that up with her favourite Diana Ross album, the one all the older girls had in school, *Touch Me In the Morning*. Bet every girl she knew had run home and played that one first time they'd done it. She knew she had. Though she'd been a good couple of years older than most of her mates when she got round to doing it. Her mum drilling it into her. You're not going the same way I did, girl, having a kid when you're sixteen. Her dad just the same. Hypocrisy of it with him took your breath away. Knocked off half Cardiff you could believe his boasting but when it came to his own dear daughter she was expected to be a bloody nun. Well, she'd shown him in the end all right. She'd actually devised a plan to piss off her father, she could hardly have done it better.

But she didn't want to think about him, her first time, now. She wanted to go back to those early teenage years, the *Jackie* years, the basketball team years, school dances when she'd be the tallest one there practically, taller than all the girls and most of the boys. Sitting on the back of the bus singing Bay City Rollers songs – yeah, well, you can laugh now but it was fun then and how old were they anyway? Eleven? Michael Jackson pictures on the wall; funny now if you thought about it, but apart from anything else he was the only black boy you ever saw in the pin-up mags. Christ, it was different back then. Now all the little girls, black or white, were wetting themselves over some obvious badman like R Kelly or those fucking rap guys she couldn't even be bothered to remember; back then you got your gran calling to watch the telly cause Hot Chocolate were on *Top of the Pops*. They were good, though. Not just that *Full Monty* one; she loved those slow ones. *Emma Emmeline* – she knew she had it somewhere – *gonna make you the biggest star this world has ever seen*. Dreams you have when you're a kid. Christ, she was definitely getting drunk now.

4

THE ASSEMBLY

1999

As it turned out, the funeral was the same day they launched the Assembly. Wasn't planned like that or anything, just the day suited the crematorium.

Tyra didn't know whether she was coming or going. The arrangements should have been down to her but somehow she'd lost control of the situation. This feller Big George – community leader they'd call him whenever he turned up in the *Echo*, which was as often as he could manage; you know, objecting to this or that bit of the bay development, demanding more local boys got jobs on the sites. All fair enough stuff, like, except you couldn't help feeling like the main thing was getting in the papers not getting anything done. Anyway, this feller comes round saying how he was Charlie's best mate and how this local developer feller wants to shell out for a big funeral for Charlie, big procession and all just like the old days, and Tyra really wanted to say fuck off. But she supposed it was just guilt that made her say yes. Like, she hadn't paid enough attention to Charlie while he was alive, so how could she deny him a big send-off now he was dead?

So that was the start of it and somehow George seemed to have taken over everything, to the point that on the morning of her father's funeral, Tyra was standing around in her own front room wondering what the hell she was supposed to be doing. When the hearse arrived at eleven she was sitting on the sofa, arms round the kids watching *Nickelodeon*, trying to shut out the noise of her mum fussing round in the kitchen.

She realised the dress she was wearing – her only black one – was a bit too sexy when the undertaker started peering down her front even as he was asking if they were ready to come to the church now.

'OK,' said Tyra, gathered her mum and the kids and got into the back of the hearse, feeling weirdly disconnected from everything.

Felt weird for starters sitting in this huge great car just to travel a hundred yards round the corner. As soon as they got close she could see it was going to be a circus. There were people milling around all over James Street. There were police, photographers, even a TV crew, plus a bunch of Kenny Ibadulla's Nation of Islam boys stood around in their bow ties.

'Mum,' said Tyra, 'did you know about this?'

Her mum, Celeste, didn't say anything. Tyra turned round to look at her and, to her amazement, saw tears streaming down her face. She didn't think she'd ever seen her mum cry before. Not even when Tyra came back from Bristol all those years ago. Just shouted at her then for bringing shame on the family. But she was crying all right now and Tyra couldn't believe it. In fact it made her bloody furious. Her mum had never had a nice word to say about her dad her whole bloody life growing up, not one nice word, and now here she was sobbing her heart out before they even made it to the church.

Then the car pulled up outside the church and the undertaker came round to open the door and Tyra stepped out and it was pure craziness, flashes going off, TV cameras coming up close like it was the Queen bloody Mother had died and not Charlie Unger who everyone cared about so much they'd left him there to rot for a bloody week. Her included, her the worst of the lot, but then it wasn't her making a big bloody pantomime out of his funeral. Hypocrites, stinking bloody hypocrites.

The service passed in a blur. Few old boys got up to say a few words; reverend who can't have seen Charlie in church in thirty years got up to say the usual shit. Big George got up and made a bloody political speech about the development, had people muttering shame well before he finished. They'd asked Tyra to say a few words, and she'd said no thanks, but suddenly she couldn't stand it and, just as George finished, and the reverend was about to announce the final hymn, she got up and walked to the front of the church, whole place suddenly buzzing with whispers.

'Look,' she said, 'it's nice of you all to come but who are we kidding? We didn't look after Charlie when he was alive and it's too late now. So let's just say goodbye to him and get out of here.' Then she almost ran back to her pew, the sobs welling up in her throat, determined not to cry in front of these vultures.

It was only walking out of the church, following the rev, the kids next to her, that she started to notice some of the people who'd shown up. Gave her a start to see some of them: Bobby Ranger, Kenny Ibadulla, for fuck's sake. Still didn't prepare her for the shock of seeing him, right at the back, like he was trying to hide behind a pillar. Mazz. Bloody Mazz, large as life and twice as pale. She knew it was nothing to do with seeing him, just the whole occasion, but she almost fainted on the spot. Felt her legs start to go but somehow caught herself. Willed herself out of the building and into the waiting car. Christ, you try to bury a man and there's no one there but ghosts.

Afterwards the car went to the cemetery and some words were said and someone pressed the little button that commended Charlie's body to the incinerator and Tyra stood outside in the spring sunshine feeling utterly numb, her mum next to her sobbing continuously. All the old aunties and church women came up to Celeste then and hugged her but it was like Tyra had a force field around her. People smiled nervously towards her, mumbled about how sorry they were and what a lovely man Charlie had been – not that most of them would have let him into their houses state he'd been in this last ten years, but still. And it was like she was just floating up above it all, watching.

'Will you be wanting the car to take you to the wake?' The undertaker's voice startled her. All of a sudden she realised it was just her, her mum and the kids standing there.

'Wake?' she said, turning to her mum. 'You know anything about a wake?'

'Course there's a wake, what's the matter with you, girl? Mr Ibadulla kindly offered to have it.'

'Mr Ibadulla, Mum? When did you start calling Kenny Mr Ibadulla?'

'Never you mind how I speak, girl. Now, we getting in the car?'

Tyra nodded and sat back in the hearse, her head spinning. Hell did Kenny Ibadulla care for Charlie, these last years, or for her come to that? Less than a year ago he'd been threatening to take her TV away over some poxy little loan. Money she owed while Tony was in prison the last time.

Tony. All of a sudden the tears came. Tears for Tony. Took her dad's funeral to cry for Tony. And he wasn't even dead. Just gone. Gone to Spain, she'd heard. Looking for his mum. And why had he gone? 'Cause she'd kicked him out. The father of her kids. Christ knows, she'd had her reasons but right now she missed him. Oh God, she missed him. What she wouldn't give to have him there now, his arms round her, taking her home. She had the kids, of course, had her arms round them now, even as she was crying. Poor little things, their mum going to pieces in front of their eyes. And that was it. She was tired of being strong for everyone else. Why couldn't anyone ever have been strong for her?

Mazz didn't go straight to the wake. He'd bumped into Col, coming out of the church, and been amazed how pleased they were to see each other. So they went over the Baltimore for a quick one before heading up the road to the do.

'So what's happening, bra?' said Col once they were sat in the corner with a couple of pints of Guinness.

'Same old, same old,' said Mazz.

'Still in the music business, yeah?'

'Yeah,' said Mazz, 'twenty years' hard guitar-playing served.'

'You're not playing in the thing tonight then?'

'What thing?'

'The Assembly concert. Just in the bay by here. Didn't you see the security? Serious business, bra. Shirley Bassey, Tom Jones, all of them, and some of them rock boys, Stereophonics and that, I expect.'

'No,' said Mazz, 'didn't know a thing about it.'

'Charlotte Church, that little girl, you know sings opera.'

'Jesus.'

'Nah, man, she's lovely. Her dad used to play in bands, you know.'

Mazz shook his head. 'Dunno. How about you, you still playing?'

'Yeah, well little bit. Was playing with this little girl-band thing Mikey put together. You remember Mikey?'

Mazz shook his head again, feeling jaded and out of touch. He picked up his pint, took a good long pull on it. 'You see much of Charlie then, these last few years?'

Col went quiet. 'Yeah, well, now and again, like,' he said eventually. 'It wasn't good, Mazz, way he went.'

'No, I heard.'

'Yeah, well. Thing about Charlie, you asking me, is he was always someone. He was a boxer, he was a musician. All the way up to our band, like, he always had something going, had a bit of respect. After that, though, y'know, what happened, well he wasn't the same really. Just another old geezer goes down the bookie's, goes down the pub, chopsing on about the old days. Young brers now they didn't know who he was, didn't give a fuck either. Y'know what I'm saying?'

Mazz nodded. 'None of us getting younger.'

'That's the truth, bra,' laughed Col, his hand going instinctively to his greying locks. 'But with Charlie, it was like he was shrinking.'

They sat there is silence for a while, both contemplating the abyss, then Mazz shook himself, lit up a fag and said, 'You ever see anything of Emyr?'

Col laughed. 'Ed, not since long time. Year or so after the band maybe, he'd come by, have a little smoke and a chat, but then he got into his rock'n'roll thing and . . . Nah, how's he doing these days?'

'What, you haven't heard?'

'Heard what?'

'Christ,' said Mazz, shaking his head, and launched into the whole strange tale of how Emyr, onetime drummer in the Wurriyas, had over the years transformed himself into an indie icon and now a rock'n'roll lost boy. After the band had split Emyr and Mazz had both headed up to London and tried to work together, but too much bad feeling remained and they went their different ways. Couple of years later Mazz had been stunned to see a picture of Emyr in the *NME*, no longer a drummer but a guitar player in some post-Smiths bunch of indie miserabilists. The band had been nothing much, far as Mazz could see, but Emyr with his blond hair grown and his puppy fat gone was an undeniable icon. His celebrity started outstripping the rest of the band; you'd see him modelling clothes in the *Face* or on the front of Japanese teen magazines, always with that look like he wasn't really there. Mazz just assumed it was 'cause he was still as stoned as ever, but sixteen-year-old Goth girls the world over seemed to see it as a sign of spiritual depth. Eventually he moved to Berlin and started making solo albums – Nick Cave without the sense of humour you asked Mazz – but still the Goth girls lapped it up.

And then he disappeared. Walked out of a sound check in Utrecht one day saying he was going to get a packet of fags and never came back. Made the cover of the *NME* three weeks running. People said he'd committed suicide, lot of stories about a blond man seen walking to the end of the pier in the Hague. Claims on the net that he'd ODed in his hotel room and the record company had hidden his body to create a mystery. Meanwhile there were sightings of him everywhere from Barry Island to Bali.

'Emyr?' said Col, looking utterly bewildered as Mazz wound up the tale. 'What d'you reckon happened, then?'

'Christ knows.'

'I saw him,' Col said suddenly.

'What?' said Mazz, stunned. 'Recently?'

'No,' said Col, 'couple of years ago easy. I'm down by Mount Stuart Square, having a little drink, just standing on the pavement outside the Ship, talking to a couple of little girls, like, and you can see there's a band playing at the Coal Exchange, couple of trucks unloading gear and that, and there's this blond feller, thin, wearing the whole black-leather thing. Thought to myself he reminded me of Emyr. Might have gone over to check him out that fat fuck hadn't been there.'

'Which fat fuck?'

'Flaherty. Jason fucking Flaherty.'

'Oh,' said Mazz, laughing, 'that fat fuck.'

Col stood up. 'Let's go to the wake, boss. Have one on Charlie.'

The wake was being held in Black Caesar's, Kenny Ibadulla's club in West Bute Street. There was a Nation of Islam mosque and storefront downstairs, window full of pictures of Louis Farrakhan and Muhammad Ali, while the other two floors of the building were firmly devoted to Mammon. The contradiction summed up Kenny Ibadulla perfectly. He wasn't a gangster with a heart of gold, but he was a gangster with a philosophy of life. And that philosophy was simple enough: it's a jungle out there and if a black man wants to prosper in the jungle he'd better work hard, not sample his own product, and carry a damn big stick.

Which was pretty much the opposite of the way Charlie Unger had lived his life, so what the hell Kenny was doing hosting the wake was something Charlie's daughter Tyra found hard to figure out.

And being a direct kind of girl herself, it was the first thing she said when she walked into the club and found it rammed with everyone she'd ever met in her life, drinking Kenny's booze and eating rice and peas and patties and chicken on paper plates.

'What you doing this for, Ken?' she asked, right up in his face.

'Easy now, sister,' said Kenny, his palms raised to pacify her. 'Just showing a little respect. Your dad was one of the guys, you know, back in the day.'

'Don't bullshit me, Kenny,' said Tyra. 'Last few years you wouldn't have crossed the road to piss on him. None of you would,' raising her voice now, waving her arm to indicate the crowd around them.

'Hey, sister,' said Kenny, his voice sounding genuinely sympathetic. 'We all' – and he held her eyes with his as he said *all* – 'know what happened to Charlie the last few years. But that don't mean we forget how he used to be.' He put his hand on Tyra's shoulder then and she felt ashamed. Felt like all she was thinking about was herself, forgetting about her dad.

'All right, Ken,' she said, 'and thanks.'

A little while later Tyra found herself in the middle of the packed club, completely alone. Her mum was still playing the role of chief mourner surrounded by all the old-timers, bursting into sobs at regular intervals and – if you asked Tyra – having the time of her life. These were probably the happiest moments she'd ever had with Charlie, least in Tyra's memory. The kids were running around with their friends, stuffing their faces with crisps, and Tyra was standing alone, an untouched glass of white wine in her hand, scanning the room for any sign of Col.

Unable to see him anywhere, she walked over to the bar to change her wine for a glass of water. Lloyd was there, pouring out a couple of bottles of wine into glasses, started saying how sorry he was and all that. Tyra waved his condolences away.

'Must be costing Kenny a fortune, this,' she said, as he dug out a warm bottle of Perrier from a dusty shelf.

'Yeah, well,' said Lloyd, 'it's not Kenny paying for it, is it.'

'What?' said Tyra.

'Nah,' said Lloyd, 'I'd have thought you knew. It's this developer guy, you know paid for the church and that and he's paying for this and all. Knew Charlie from the old days, I suppose.'

Tyra shook her head. 'He got a name, this developer?'

'Yeah,' said Lloyd. 'Flaherty, they call him, Jason, big feller.'

'Oh,' said Tyra, 'right, thanks,' and turned back towards the room, feeling more confused than ever. Jason Flaherty. She couldn't figure it at all. Far as she knew, last time Charlie had seen Flaherty was the same as her, the day the Wurriyas split up.

Just then she spotted Col over by the entrance and she was three-quarters of the way across the room towards him before she noticed who he was with, and by then Col had seen her and it was too late.

'All right, girl,' said Col, folding her in a hug. Then he stepped back and said, 'Look what the cat dragged in.'

'Mazz,' said Tyra.

'Yeah,' said Mazz, and they stood there for a couple of seconds in silence.

'Well fucking hell,' said Mazz then and he stepped towards her and hugged her too, quickly but firmly.

What was the matter with her? It was all Tyra could do not to grind up against him. Up against Mazz after what he'd done to her and all these years gone by. Your mind's saying fine, say hello, he was a friend of your dad's after all, it's nice he's here, now say goodbye and walk away, any luck you won't see him again for another eighteen years. Eighteen years . . . she'd had the baby, he'd be in college now – she knew it was a he, they'd told her after the abortion. All right then, really what her mind was saying was screw you for what you did. But her body was singing a different tune.

She was proud of herself how she coped, though. 'Good of you to come,' she said, cold as you like, 'Charlie would have appreciated it, I'm sure.'

'Yeah, well,' said Mazz, 'I'm sorry I haven't seen him in so long, like.' He paused. 'I loved your dad, you know.'

Tyra softened a little; she couldn't help it. 'Yeah,' she said, 'I know.' Then she saw that Mazz's attention was distracted; he was looking past her at someone. Tyra turned to see who it was.

It was Jason Flaherty, walking through the middle of the room, deep in conversation with Big George, who, by comparison with the behemoth Flaherty had become, looked more like Medium-Large George.

'What's he doing here?' asked Mazz.

'I dunno,' said Tyra, 'Lloyd told me he was paying for all this.' She turned to Col. 'You heard that?'

'Yeah,' said Col, 'I heard that. Dunno if it's true but it's what I hears people saying.'

'What,' said Mazz, 'old Jase got religion, has he?'

'No,' said Col, 'not what I heard. He's made a lot of money, mind. Lot of the new stuff you sees down the bay, those are Flaherty sites. But I ain't heard he's doing a lot for charity, like. He seen a lot of your old man these last few years, has he?'

'No,' said Tyra. 'I don't know what the fuck's going on. I'll go and ask him.' And with that she walked off towards Jason Flaherty who was by now settled at the bar, book-ended by the only slightly less imposing figures of Big George and Kenny Ibadulla.

Mazz and Col watched Tyra go, Mazz happy to see she still walked as upright and purposeful as he remembered, back then when he used to think of her as his girl. He watched her go right into Jason's face, saw Jason smile then frown then smile again, a big bullshitter's smile that said don't worry, little girl, I'm just a nice friendly old wolf out for your best interests. Saw Tyra shake her head and walk away, heading for the toilets until she was intercepted by Jermaine and Emily.

'Who are the kids?' Mazz asked Col.

'Hers, innit. Hers and Tony's.'

'Christ, she's married.'

'Nah, well he's not around. You ever meet Tony?'

'Don't think so.'

'Docks boy. Used to come to the gigs, like. Tall, skinny guy, Kenny's mate.'

'Oh,' said Mazz, vaguely conjuring up the image of a dangerous-looking guy with shortish dreads. 'He's not around, though?'

'No,' said Col, 'and he's not a name to mention too much these days, specially not around Kenny.'

'And two kids,' said Mazz.

'Yeah, well,' said Col, 'life goes on, you knows what I mean. You goes away for ten years or twenty years or whatever, it don't all stay the same waiting for you to come back, like. You got any kids yourself?'

'No,' said Mazz, 'not as far as I know. How about you?'

'Well,' said Col, 'two that I knows about. A boy from when I was young – he's nearly grown now – and another little one with another girl, live round the corner.'

'Shit,' said Mazz, shaking his head.

'Yeah,' said Col, laughing and lighting up a spliff.

Mazz shared the draw with Col and then Col moved off doing his rounds and Mazz found a space at the bar and leaned there for a while just watching the people and wondering how it might have been if he'd made a life there with Tyra.

Couple of people came by and said hello. Bobby and her girlfriend, then Jason Flaherty. He acted amazed to see Mazz there, but somehow Mazz felt like Jason knew already. Anyway he was friendly and asked Mazz to drop by the office sometime, have some lunch, catch up. Yeah, said Mazz, sure.

He was just about ready to call it a day when another ghost from the past slipped in beside him at the bar.

'Man, how you doing? Listen, I'm sorry about last night. Business, you know.'

It was Lawrence. He looked different, though it took Mazz a minute to figure out what it was. Well, partly he didn't have locks any more, had a little goatee and round glasses, his hair cropped short. But the way that the new look combined with the jaundiced complexion of the heroin aficionado meant that instead of looking mixed race going on black, he now looked mixed race going on white.

'Lawrence, man, what are you drinking?'

'Brandy, man, with a little bit of soda. Don't let them fill up the whole glass, though. No ice neither. So how are you doing, Brer Mazz?'

'Yeah, good,' said Mazz, waving to get the barman's attention and weary of retelling his tale of rock'n'roll woes.

'Good, good. Old Charlie, eh?'

'Yeah,' said Mazz, 'Charlie.' And was about to leave it there but then decided to go on with what seemed to be a ritual exchange: Did you see much of him lately? No. You? No. Shame, eh? So Mazz kicked it off. 'See much of him lately?'

'No,' said Lawrence, right on cue, but then he went on, 'Didn't see much of him, but I did see him lately. Just a couple of weeks ago, as it happens.'

'Yeah?'

'Yeah, it was Charlie, the big man over there, Flaherty, and another guy coming out of the snooker club on Broadway. Late, you know, I was just in the all-night garage over the road, buying some fags, and I saw them come out. Remember thinking old Charlie was starting to look his age. Had a big coat on but he looked cold.'

'Strange,' said Mazz.

'Yeah, what I thought,' said Lawrence. 'Flaherty's a big man these days and Charlie, well you know Charlie hadn't been too good for a while – not that I'm like, one to talk. Anyway, s'pose I just figured Charlie was after him for a loan or something.'

'Yeah,' said Mazz, 'sounds about right.' And with that they dropped the subject, started on the catch-up questions. Few minutes of that and Lawrence started looking uncomfortable.

'Tell you what, man,' he said. 'You mind if we step outside for a bit? Don't like to be in a room with so many people.'

'Sure,' said Mazz, feeling about ready to head off anyway.

Outside, West Bute Street was alive with people. Which was strange as usually by this time, seven or so, of an evening the commercial part of the docks was generally as dead as anything. Instead it was full of people walking purposefully towards the bay.

'Ah shit, man,' said Lawrence, 'it's this Assembly business.'

'Oh yeah,' said Mazz. 'You want to check it out?'

Lawrence shrugged and they started to walk down towards James Street. Lawrence pulled a spliff out of his pocket and lit it up and they passed it back and forth in companionable silence till they reached the edge of what turned out to be a huge crowd assembled in the bay.

There were two stages and a giant TV screen set up in the vacant lot where Lawrence told Mazz they were meant to be putting the Assembly building. In front of the bigger stage there must have been a good thirty thousand people. And there on the stage – you had to see it to believe it – was Shirley Bassey wearing a dress that appeared to be made out of the Welsh flag.

Don't know which one of them started laughing first, Mazz or Lawrence, but after a moment they were both in hysterics, holding on to each other to keep from falling over. Then they started to notice the dirty looks they were getting from all the born-again Welsh patriots around them and that just made things worse. Finally Shirley stopped singing and swept offstage just in time to save Mazz and Lawrence from a good kicking from a bunch of rugby boys.

Mazz inclined his head back away from the crowd and Lawrence nodded and a couple of minutes later they were sat in the Packet still shaking with laughter.

Inside, surreally enough, the shebang was on the TV and there were a good twenty or so people clustered around it watching, even though they could be seeing it for real simply by walking out the door.

The next couple of hours Mazz just couldn't stop laughing, watching this absurdist panoply of Welsh cultural life unfolding in front of him. Tom Jones of course. Well, at least big Tom knows he's funny these days. But still, 'The Green, Green Grass of Home' – if the sight of Wales welcoming the brave new world to the sound of 'Green, Green Grass' didn't make you laugh, your kitsch bullshit detector had to be well out of order. And the rest of the stuff – well, it was hard to choose between the ghastly reading of *Under Milk Wood* by some terrible old ham and the bunch of, ahem, hip Welsh actors making complete tits of themselves doing some kind of rock poetry, until the outright winner came along in the shape of the bloke with the big hair from the Alarm doing some kind of cod folk song with a male-voice choir backing him. And then came the grand finale, the whole bloody lot of them singing 'Every day I Thank the Lord I'm Welsh', which Mazz had kind of assumed was meant to be funny more or less but was here being done in deadly earnest.

'Fuckin' hell, butt,' said Mazz once he'd recovered himself. 'Glad to be Welsh then?'

'*Was ist das?*' said Lawrence in a dumb German accent and Mazz started laughing again.

'Christ,' he said eventually, 'great to know you've got a culture boils down to one famous play, two sixties cabaret stars, a male-voice choir and a twelve-year-old opera singer, innit?'

'Should have got the Wurriyas back together again for it, mate. Legends of Welsh ska, you could have done "Cwm Rhondda".'

Mazz made to punch Lawrence who ducked then came up frowning.

'Hey,' he said. 'That's who that guy was.'

'Which guy?'

'The other guy. You know I told you I saw Charlie with Flaherty and another guy? Now I remember who the other guy was. It's just he looked different, but it was that guy from your band.'

'Which guy?' said Mazz, quickly taking an inventory of who'd been in the Wurriyas – the only guys were him, Charlie, Col and Emyr. 'Col?'

'No, the drummer guy.'

'Ed. Can't have been.'

'Why not?'

'He's vanished. It's been all over the papers and that. Missing rock star Emyr.'

'Shit, that's the same Emyr? The missing guy?'

'Yeah, what I said.'

Lawrence frowned, then scratched his head. 'It was him, though, I'm sure. He's got long hair. Really white blond. Looks a bit like that albino guitar-player guy.'

'Johnny Winter.'

'Yeah, yeah. Wearing, like, surfer clothes, you know, those baggy trousers and a Hawaiian shirt, I remember, looked weird in the middle of the night.'

Mazz nodded non-committally. Sounded possible. One thing about Emyr was he had a knack of looking, like Chandler said of Moose Malloy in Mazz's favourite road book, 'about as inconspicuous as a tarantula on a slab of angel cake'. And a Hawaiian shirt on a cold spring night in Splott sounded about right to Mazz. But what would he have been doing with Flaherty and Charlie?

It was late and Tyra was drunk. She was walking down the street, holding her heels in one hand, weaving between the cans and bottles strewn around the place in the aftermath of the Assembly do. Her mum had taken the kids off hours ago, must have sensed what was coming. After she'd talked to Jason Flaherty, who'd just brushed her off with some bullshit about what an inspiration Charlie had been and how it was the least he could do, she'd just thought fuck it, grabbed a bottle of wine and a glass from the bar, sat at a table in the corner and started drinking. It's what her dad would have wanted. Hah!

So she'd been sitting there thinking bad thoughts about everyone in the room, and about Charlie and about herself too, don't worry, when Bobby Ranger came over.

They hadn't had much to do with each other, all the years since the band. Tyra'd gone one way – jobs, husband, children; Bobby'd gone the other way – into the life. She'd been hanging round with the Custom House girls even back then. Tyra'd supposed you were a lesbian you didn't have much choice. Not the kind of lesbian Bob was anyway, wasn't a student lefty like the other lesbians Tyra knew; Bobby was just a little hooligan from Ely. So, yeah, it wasn't surprising Bobby ended up in the life, pimping and that. Tyra didn't know the details but she knew enough.

And Tyra, well, after the first year or two when she'd gone to pieces, she'd done her best to stay on the straight and narrow. Wasn't easy being married to Tony but, whatever he'd done, she'd been straight and she was proud of that and she did her best to keep herself and her children away from the life.

Bobby she'd see once in a while maybe walking into town or at the carnival, but it was a surprise when she came over and sat herself down next to Tyra.

'All right, girl?' she said.

'No, not really,' said Tyra.

'Nah,' said Bobby, 's'pose you wouldn't be.' She paused for a moment. 'Me either, really. I loved your dad, you know.'

'Yeah,' said Tyra, remembering then how close Bobby and Charlie had been in the band. 'Yeah, well he liked you too. In fact,' she said, and where the hell was this coming from, 'I used to think he liked you better than me. Like you were the kind of daughter he wanted.'

Bobby went very quiet, made a kind of choking noise in her throat. Christ, thought Tyra, what's that about? Then it struck her: of course Bobby grew up in a home – or bunch of homes more like. Didn't have a clue who her dad was.

'Sorry,' said Tyra. 'Didn't mean . . .'

'No,' said Bobby, putting her hand on Tyra's knee and squeezing. 'Not your fault. It's just, like, you're right. I used to think, you know, what it would be like if Charlie was my dad. He was the right age and everything . . .' Bobby sniffed hard and straightened up. 'Fuckin' hell, Bob, pull yourself together.'

Then Bobby'd gone and grabbed another bottle of wine and they'd sat there, the two of them getting drunker and drunker, and suddenly Tyra was able to talk about Charlie and funny thing was it was a cliché but it was true talking did make her feel better and after a bit she'd been up and dancing with Bobby. People probably saying all sorts about her blind drunk dancing with Bobby Ranger but fuck 'em. Least Bobby was straight with you.

And after that it had all got a bit blurry and now here she was, no shoes on, walking down James Street with a car slowing down and drawing up just behind her.

She turned round ready to give whatever kerb-crawling slimeball it was a good slagging when she saw it was a police car. Great, bloody great, going to spend the night of her father's funeral banged up drunk in the cells.

Jimmy Fairfax got out of the car, walked over to her and took her gently by the arm.

'You all right, love?' he said.

'Fine,' said Tyra.

'Yeah,' he said, looking at her and smiling, 'I can see that. C'mon, let me give you a lift home.' And he guided Tyra into the passenger seat, Tyra showing the first signs of making a fuss then subsiding.

What happened next she could piece together approximately. She must have fallen asleep on the brief ride home. Then she distinctly recalled inviting Jimmy in. And then what she wasn't too sure. But when she woke up about four in the morning desperate for a pee and a glass of water, she was fully clothed and lying on the sofa so it couldn't have been anything too outrageous.

Christ, though, she felt miserable the next morning. Couldn't believe it. Her dad's funeral and what does she do but get pissed and dance around like an idiot with Bobby Ranger. She called her mum to ask her to bring the kids round. Her mum sounded typically bloody snotty, said they were happy watching the Saturday cartoons and she'd bring them over a bit later. Tyra put the phone down and started crying the way you do over nothing when you're hungover.

Then the bell rang. Tyra walked over and opened the door thinking her mum wasn't so bad after all. But it wasn't her mum and the kids; it was Mazz.

She just stood there staring at him for a moment, her mouth open.

'Can I come in?' he said eventually.

'Yeah,' she said, 'all right.' Then, 'How d'you know where I live?' She knew even as the words left her mouth that this was a stupid question. Nothing was secret in Butetown; ask anyone they'd tell you where she lived. People, the police and that, used to talk about a wall of silence any time there was crime they couldn't solve. Bollocks, the real problem you had round here was too many people chatting at you, all getting it wrong.

'Oh,' said Mazz vaguely, 'Col.'

Tyra led the way into the kitchen and Mazz, looking, she noticed now, no better than she felt, collapsed on a stool by the breakfast bar.

5

THE COTTAGE

1980

A Tuesday lunchtime Mazz was walking through town, just been to Kelly's in the market and picked up a couple more compilation albums looked quite decent, and he was just about to go into the Hayes Island Snack Bar when Kate spotted him.

Minutes later they were sat down, egg sandwich for her, bacon roll for him, and she was doing her best to jerk him about.

First she said the black thing, like she understood his urge to check out some jungle pussy. All he could do not to chuck his tea in her face; only thing that stopped him was he wasn't quite sure who she was being more offensive to – him or Tyra. Anyway she must have noticed that this didn't go down too well 'cause she changed the subject for a bit, asking about the band and that, using this snotty tone like oh yes, your amusing band, course we all know which one of us is going to end up with the money in the bank. But he sat there and listened to it, taking the path of least resistance, then she went back to her favourite subject – obviously smarted like hell seeing Mazz with Tyra.

'Oh,' she said, 'I was talking to Margot. From the SWP, yeah.'

'Mmm,' said Mazz, vaguely.

'Tall girl, spiky hair.'

'Mmm,' said Mazz again, vaguer still.

'Well anyway, we were having a little chat and she was telling me about your girlfriend.'

'Yeah,' said Mazz in a tone of complete disinterest that might have told a more sensitive or less determined soul to drop the subject now.

'Yeah,' said Kate. 'You know she's a lesbian, of course?'

Mazz, to his credit, didn't react at all for a moment, just carried on letting his eyes follow the passers-by. Then he stood, picked up the last of his bacon roll and popped it in his mouth, said 'See you then' to Kate and walked off up the Hayes towards Bridge Street.

Kate's words came back into Mazz's head, though, when he was in bed with Tyra again, Thursday night after the rehearsal. They'd all gone down the Panorama after. Emyr and Col wanted to go over to Monty's next, meet up with a couple of nurses. Tyra said she was tired and Mazz said he'd walk her home. Which he did, but his home not hers. And . . . and it was the same again really. The sex was fine, no complaints there. But afterwards, Christ, she just looked so miserable, and that's when the lesbian thing popped back into Mazz's brain. Was obvious something was bothering her to do with sex anyway. He was wondering whether he should bring it up when she started to talk.

'I'm sorry,' she said.

'What for?' said Mazz, turning towards her and stroking her back, something she accepted for a couple of seconds before rolling away.

'It's just,' she said, faltering, 'it's just afterwards I feel so . . .'

'Guilty?' offered Mazz.

'Yeah, well, I was going to say miserable,' she said, half smiling, 'but guilty, yeah. I suppose that's it. It's like my mother's in the room watching me. You ever feel like that?'

'No,' said Mazz, laughing and shuddering at the same time.

They lay there in silence for a little while, easier now than they had been together. Mazz lit the traditional fag and passed it to Tyra who took it gratefully.

'You had a lot of boyfriends then?' he asked, casually as he could.

'No,' said Tyra, turning to look him straight in the eye, 'a couple, like. Delroy was the longest.'

Mazz stared at her, raised his eyebrows in an interrogative kind of way.

'Six months,' she said, 'something like that.'

'And before him?' Mazz asked, idly now, drifting towards sleep.

'Before that,' said Tyra slowly, 'before that I was going with a girl, like.'

'Oh yeah,' said Mazz, no longer heading for sleep.

'Yeah,' said Tyra, 'Maggie, Mags. We was in school together. She's in the Party. You remember that march? You might have seen her there.'

'Hmmm,' said Mazz non-committally, half wanting to drop the subject utterly, half wanting to know every detail. Part of him, to be honest, wanting to smack her one, like she was making a fool out of him.

'You think about him at all?' said Tyra suddenly.

'Who?' asked Mazz, wondering what the hell she was going to drop on him next.

'Bobby Sands, the feller on hunger strike.'

'Yeah,' said Mazz, surprising himself, 'yeah, I had a dream about him the other night.' It was true; he'd forgotten it but it came back to him now. He'd been in this recording studio and suddenly he'd realised the walls were covered in shit and then it wasn't a recording studio at all, it was Bobby Sands' cell in the H Blocks, and at first he'd thought he was going to throw up but then Bobby Sands was talking to him and he didn't notice the smell any more – good thing about dreams, really, you couldn't smell too much – and Bobby Sands was telling him to be careful what he signed. They'll stick all kinds of pieces of paper in front of you and expect you to sign them but don't, he said. Don't let them take your name away from you, he'd said, and then Mazz had woken up, or maybe the dream had gone some place else, but anyway that was the end of the Bobby Sands bit of the dream.

'Me too,' said Tyra, 'I think about him a lot. Sitting in that cell covered in his own shit, starving himself to death. And all you read in the papers here is how he's just a common criminal. That make sense to you?'

'No,' said Mazz, who never read the front part of the paper much, and then Tyra turned towards him and let him take her in his arms and they said nothing for a bit till Mazz realised she'd gone to sleep. He didn't move for a little while, made sure she was soundly out, then carefully extricated his arm from underneath her head and lay there, not sleeping just staring up at the ceiling, thinking about the future, suddenly filled with a conviction that the Wurriyas were going somewhere.

Mazz woke at six to find Tyra getting dressed. He half-heartedly offered to walk her home but didn't protest when she said she'd be fine. As she left she wrote down a number on a piece of paper. My mum's, she said. Call me tomorrow, maybe we could go out. Great, said Mazz, and was asleep before she was out the front door.

He was having a bath later that morning when the lesbian thing came back into his mind. His first thought was he should be angry about it; she was taking the piss. But really he couldn't get angry about it . . . Came down to it, he couldn't see much difference – old boyfriend, old girlfriend, what did it matter who your girlfriend's exes were – so long as they weren't still seeing them. Thing was, too, and he couldn't explain it really but there it was, it didn't seem like such a big deal, a girl copping off with another girl. Two blokes were at it together, well, that was that, you were a queer any way you looked at it, and, be honest again, Mazz knew you weren't meant to mind and everything but he still didn't feel at all comfortable around queers. Two girls, though, it didn't seem too bad. He didn't mean like he wanted to watch or any of that crap, it just, well – when it came down to it he couldn't take it that seriously he supposed. And, anyway, he hadn't come down to Cardiff for everything to be just the same as the valleys, had he?

Saturday afternoon Mazz called the number Tyra had given him. It rang half a dozen times, then a woman with a strong West Indian accent picked up the phone.

''Scuse me, is Tyra there, please?' said Mazz.

'She's gone out,' said the woman.

'Oh right, thanks,' said Mazz and was about to put the phone down.

'Hold on now,' said the voice. 'They call you Mazz?'

'Yes,' said Mazz.

'Right, well she leave me a message. She wants you to come round at eight o'clock.'

Mazz turned up at the house around ten past eight. This time of a Saturday evening Angelina Street was full of people, all of whom seemed to be staring at him. A couple of teenage rastas on the corner started to say something to him but stopped when they saw him heading purposefully towards Tyra's place. He knocked on the door and immediately saw the front-room curtains twitch and two girls' faces, looked about twelve, peered out at him, giggled, and closed the curtains again. Another thirty seconds or so passed, Mazz sure the whole street was staring at him now, wondering when bailiffs started dressing like that, and then, finally, the door opened.

A tall fortyish woman in an African print dress, the spit of Tyra only a little darker complected, was standing there. She looked Mazz up and down – literally started off looking at his face, let her eyes travel all the way down to the DMs on his feet and then come back up. She didn't bother to look anything but unimpressed, didn't say a word, just turned back into the house and shouted.

'Tyra, girl, someone here for you.' Then she walked off, leaving Mazz still stranded on the doorstep.

Another thirty seconds passed and Mazz was on the point of saying fuck it and going, when Tyra came down the stairs wearing pedal pushers and a white Fred Perry, her hair up and wrapped in a towel and looking like the finest thing Mazz had ever seen. Suddenly, just like that. Up to that point he hadn't really thought too much about how she looked. Well, he wasn't blind, he knew she was a good-looking woman all right, but seeing her then he just thought fucking hell she's beautiful, almost said it out loud which would have been just a bit embarrassing . . .

Tyra saw Mazz standing on the front step and her face darkened instantly. 'Mum,' she yelled, 'what are you doing leaving him standing outside?'

'I don't know, girl,' came the reply, 'who you wants to bring in my house and who you don't.'

Tyra shook her head furiously, grabbed Mazz by the hand and pulled him through the hall and upstairs after her. As they turned the bend in the stairs, the two girls Mazz had seen looking out the window popped out of the front room and peered up at him.

'He your new boyfriend?' said the skinnier one to Tyra.

Tyra sighed. 'Mazz,' she said, 'this is my little sister Corinne and this is her friend Gemma.' The two girls giggled some more and Mazz waved at them. Tyra waited a couple of seconds then said, 'Piss off, you two, I'm getting ready to go out.'

With that she led Mazz into her bedroom. She pulled out a chair for Mazz to sit on, said, 'Sorry about this, I'll just be a sec,' and turned on the hair dryer. Mazz looked around the room. It was spotlessly neat. He checked the bed for any sign of piles of cuddly animals and was relieved to see none. He checked the posters on the walls – Bob Marley, of course, one from the big Rock Against Racism Carnival, an abstract art thing from some exhibition at the museum, Joan Miró, didn't mean much to Mazz. He looked around a little more, spotted a picture on the mantelpiece, a fifties portrait of a young boxer holding up a Lonsdale belt – Charlie in his prime.

Tyra stopped the dryer for a moment. 'Put a record on if you like,' she said.

Mazz stood up and walked over to the music centre, perched on the window ledge. Next to it was a pile of albums. He started flicking through them. Took him aback slightly. Didn't know what he was expecting – a load of reggae and funk records he'd never heard of maybe – but actually she just had a typical girl's record collection – that's typical white girl, he supposed. All present and correct were Fleetwood Mac's *Rumours*, lying there, the disc out of its sleeve and scratched all over, the usual thing; three Elton John albums; Stevie Wonder's *Talking Book*, which he thought he'd put on if nothing better showed up; the first Jam album, felt-tip scrawl on the front, must have got one of them to sign it; Joan Armatrading, the one with 'Love and Affection' – was it, like, compulsory to have that record if you were a girl? – and, yep, there it was, Cat Stevens' *Tea For the Tillerman*. Then he got to a bunch of classical records and he gave up, pulled out the Stevie Wonder, checked he'd got the side which didn't have 'You Are the Sunshine of My Life' on and stuck it on the record player.

Moments later Tyra stopped drying her hair, checked herself in the mirror, then leaned over and kissed Mazz hard and deep as the strains of 'Maybe Your Baby Done Found Somebody New' burbled away in the background.

'Right,' she said, coming up for air one and a half songs later and removing Mazz's hands from under her Fred Perry, 'time we were going out.'

'Mmm,' said Mazz, giving every indication he was quite happy staying in.

Tyra stood up, straightened her clothing. 'No, really, we should have been in the pub half an hour ago.'

'Oh yeah,' said Mazz. 'Where are we going?'

'Oh,' said Tyra, 'didn't I tell you? There's a benefit night for the Party on, over in Roath somewhere. I said we'd meet some of the others in the Cottage before.'

'Oh,' said Mazz, a little less than fully enthusiastic, but still happy enough just to be close to Tyra at the moment.

It took another half hour to get out past Tyra's over-excited little sister and blatantly disapproving mother, who wanted them to get a cab into town, but Tyra thankfully told her not to be stupid, it would be quicker to walk. Which it would have been if they hadn't kept stopping every hundred yards or so to get some serious snogging in.

In the pub they met half a dozen of Tyra's Party comrades sat round a table in the quiet front bar. There was the Indian girl Mazz had seen on the march, a bloke in a leather jacket sitting next to her, a couple of obvious students in matching glasses – looked like the most boring couple on earth – a big jolly-looking girl with tons of frizzy hair, and next to her a small intense-looking girl with cropped bright red hair, looked natural to Mazz.

'Hiya, darling,' said Tyra to the red-headed girl and bent down to kiss her, something in Mazz's experience Tyra generally didn't do. 'Mazz,' she said then, 'meet Maggie.'

Mazz was smiling and sticking his hand out before the information computed. This was Tyra's girlfriend. Ex-girlfriend. Funny thing was, even as he was realising this and ready to be thoroughly fucked off, Maggie was smiling back at him and shaking his hand firmly and his first reaction was he liked her.

An hour or so later they were all in the upstairs room of a pub on City Road. A bloke in full skinhead Harrington and crop was behind the record decks playing a mixture of old ska tunes, early James Brown and a bit of Motown. Mazz went over to have a word, ask him what one of the ska tunes was, and was gratified to find that the bloke, Nicky, had seen the Wurriyas at the University.

'Fucking great, man,' he told him repeatedly and suggested the band should play at the Rock Against Racism thing the Party was organising next month. Mazz said sure, sounded good to him.

Nicky was not the only one there who had seen the Wurriyas. All evening people kept coming up to Mazz telling him how good the band was or asking when they were going to be playing next. In fact he was having a thoroughly good time, showing off, feeling like life was going his way. He could see Tyra was feeling the same; she was mostly off with her crowd of mates but now and again their eyes would meet across the room and she'd give him this smile sent shivers down his spine. Christ, he thought, he was close to losing it over this girl.

Then, just as the night was building up nicely, someone turned the lights on. Literally. No way you could trust Trotskyists to run a proper party. Coming up to midnight on a Saturday night, room full of young people getting stuck in to each other, and what d'you do – bring up the house lights and make a speech. The weird, if not downright creepy, thing was, far as Mazz was concerned, that everyone clapped in what seemed to be genuine enthusiasm when this fortyish bloke, with John Lennon glasses, a high forehead and long hair round the sides and back, stood up and started talking.

'That's Derek,' whispered Tyra, who'd suddenly materialised at Mazz's side.

Derek waffled on for about ten minutes about how, thanks to the Party, the British State was on the point of collapse. The riots in St Paul's showed how the conditions for revolution were ripe – everyone stomped and cheered at this bit – and then he went on to say that next Sunday's hunger-strike support march had been called off – puzzled grunts from the audience – because the hunger strike had been called off! Bobby Sands has won! – cheers from everyone – the British State – now faltering on its last legs – has made historic concessions – he didn't say what they might be but it didn't matter – the whole room was cheering and hugging each other now. Mazz turned to clutch Tyra and was a little put out to find her already gripped in a fierce embrace by Maggie.

Then the music started up again. DJ put on 'The Whip' by the Ethiopians – the number that always stuck in Mazz's mind in the years after as the absolute archetypal ska dance tune – and suddenly everyone was dancing, Tyra and Maggie right in the centre of the floor together.

And Mazz was cool about it. He could give Tyra her space. Maggie seemed like a nice enough person, your regular fiery young Irish lefty. So Mazz headed over to the bar, got himself a pint and a whisky, chatted to a couple of girls came up asking about the band. Cool.

He hardly even understood it himself when forty minutes later, after the do had finished and everyone had hugged everyone else in sight, and Mazz and Tyra were walking back through town heading for his place, he suddenly went for her. What the fuck she think she was doing showing him up like that? Like what? she said, her face cheery enough at first, like he was just playing around. Like, like dancing with your fucking lezzo girlfriend right under my nose. Tyra tried to laugh at this, show him how ridiculous he was being, make it go away. But instead something – the whisky, his bad self – was infuriated by her laughter.

'Fuck's so funny?'

'Nothing,' said Tyra, her face falling now.

'You think it's funny, make me look like a dickhead? Your lefty mates laughing at me 'cause I'm the only one doesn't know what's going on? You think that's funny?'

Tyra just shook her head and picked up her pace. Mazz speeded up too. Caught Tyra by the shoulders, pulled her round to look at him.

'I asked you a question. You think I'm a joke or what?'

Tyra stepped back smartly, disentangling herself from Mazz in the process. Angry now, as well as visibly upset.

'Don't you put your hands on me,' she said. 'And don't give me this shit, you hypocrite. Like, I'm expected to have been a bloody nun but you, every time we go out you're rubbing my face in it, all these stupid girls going "Ooh, Mazz, you haven't phoned; Ooh, Mazz, your guitar playing's really great; ooh, Mazz could you teach me to play guitar." '

She stopped in mid-rant, suddenly overcome, then she stepped back another couple of paces, pointed at him and said, 'I thought you were better than this but you're not. You're just full of shit.' Then her voice broke, she looked around wildly, saw they were outside the castle and, instead of carrying on towards Riverside and Mazz's place, she just ran across Castle Street, not even glancing around to see if there was any traffic heading for St Mary Street and the way home to Butetown.

Mazz stood then, half stunned, half still angry, and watched her go, heading up St Mary Street past a few drunken office types coming out of Bananas. He shrugged his shoulders, straightened his jacket round his shoulders and headed for home. Fucking bitch going into one like that, who did she think he was?

He was on the Taff bridge, stopped for a moment looking down at the water, when his attention was gripped by a couple of dossers sitting down almost underneath the bridge sharing a couple of cans of lager, and for an instant he had a presentiment of himself there in years to come. A total screw-up. And in that same instant he realised that he was screwing up right there and then. And he turned and he ran.

Ran back across the bridge past the Post House Hotel. Ran over Westgate Street and turned right at the Angel, down past the Arms Park till he got to the new burger bar. He turned left there and cut back up to St Mary Street, running slightly slower now, scanning the late-night stragglers as they came out of Les Croupiers and Qui Qui's. He saw her just past the Taurus Steak House, and caught up with her by the monument outside the Central Hotel, just about to head under the railway.

She heard his footsteps first, running footsteps right behind her, and turned fearfully, a girl alone on the streets at night. She started to smile when she saw it was Mazz then almost instantly set her face into a frown.

'Sorry,' he said, 'sorry, sorry, sorry.'

'Yeah,' she said, looking at him hard. 'So you're sorry. I'm going home.' And she turned and walked on under the bridge.

Mazz paused for a moment then ran after her again. 'I said I'm sorry,' he said when he caught up with her once more, on East Canal Wharf now.

'I know,' she said, 'I heard you and I'm going home.' Then she softened a little. 'Listen, we'll talk about it tomorrow, yeah.'

'No,' said Mazz, a new tone creeping into his voice. 'No, please. I'm sorry I was being a dickhead. I was just, just . . . jealous.' It surprised him as the words came out of his mouth. He'd never been jealous before, not so he could remember anyway. It surprised Tyra too, he could see. She had stopped now and was looking at him closely. Still it didn't surprise either of them half as much as what he said next.

'It's 'cause I love you.'

The words just hung there for a few moments. Mazz shook his head, amazed at himself. Tyra whistled, then she moved towards Mazz, touched his face tentatively like she was seeing him for the first time, like she was a blind girl looking to know him by feel.

'You mean it?' she said softly, in a voice apparently devoid of emotion.

'Yeah,' said Mazz, and suddenly Tyra was all over him, and he her.

A little while later Tyra looked around her and then pulled Mazz by the hand towards the railway arches, Mazz wondering what the hell was going on. Most of the arches were bricked or boarded up, a couple had the inevitable car-related activities, but Tyra made for one said City Skates and sported a very badly painted mural of a skateboarder daubed across its doors. Getting close to it, Tyra suddenly ducked down and examined the wall to the side of the arch. Seconds later she removed a loose half brick, felt around behind it and pulled out a key. Mazz started to ask something but Tyra put her finger to his lips and smiled. Moments later they were inside the skateboard shop and Tyra was laying a big roll of plastic down on the floor. Precious few seconds after that she was naked beneath Mazz, pulling him on to her.

Three times they did it before they left the skate shop, and when they left Mazz had a chain of love-bites on the right side of his neck and blood and skin from Tyra's back beneath his fingernails.

For her part, Tyra was pregnant, but they didn't know that till later.

6

TECHNIQUEST

1999

Mazz couldn't stop staring at Tyra. Stood there making the tea wearing a faded old dressing gown, she still just looked great. It's weird seeing people you've slept with twenty years ago, and haven't seen since. On the one hand there's these flashes of intimate memory, skin on skin, all of that; on the other hand there's the here and now and a person you just don't know any more. So close and so far. Even the memories seem hardly more real than dreams or fantasies, things from another lifetime. Which is what it felt like now to Mazz, that time in Cardiff, separated from the present Cardiff by year after year of Camden rehearsal rooms, mid-American Holiday Inns, Transit vans and tour buses, floors in Krakow, pensiones in Italy and those weird French motorway hotels where you don't ever see a living person, just get a key card from a machine, spend the night in a box, about the right size for a battery human.

And Tyra? He didn't know, couldn't guess. Was staying here all this time just as weird as leaving? Growing into kids and husband just as strange as running as fast as you can just to tread water in the music business? Seemed to him she was different, like she was – well, not exactly blacker 'cause that sounded terrible – more docks, he supposed. Like when they met he knew she lived in the docks and that but he supposed he'd seen her as just another student-type serious girl, only a bit more streetwise and that. But now, seeing her in her own house, her kids' toys around the place, and having heard the stories about her man Tony, some gangster who'd fled the country, he could see she'd grown up into a life he didn't really comprehend at all.

Still, you get older you can handle these situations easier. So they sat there both nursing their hangovers and talking about nothing for a few minutes before Mazz decided to broach the reason he'd come. Apart from the chance to feast his eyes on Tyra one more time.

Mazz had been up most of the night. After the pub he'd phoned the Colonel and dragged Lawrence over to the late-night drinker in Penarth. And over the next few hours, aided by drink and the last of Mazz's cocaine, they'd worked Lawrence's alleged sighting of Charlie, Emyr and Jason together into an epic conspiracy theory. Why would Charlie have been seeing Flaherty? Jason wouldn't have given the time of day to Charlie these days. What had Charlie got that Jason wanted? Or was Charlie blackmailing Jason? The Colonel said Jason was getting to be a big man in the city and God knew he must have enough skeletons in his closet. And Emyr – if it was Emyr – something strange had to be going on there.

Mazz woke up on the Colonel's spare bed at nine unable to go back to sleep and filled with a sense of purpose he hadn't felt in . . . years? He was going to dig a little. May not have done much for Charlie while he was alive but the least he could do now was follow this thing up.

He hadn't been so hungover, he'd have tried to introduce the subject sensitively into the conversation. As it was he just blurted it out into the silence as he sat there dipping a digestive in his tea.

'You thing there was anything funny about Charlie's death?'

'Funny!' For a moment Mazz thought Tyra was going to hit the roof. Then she caught herself and stared at him. 'What d'you mean, funny?'

'I dunno,' said Mazz. 'It's just there's a few things seem a bit strange about Charlie's last few weeks. I mean, he wasn't in too good a state these last few years, that's right?'

'Yeah,' she said, and he could see her wondering if she had the energy to have a go at him but instead she just shook her head wearily. 'Not too good at all.'

'Well,' said Mazz, 'you got any idea what he'd been doing with Jason Flaherty lately? Two different people have told me they saw them together the last few weeks.'

Tyra frowned and hesitated, then she said, 'He paid for the funeral too, you know. And the wake. I thought that was weird myself. But so what?'

'I dunno. It's just it seems really kind of odd. And I tell you the strangest thing. Someone told me they saw Charlie, Jason and Emyr together.'

'Emyr the drummer?' Tyra said. 'Isn't he meant to have vanished?'

'Yeah,' said Mazz. 'You knew that already?' He looked at her closely. 'You still interested in music then?'

Tyra smiled – the first time he'd seen her smile. 'Yeah, you know, old stuff mostly. But there was a documentary about him a little while back. I saw that. Couldn't believe it really. Emyr. She smiled again. 'Dark horse that one, wasn't he?'

'Yeah,' said Mazz, 'a dark horse, or a pale horse, more like.'

'Well, that's weird too,' she said, 'but I still don't see . . .'

'Me either,' said Mazz. 'But still I don't know, the way he died and everything, that was all straightforward, wasn't it?'

Tyra frowned. 'I think so. They had an inquest the other day so it must have been all right or the police would have said, I s'pose.'

'You haven't seen it then?'

'What?'

'The autopsy report.'

'No.'

'Might be worth just having a look, you know.'

Tyra shivered at the prospect of reading the details of her father's death and decay. 'Christ,' she said, 'no thanks.'

'Oh sure, sorry.' Mazz fell silent.

Tyra shrugged. 'Tell you what, I'll have a word with the police, find out if there was anything strange about it.'

'Great,' said Mazz, and they both lapsed into silence now. Before either of them could break it there was a knock on the front door.

'Oh Christ,' said Tyra. 'That'll be my mum.'

Mazz considered jumping into a cupboard for a moment but, tired as he was, opted for just staying put. Tyra opened the door and in walked Celeste accompanied by a couple of kids, a boy and a girl, who yelled perfunctory hiyas before disappearing into the front room. Celeste stayed in the hall talking to Tyra, and Mazz thought he might escape unobserved. But just as she was preparing to go Celeste's eyes swivelled right into the kitchen and she caught sight of him. Gave Mazz a look that instantly made him feel nineteen again.

Celeste turned to Tyra. 'What's he doing here?'

'Nothing, Mum,' said Tyra, sounding like a teenager again too. 'He just came for Dad's funeral. Just came round this morning for a cup of coffee.'

'Mmm hmm,' said Celeste and moved towards the door. 'You call me later on, girl,' she ordered as she left.

Mazz and Tyra waited a few seconds then looked at each other and burst out laughing. Both nineteen again and together, just for a moment.

'Oh God,' said Mazz eventually, 'she always liked me, didn't she?' They both cracked up again, but then Mazz could see Tyra's face tighten up, sure he could read what was going on behind her eyes, something along the lines of 'And she was damn right to mistrust you'. He leaned forward and said, 'Sorry.'

It hung there in the air.

'Sorry,' she repeated, 'yeah, sorry . . . Look, Mazz, just leave it, OK? Long time ago. Different people, you know what I'm saying?'

She stood up, made it clear it was time for him to go. At the door she said. 'Thanks for coming round. Give me your number and I'll let you know about the autopsy. OK?'

Mazz nodded, smiled weakly, scribbled the Colonel's number on the back of a bus ticket and headed off towards the bay.

Monday morning and Tyra had pulled herself together. All weekend she'd been weepy as hell. Just anything would set her off. The kids, the telly, her book, some blind lady walking down the street. Kids didn't seem to notice much, thank God; you worry you're going to disturb them or something but mostly they don't pay any attention. One time Emily saw her in the living-room sobbing in front of the afternoon film, she was sweet as anything, came up and said, 'You sad about Charlie dying?' – everyone called him Charlie, even his grandkids – and when Tyra nodded she just hugged her and said, 'Don't worry, Mum, he's in heaven now.'

Which must have been her own mum's influence – the heaven bit not the Charlie bit.

Anyway it was Monday now and the kids were off at school and she was feeling, well, not great but better. And she'd been thinking about what Mazz had said about Charlie and Jason. Well, she was sure it was nothing but it didn't hurt checking it out a bit, did it? Yeah, well, she knew it was her own guilt really and to be honest she wasn't sure if it would make her feel better or worse if he had been murdered. Murdered? What the hell was she talking about?

So she'd called Jimmy Fairfax. And maybe that's what it was all about, maybe she was just after Jimmy Fairfax. Way she was feeling at the moment, sobbing one moment, horny as hell the next, she didn't trust herself an inch. So, yeah, so she'd spoken to Jimmy and he was nice enough, but sounded like he was in a bit of a hurry. Told her to come down the station at twelve, they'd have a chat.

He was waiting for her by the desk when she came in.

'All right,' he said, 'nice day out there so I'm told.' He turned and winked at the chubby blonde on the phones. 'Fancy a little walk?'

Tyra nodded and they crossed the road and headed down towards Techniquest.

'Uh, the other night . . .' Tyra started.

'Don't worry,' said Jimmy. 'Got your key in the door, over to the sofa and out like a light.'

'Yeah?' she said.

'No, not really. You had me on the go all night long.'

Tyra looked at him, speechless for a second, then he started laughing and she said, 'Bastard.'

'Yeah, sorry,' said Jimmy, not looking a bit sorry, 'couldn't resist it. Still, like I said before, sorry about your dad.'

'Yeah,' said Tyra, 'so the inquest or whatever – all right, was it?'

'Well, no big surprises, like. Be honest, someone's been dead a week like that, there's not a hell of a lot you can be sure about.'

Tyra swallowed.

'Sorry,' said Jimmy, 'but you did ask. You sure you want to hear any more?'

Tyra nodded.

'All right, well there were a few little things. There was a certain amount of bruising on his arms and body, but it's impossible to say how long before he died it was inflicted and, be honest, the way Charlie was the last . . .'

'Few years, yeah. Could have happened any time.'

'Yeah, well, sorry again, but that's the truth. Other funny thing is – and, look, again I'm sorry – did you know your dad to take much cocaine?'

'Cocaine? Hardly. His pension barely covered the Special Brew.'

'Yeah, that's what I thought, but the doc reckoned he'd taken a good bit shortly before he died.'

Tyra frowned. 'Doesn't make sense, that.'

Jimmy shrugged. 'Someone must have given him some, I suppose.'

They walked on together in silence for a while past Techniquest and the Sports Café till they came to the edge of the bay itself, still a gigantic rather ghostly mud-bath waiting for the barrage to come into operation and turn it into a bustling marina. Tyra pondered who might have given her dad some coke before he died. Far as she knew, he mostly just hung around with a bunch of fellow deadbeats doing the pub, bookie's, Spar shuffle. Then a thought hit her.

'You hear anything about Charlie hanging round with Jason Flaherty at all?'

Jimmy didn't answer the question, just fired one straight back. 'Where d'you hear that?'

'Oh I dunno, couple of people said they'd seen them together. And Jason paid for the funeral.'

'Yeah?' said Jimmy. 'Did he?' And his brow creased. Then he smiled. 'Course, Jason' – not Flaherty, she noticed, Jason – 'used to manage Charlie's band, that ska band, the Wurriyas, you remember?'

'Course I remember,' said Tyra, 'I was in it.'

'Christ, you were and all.' Jimmy turned round to stare at her. 'Course you were. It's just like . . . You ever think we were different people when we were younger?'

Tyra couldn't help laughing. 'You certainly were, Fairfax.'

'Yeah,' said Jimmy, smiling, 'that's what I was remembering. Went to see your band once down the Top Rank, whole bunch of us City boys went down, 'cause you had Bobby in the band, like. And a load of Bristol Rovers came over, terrible ruck.' He shook his head. 'And now look at me.'

Tyra smiled too, thinking of herself back then: short skirts, black tights and DMs, hair tied up in a polka-dot bow. And Mazz. She shook her head, trying to banish the thoughts of the old days. She couldn't believe seeing Mazz the other morning had been such a non-event. There he'd been in her kitchen and she wasn't angry, wasn't happy, wasn't anything. Same for him, far as she could see, and yet back then it had been wild, way she remembered it. Times she'd been out of control. And now nothing. That was passion for you, she supposed. And time.

Didn't know how long she'd drifted off on this train of thought but suddenly she was startled by Jimmy coughing.

'Look,' he said, 'got to get back to the station now. And sorry not to be more help, like, but anything I can do, yeah, just let me know.'

'Yeah,' said Tyra, 'thanks,' and smiled at Jimmy but didn't follow him back to James Street. Instead she stood there a while longer looking out at the bay wondering what to make of what Jimmy had told her. Three strange things. Charlie got beaten up before he died, Charlie took some cocaine before he died, Charlie met up with Jason Flaherty before he died. Any of them could be explained easily enough, but all three together? Maybe Mazz had a point; maybe there was something going on.

Later that evening Tyra was sitting at home, trying to take it easy. She'd got her feet up, the kids in bed, glass of wine in her hand watching *Who Wants to be a Millionaire?*. She was just up to thirty-two grand and was wondering whether to phone a friend to find out which American state somewhere called Cape Cod was in when someone came knocking on her back door.

She opened the door and there was Bobby Ranger standing there, gap-toothed grin in place, but a definite urgency about her stance.

'Hiya,' said Tyra. 'C'mon in.'

Inside she offered Bobby a glass of wine.

Bobby shook her head. 'Got some pop or something that'd be nice, though.'

Tyra went to fetch a glass of Coke from the fridge and when she came back Bobby was sat there in front of the TV shouting, 'Massachusetts, you silly cunt, Massachusetts.'

'Yeah,' said Tyra, 'you sure?'

'Course I'm sure,' said Bobby. 'Where the President and that goes for their holidays, Cape Cod.'

'Oh,' said Tyra and sat back in her chair with her drink.

They stayed there till the show finished, Tyra not saying anything much at all, Bobby calling out the answers, getting them right three times out of four, the fourth generally being very confidently wrong.

Tyra was sitting there watching Bobby, wondering why she was here. 'Bob,' she said when the credits started rolling and she'd turned down the sound with the remote, 'something I can do for you?'

'Nah,' said Bobby. 'Well, I was just wondering, like, if you've been through Charlie's flat yet.'

Tyra stared at her, perplexed. 'How d'you mean?'

'Through his things, like.'

Tyra was on the point of saying what's it got to do with you, but her curiosity got the better of her. 'Why? He got something of yours?'

'No,' said Bobby, 'it's not that. You haven't heard the rumours, then?'

'Rumours?'

'Yeah, that Charlie had something stashed away. Lot of the old-timers – Charlie's mates – been talking about it. Apparently Charlie was going on about it before, before he died, like, how he had this stuff stashed away. Being very mysterious about it, what it was exactly. No one thought much about it at the time, like, but now he's dead people are talking. Probably making it up as they go along, you know. But I'd tell you.'

Tyra frowned. 'First I've heard of it,' she said. 'Be honest with you, I've been putting it off, like, going round there. Seeing his stuff . . . And knowing he was lying there all that time . . .'

'Course,' said Bobby, 'course. I'll come round with you if you like.'

'Yeah?'

'Yeah, no problem. Do it tomorrow, yeah?'

Tyra nodded. It was agreed. Bobby stayed a little while longer then said she had to go pick her girl up from work. Tyra said all right she'd see her tomorrow then. Who was she to judge?

Mazz had spent a shitty night on Lawrence's sofa, after a long night out at the Oak, listening to Big Mo sing the blues. Eventually, around eight, he'd had enough, got off the couch, put his jeans on, rinsed his mouth out under the tap and headed out.

Walking into town, he clocked for the first time just how much the new rugby stadium was dominating the skyline, changing it radically from the cityscape he remembered. He shook his head, feeling like everything he knew and had hoped for in this city was long gone, while other people's dreams, the grand development dreams of the Jason Flahertys, carried on apace.

As if looking for reassurance that not everything had changed, his feet led him into the old Victorian covered market in town, past the fishmonger and through the ranks of haberdashers and cheese sellers, watch repairers and sweetshops and then up to the gallery and the cheapest greasiest breakfast left in captivity.

Sitting there over successive cups of sweet stewed tea, Mazz reviewed his options. He could go back to London. His stuff, what there was of it, was there, if Susie, his ex, hadn't thrown it out on the street yet. Probably she'd let him stay for a couple of weeks while he found another gig. Worst case he could eat humble pie and get back with the fat Yank. Or he could get a few guys together and call them the Wurriyas, go off and play the American ska circuit. Word was there was plenty of work to be had out there, specially since 'Lick Her Down' had been stuck on some *20 Ska Greats* CD lately. But that just felt too depressing. In fact all of option one sounded too damn depressing.

Option two then. Stay in Cardiff. And do what? Run some half-arsed investigation into why Charlie died. Uh huh, and for whose benefit would that be? Certainly not Charlie's. Charlie was dead. For Tyra then. He didn't want to go there at all. But . . . but, but, but. He did want to know what had happened. What had happened to Charlie, what had happened to Emyr.

Face it, he thought, mournfully eyeing the world from behind the remains of a bacon roll, he wanted to know what had happened to himself, brought him to this stage in his life with so little to anchor him to the world. And unbidden he found himself humming the theme to *Whatever Happened to the Likely Lads?*.

He smiled and stood up. Decision made. He was going to hang about. Next question: where to start? Didn't take long to figure that out. There was one man seemed to be most involved in whatever it was that was going on, and that same man was the one person Mazz knew in Cardiff who might have some work for him. His old mate and manager Jason Flaherty.

Bobby came round about twelve. Tyra asked it she wanted a drink but Bob shook her head and said why didn't they get on with it, which was nice of her – she could probably see how nervous Tyra was. Stupid, really, it was only a couple of hundred yards and she must have walked them about a billion times but today she was dreading every inch of it.

Charlie's flat was on James Street just above a newsagent's. Horrible flat at the best of times. She'd hardly ever been there; too depressing to see how far her dad had fallen. There was a street door next to the shop and Charlie's flat was on the first floor. She dug out the keys he'd given her, years ago when he first moved in there, and opened the door. The light wasn't working inside so she picked her way up the filthy stairs, round the bend and on to the first-floor landing. No light here either and Tyra fumbled about for a minute before she got her key in the lock. She opened the door, turned the light on in the hall with a sigh of relief when it worked, then walked into the front room.

'Oh my God,' she said as she looked around the place.

'Fucking hell,' said Bobby as she pushed in beside her.

The room was trashed. It wasn't like Charlie had been Mr Houseproud or anything but this was different. The ratty old sofa was tipped upside down, the cushions slashed on the floor next to it. The pictures were off the walls, frames smashed; the table he ate on and kept his bills and stuff on was upturned and the papers all over the place; the back was hanging off the TV. His stash of racing form guides were scattered around by the fireplace. God knows what the rest of the chaos was.

Tyra couldn't take it; she just sank to the floor and started sobbing.

'C'mon,' said Bobby, sitting down next to her, putting her arms round her, 'c'mon,' and after a while Tyra's sobs subsided.

She turned to Bobby and said, 'What's going on, Bob?'

Bobby shook her head. 'Dunno, girl.' She frowned then looked up. 'Tell you what, I knows the girls live upstairs. Why don't I go up, have a little word, see if they know anything about it?'

'All right,' said Tyra. 'But, Bob . . . don't be long, yeah? Place is giving me the creeps.'

Bobby went upstairs and Tyra took a deep breath then started exploring the rest of the flat. Same story in the kitchen and the bedroom – totally ransacked. The bathroom even: they'd ripped the top off the toilet, pulled off the cladding round the bath. No getting round it, someone had been searching the place for something.

What? And had they found it? No way of knowing, though she supposed the fact they'd ransacked the whole place, instead of stopping halfway through, suggested that maybe they hadn't. What the hell they could be looking for she couldn't imagine. It beggared belief that Charlie had hold of anything worth having. Anything Charlie'd had had been sold off years ago. Records, boxing mementoes, you name it. Still, you didn't go to these kind of lengths to find someone's last bottle of White Lightning. Maybe he had had that winning lottery ticket after all. She almost laughed then stopped herself, realising how close she was to total hysteria.

'Bobby,' she called, walking out on to the landing. 'Bobby!'

'Just coming, doll,' shouted Bobby from the floor above, and Tyra went back into the living-room and started aimlessly tidying things up, drop-in-the-ocean time, till Bobby reappeared.

'Say they don't know nothing about the break-in,' said Bob, 'but I dunno. Pair of lying fucking slags, you ask me. One thing they did say, though, was the landlord wouldn't be pleased. And you know who he is?'

'Who?' said Tyra.

'Nichols, Vernon Nichols,' said Bobby. 'You know him?'

'Know the name,' said Tyra. She'd known it most of her life, in fact. These days he was some big developer. Any of these big buildings – the stadium, the Assembly – people'd mention him. But she'd known his name for longer than that.

'Yeah,' she said, 'my dad knew him, something to do with the boxing. He used to be a promoter or something. S'pose that's why Charlie was living her, a favour from some old boxing guy.'

'Mmm,' said Bobby, 'maybe. Though, what I hear, Vernon Nichols doesn't do a lot of favours. Anyway, what're we going to do about all this shit? You think they found anything?'

Tyra looked around helplessly. 'I dunno, Bob. If they did they made a hell of a mess doing it.'

'Yeah, you know where he kept his papers and stuff?'

'On the table by the window.' Tyra pointed at the upturned table and the pile of crap surrounding it. Then a thought stuck her. 'And he had a box he kept a lot of his precious stuff in. His boxing things, old photos . . .'

'What sort of box?'

'Just an old shoebox.'

'Any idea where he kept it?'

'I dunno. In the bedroom, maybe?'

The two women walked into the bedroom and looked around. Tyra gingerly lifted up piles of clothes. Nothing. Then Bobby opened up the cupboard and there it was: an upturned shoebox and a bunch of papers underneath it. Bobby picked them up carefully then went over to the bed and sat down. She started looking through them with an eagerness and care that surprised Tyra.

'What you searching for, Bob?'

Bobby looked up, startled. 'I dunno, nothing really . . . Just, you know, something might explain what's going on here.'

Tyra sat down next to her and had a quick shufti but it was just a bunch of old papers, a building society bank book that hadn't been touched in years, his NHS card, a few boxing certificates. It was all Tyra could do not to start crying at the pathetic sight of it all.

'C'mon,' she said. 'Better go and report this to the police.'

★　　★　　★

Jason's office was on Windsor Terrace, a classy little street just off the city centre, Italian restaurants at one end, lawyers at the other. Jason had a whole building, a discreet brownstone halfway up on the left. The foyer was expensively minimalist, dominated by a hugely blown-up photo of the Cardiff Docklands. Building sites all over the place, and big red circles round many of them. Jason's sites, Mazz supposed.

The receptionist, a good-looking blonde Mazz's age but doing her best not to seem it, took his name and gave him a look that sent him over to examine his reflection in the mirror, while she murmured something into a phone. Unshaven, red-eyed, clothes he'd slept in, probably whiffed a bit you got up close. Probably too you could smell the couple of pints he'd had already this morning waiting for half twelve when Jason had said he could see him. But Mazz knew he still had what it took. Outlaw charisma.

He straightened his hair in the mirror, turned to the receptionist and winked. 'Hard night last night,' he said.

'Oh,' she said, like she could really, really give a shit.

'Yeah,' he said. Then, his attention suddenly caught by a gold disc on the wall behind her, he asked, 'Whose is that?'

The receptionist ignored him. Mazz walked round her and peered at the record himself. It was one of Emyr's albums, a gold disc for Japanese sales presented to JPF Management Services. Mazz scratched his head; he didn't know Jason still managed Emyr.

'Mr Flaherty will see you now,' said the receptionist, sounding surprised and slightly offended at the news. 'Take the lift to the third floor.'

Mazz did as he was told, passed through a secretary's antechamber and found himself in Jason's office, a huge great space equal parts corporate intimidating and lads rec room. There was a dirty great desk with a computer and flat-screen monitor that must have cost a fortune, but Jason wasn't behind it: he was over by the window bending over a pool table.

'Mazz!' he said like it was an amazing surprise to find Mazz standing in his office. 'Coffee, tea? Something stronger?'

'Yeah,' said Mazz, 'OK.'

Jason walked over to the bar in the corner of the room, opened a bottle of Bell's, poured out a large one and handed it to Mazz. Mazz stood there waiting for Jason to pour himself one; when he didn't he shrugged and knocked back a healthy swallow. What did he care if Jason Flaherty thought he was an alky?

'So, Mazz,' said Jason, looking amused like Mazz was some kind of standup comic wheeled into the room for his benefit, 'how's the rock'n'roll game?'

Mazz shrugged, drank off some more of the whisky.

'Like that, yeah?' said Jason. 'Tough business, all right. So what can I do for you, assuming you're not here just to shoot the shit with your old mucker Jason?'

'No,' said Mazz. 'I was thinking of staying back in town, like, for a bit and I was wondering . . .'

'If your old Uncle Jase could sort you out with some work. That it?'

'Yeah, well,' said Mazz, trying to stop himself from shuffling.

'You an architect then?'

'Mazz shook his head.

'A hod carrier, crane operator? Didn't think so. Or did you think maybe I was looking for a forty-year-old guitar player, so's I could turn him into the new Eric Clapton? No? Well, you're right there. Christ.' Jason paused. 'He was in here too a month or so back.'

'Who?' said Mazz.

'Charlie. Came in, asked me if I needed any security. Thought he was trying to shake me down for a minute, which would have been a laugh. Then I realised he seriously thought I was going to hire a sixty-year-old alky to work security for me.'

'So what d'you tell him?'

'Told him to fuck off, of course. Same way I'm going to tell you to fuck off soon as you finish drinking my whisky.'

Mazz stood there immobile wondering what the hell he was supposed to say to that, but then Jason carried on.

''Cept one thing I told him, and I may as well tell you the same thing. I've had one or two people asking me questions about your old band. Asking if you ever thought about getting back together, like.'

'Oh,' said Mazz.

'Yeah, incredible, isn't it? Twenty years on.'

'Yeah,' said Mazz, not laughing, 'Not going to happen now, is it?'

Jason looked at him quizzically, if a man that big can ever look quizzical.

'Charlie's dead, you know. You paid for his bloody funeral.' Whisky before lunchtime; is there anyone it doesn't put in a fighting mood?

'Yeah,' said Jason. 'Poor Charlie, couldn't help feeling a bit guilty in the end there, like. But, be honest with you, Mazz, it's not Charlie you'd need to get the band back together. Feller that would make the difference would be Emyr.'

Mazz looked at Jason disbelievingly. 'Emyr? What the fuck would Emyr want to do that for? Anyway isn't he meant to have topped himself?'

Jason paused. 'You believe that?' he asked finally.

'I dunno,' said Mazz. 'Haven't seen the feller in a long time.'

Jason shrugged then and Mazz could see he was about to be dismissed so he carried on. 'Course you hear stories about people seeing him.'

Jason stared at him. 'Oh yeah? What kind of stories?'

'You know, Emyr playing snooker down on Broadway with a couple of fellers, that kind of thing.'

'Who told you that?' Jason suddenly in Mazz's face, not playing about now.

'Feller I know.' Mazz stayed put, not letting the fear show.

'Yeah, he say anything else, this feller?'

'Said Emyr was carrying a surfboard.'

'A surfboard?'

'Yeah,' said Mazz. 'Mad, innit?'

'Don't suppose he said who else was there, this, uh, feller?'

'Yeah,' said Mazz, 'he said Charlie was there' – Mazz paused, savouring the moment – 'and a big heavy feller in a suit.'

With one movement Jason had Mazz picked up by the jacket and swung him over to an open window. A slight adjustment and he had half Mazz's body sticking out of the window, his face looking fifty foot down at the concrete below.

'Failed rock star commits suicide by jumping out of manager's office – that the story you want to read in the *Echo*?'

Mazz managed to grunt and shake his head.

'Then quit fucking me around,' said Jason, pulling Mazz back into the room and handing him a fresh glass of whisky.

'So what did you think you were going to do? Blackmail me? That the idea? You think I've got Emyr stashed here in the cupboard, is that it?'

Mazz had his head between his knees and was concentrating on taking deep breaths, keep the panic under control. He knew Jason did things like that. Back in the day they used to laugh about Jason and Kenny pulling those kind of stunts. But when it happened to you, fucking hell. Finally the panic rolled back a little and he raised his head. 'Just thought you might know where he is, like.'

Jason stared at Mazz some more, like he couldn't bring himself to believe that Mazz was as dumb as he was playing. Finally he sighed. 'Charlie didn't call you then?'

'Charlie?'

'Yeah, he didn't call you a few weeks back?'

Mazz shook his head. 'I was on a tour.'

Jason poured himself a glass of whisky, then motioned to Mazz to sit down and plonked himself down behind his desk. 'Fair enough,' he said. ''Fraid I may have been reading this situation all wrong. Best thing is I explain what's been going on. I told you Charlie came to see me, right. Well, you could see he was desperate, right, all this crap about security. No way I could have him working for me, the state he was in. But then, like I said. I told him the same thing I told you, you could get the Wurriyas back together again, there'd be a little bit of money in it. Lot of money maybe if you could get Emyr involved. Now I don't think much of it, just something to say, really, get the poor sad old bastard out of my office. But a couple of weeks later he phones me up, out of the blue, like, and asks me to meet him in the snooker club, over on Broadway. Says there'll be someone there be worth my while to meet. Same again, I don't expect much of it really. Be honest, I thought he'd probably dug you up from somewhere. But last minute I decide to head down there, and there's Emyr, large as life and carrying – your mate's right about that – carrying an effing surfboard.'

'Shit,' said Mazz.

'Yeah. Couldn't believe it. Emyr, who I've had bloody private detectives chasing from here to Bali, 'cause the little twerp walked out on contracts worth a bloody fortune, he has the nerve to come up to me in the Broadway snooker club saying he'd like to do a couple of gigs with the Wurriyas. Benefits for Charlie, like.'

Mazz shook his head, bewildered, not sure whether to believe a word of it. 'So?' he said finally.

'So I told him that's fine. He can fit them in between the German tour and recording the new album and giving about five zillion interviews to the media explaining how come he's not dead.'

'Bet he liked that.'

'Yeah, well,' said Jason, sighing and taking a goodish slug of his whisky, 'didn't smack him one, did I?'

Mazz couldn't help laughing. A minute ago he'd been scared out of his wits and now he was amused by the bloke. That was the thing about Jason; he was like a cartoon character – Taz, the Tasmanian Devil from *Bugs Bunny* sprang to mind – that seemed to operate perfectly well in two dimensions while the rest of us tried to struggle along in three. Mazz couldn't image how Jason dealt with all the corporate shit he must be involved in these days; the bloke was still just a football hooligan at heart. Probably that was the secret of his success, though. Those kinds of guys in suits didn't usually mix with people who'd hang you out the window soon as look at you. 'So, then what?' he asked once he'd recovered himself.

'That's what's weird,' said Jason, 'then nothing. We walk out of the snooker club. Fucking Mr Emyr there says he's got somewhere he has to be and he'll be in touch, walks off into the middle of the night carrying this bloody surfboard. Charlie puts the touch on me for some money, so I bung him fifty quid. And that's the last I see of either of them. Apart from poor old Charlie in his coffin there.'

'And that's all?'

'That's all. I sent this wanker of a detective to check out the surfing places. Wanker spends a week in Newquay on expenses, comes up with nothing.' Jason paused, looked at Mazz carefully. 'Why? You want to have a go?'

'What, finding Emyr?'

'No, finding Lord fucking Lucan.' Jason snorted, dug out his wallet, pulled out a big wad of cash, peeled off ten fifties and gave them to Mazz. 'Here, that'll do you for a week. Just go round the surfer beaches till you find him. You don't find him, don't bother showing up here again or next time I will throw you out the window.'

Mazz took the money, stuffed it in his front pocket, then said, 'Surfer beaches, round here, like?'

'No, in fucking Hawaii. How far d'you think five hundred gets you? Course I mean round here. You been away too long, boy. 'S'what people do down here these days. Surfing. There's some shops in town, they'll tell you where to go.'

Mazz stood there for a moment, trying to think what to ask next.

'Didn't I tell you to go?' said Jason. 'Go on. Fuck off. Now.'

7

THE STOWAWAY

1981

Six weeks later things were starting to move fast. It was the beginning of February 1981 and Bobby Sands had announced that the British government had reneged on its promises and he was going back on hunger strike. Christmas had been and gone. The band had recorded a single, played in London, acquired a manager, and a road manager.

The road manager was a feller called Kenny Ibadulla. Round Christmas the band were playing practically every night – parties, pubs, clubs, Cardiff, Newport, Bristol – and had found themselves all of a sudden with a following. Well, two followings really. There were a load of student types would come and see the gigs in town or at the Uni, and then there were the docks boys. They'd played at Mel's, at the Casa, at the Dowlais, and people started coming out – younger kids in little two-tone outfits like they'd seen the Specials wearing on *Top of the Pops* and older ones too, scary skinhead types like Kenny Ibadulla. Mazz never knew you got black skinheads. Mentioned it to Charlie one time, though, and Charlie set him right: 'The whole thing, man – Crombies, braces, Ben Sherman's – pure rude boy.' Way Charlie told it, back in the late sixties all the black boys were dressing like that. Same time the hippy thing was going on so all the mods they either changed into hippies or the hardcore ones – the working-class ones you like to use that kind of a term – they starts dressing like rude boys, right down to getting their hair cut off, pissing the hippies off like hell. 'Yeah, man,' said Charlie, 'skinheads were a black thing first.'

Whatever the history, the reality was Kenny Ibadulla, hulking twenty-year-old light-skinned black guy just out of prison and the scariest person Mazz had ever met. Also his biggest fan. Kenny loved the Wurriyas and any time there was trouble Kenny would sort it out. Least he would if he wasn't starting it himself.

Plot complicated further when they started playing away; Newport, Bristol. Whole bunch of docks boys would follow the band over there, and you'd better believe they didn't take any shit from any local posses. Made for some scary atmospheres from time to time, specially over Bristol where the boys would bring their football colours and the Rovers boys would feel honour-bound to get stuck in – Cardiff City and Bristol Rovers, they fucking hated each other, from time. So the band started getting a little fearful and Kenny noticed this and offered to take over their security. Which was kind of ironic 'cause without Kenny and his mates they probably wouldn't have needed any security, but there you were. So Kenny came on board as road manager. And, be fair, he did a decent job. Had hidden organisational talents did Kenny.

In fact Mazz and Charlie – who had become the kind of ruling duo in the band – were seriously thinking about getting Kenny to be the band's manager full stop. Way Mazz saw it, what they stood to lose in Kenny's lack of knowledge of the business they'd gain in the sheer force he would lend to the role.

But that was before Jason Flaherty came back on the scene.

Mazz hadn't seen Jason since Venomous fell apart. He'd assumed Jason must have gone up to London, started playing in the big leagues. So it was a bit of a surprise to see him looming out of the darkness one night just after a show at the Newport Stowaway, wearing what looked like a bouncer's tuxedo.

Most people Mazz knew he'd seen them dressed like that he'd have taken the piss. Not Jason Flaherty. Come to think of it, when Mazz had rated Kenny Ibadulla the scariest person he'd ever met he couldn't have been thinking. Kenny was scarier first off, in the sense you could feel his capacity for violence right up near the surface. But with Kenny you knew it could come and go in a flash. Jason Flaherty, though, was a man you just knew you didn't want to piss off, not even once. 'Cause he'd never forget.

Still this time it was all silken glove and no iron fist; Jason picked out Charlie from the start, gave him the spiel. The Wurriyas needed management, needed to make a record, needed to play London. They had to move quick; ska wasn't going to be around for ever. So what plans did they have? Charlie ummed and aahed and Jason just nodded, said he figured as much and why didn't Charlie and Mazz come to his office the next day?

The office was in a warehouse on the edge of Splott where Jason was running a van-hire cum security cum property company, and the second Mazz walked in there he knew they'd committed themselves already; you just didn't say no to Jason. And the next few weeks seemed to be showing that they were right not to. Within days Jason had them in the studio, recording 'Lick Her Down'; within weeks he'd had the tape up to London and got a copy to the Specials' own label, Two-Tone. They got a gig in the Rock Garden and a bunch of record-company people came down. Jason told them all to get lost and put out the single with his own money. Two weeks later they sold ten thousand copies independently, Andy Peebles was playing it on daytime Radio One and the record companies were back and begging.

So everyone was happy with Jason. Even Kenny, whose nose could easily have been put out of joint. But instead, after a little bit of pussyfooting around each other, like two rhinos sizing each other up, Kenny seemed to accept that for the moment Jason was the bigger of the two. And in return for Kenny stepping aside, Jason let him into his other business, the security side in particular. Showed Kenny just how close you could go to running an out-and-out protection racket without getting caught. A couple of jobs they worked together. Persuading a car-breaker's over Tremorfa they needed Flaherty security – that was the one involved Jason taking out an Alsatian with a car jack. Collecting payments round Mount Stuart Square – that was the one Kenny held the guy out of the window just like he'd seen them do in the films. Kenny and Jason – came down to it, they were brothers. Brothers you'd cross the road to avoid. Unless, of course, they were your management team.

But still, far as Mazz could see, the thing about guys like Kenny and Jason was to have them on your side and that was just where they were.

And so there they were, February 1981 in the van on the way up to London. A record company waiting to sign them up and take over production of the single, promising to have them on *TOTP* within the fortnight; gig coming up that night supporting the Beat at the Electric Ballroom. Stuff could probably be going better but Mazz couldn't see how.

Well, not until Tyra told him her news. In a little coffee bar just off Bond Street, Tyra told him she was pregnant and Mazz just whooped for joy.

'Christ,' he said, 'Christ,' after he'd calmed down a bit and stopped leaning over the table to kiss her. 'I've got to tell the others. Does your dad know? This is fantastic.'

Mazz was half out of his chair when Tyra pulled him back. 'Mazz, no. Not yet. We've got to talk about it. You don't just say yeah, yeah, everything's cool, let's have a baby. Not you having it, for starters.'

Mazz quieted down quickly. 'You do want to keep it?' he said.

'Oh Christ. Yes. No. I mean, I don't know.'

Mazz didn't reply, just pulled her to him and sat her down on his knee, tall as she was. 'It's just great,' he said softly, 'just great,' and stroked her back and after a little while she twisted round to face him and smiled and kissed him.

'But please,' she said as she disentangled herself and stood up, 'please don't say a word to the others.'

Mazz just buzzed through the rest of the day. The record-company meeting went great. Well, the guy himself was the usual long-haired public schoolboy with a Mick Jagger mockney accent and dodgy bomber jacket, but the point was he was keen and Jason looked to have him pretty well intimidated. He even squeezed him for thirty grand up front to buy the rights to 'Lick Her Down' and then the guy started throwing around telephone-number-type figures for how much the label might invest in the next five albums. All bullshit probably, but nice to hear all the same.

Load of people from the company came down to the gig after, as did a minibus full of docks boys, which made for an interesting combination hanging round the dressing-room afterwards but helped give the band the confidence to tear into the show like they'd never done before.

'Wouldn't like to be the Beat, coming on after that,' said the record-company guy, Simon, afterwards and then he tapped his nose and inclined his head and Mazz smiled and followed him into the bogs expecting a line of speed but instead making his first acquaintance with Mr Cocaine. And maybe it's getting old but cocaine really was cocaine back then. Marvellous stuff. Mazz was buzzing all the more then. Took all his efforts not to blurt out to everyone, 'I'm going to be a daddy.'

The original plan had been to drive back to Cardiff straight after the gig, the way they usually did, and the band were all getting ready to pack up, and Kenny was carrying the gear, when Jason suddenly told them to relax, take their time, he'd booked a hotel in London for the night.

It was shortly after that that Mazz started to lose it a bit. He went out front with Tyra to have a look at the Beat, half wanting to hate them but instead his good mood winning out and he danced with Tyra to 'Mirror in the Bathroom' and 'Stand Down, Margaret' and held her tight during the crappy fast version of 'Tears of a Clown' and everything was fine and then a bunch of kids came up and started telling them how great the Wurriyas had been and that was fine too except suddenly there were loads of kids around them and Tyra had to pull on Mazz's sleeve, shout in his ear that she had to go backstage again, this was freaking her out.

So Mazz led the way backstage and, just as the security guy was waving them through, Jason was coming in the other direction and said why didn't they come to the upstairs bar, the record company was going to be having a little do there after the show. And so of course that's where they ended up and suddenly it was one in the morning and Mazz had had more than a few drinks – 'cause that's the thing with cocaine, of course: you can drink like crazy; in fact you're almost bound to drink like crazy cause of the speediness and it doesn't affect you, not till the cocaine wears off, which is what it did around one – and Tyra was saying she was exhausted and wanted to go back to the hotel and Emyr and Col said they'd had enough of being there too and Jason said he'd get a taxi and Tyra was saying to Mazz you coming then but all he could think about was he'd just spotted Simon again and probably he could get another line of coke off him and keep the buzz going all night 'cause he hadn't even really had a chance to talk to Charlie yet as the old bugger seemed to have at least three girls around him at all times, or to Bobby who was holding court at the bar telling some geezer from the record company stories that looked to have his eyes popping out, and Mazz didn't want the night to end, so he said you go on back, I won't be long.

In fact it was about five when Mazz made it back and he was drunk and Tyra was awake and more miserable than pissed off. But it wasn't as bad as all that, it wasn't like Mazz had got off with someone else or even tried to; he'd just been enjoying his first bit of the limelight and Tyra could see that and didn't blame him. And in fact now he was back she could sleep and so did he and when they woke in the morning they got it on and were the best of a bunch of tired and hungover but very happy bunnies who got in the van back to Cardiff next morning.

The next few weeks were more of the same, magnified, stretched. Now it was happening, it was incredible how fast things came. Different these days, bands have to be marketed with military precision; back then, you were riding something like the ska train you could go from nowhere to the charts in weeks. And that's how it was for the Wurriyas. After London they played Birmingham, Manchester, Glasgow – where Bobby nearly got beaten up by some bunch of Rangers supporting Nazis, before Jason and Kenny waded in and caused some serious damage to the flute-playing boys. Then came the first TV show, some youth thing on BBC2, shot in Cardiff. A couple of days being interviewed, them serious boys from the music papers coming down to Cardiff on the train. Charlie dominating the show every time – boxing stories, gangster stories, drug stories – Mazz doing his best to chip in with some right-on politics – Bobby Sands – the rest of them hardly saying a word. Picture in the *NME* summed it up – Bobby at the front, of course, being the singer; Mazz looking like he's trying to elbow his way into the limelight but failing; Charlie stage left but catching the eye none the less; Emyr and Col barely visible in a cloud of smoke; and Tyra somehow in the picture but alone.

Years after, Mazz would think it all happened too fast. There was a line from a Mott the Hoople song started haunting him – *I wish I'd never wanted then what I want now, twice as much* – like you'd never tasted a bit of success you wouldn't spend the rest of your adult life craving some more.

Instead it had come down hard and fast, hardly a second to savour it or even experience it as much more than a dream. There was a full month without anything approaching a day off as the song charted at thirty-two, went up to seventeen the next week and got them on *Top of the Pops*. That had been pretty horrendous really – Mazz could be sure of that 'cause his mam's brother who had a video had taped the thing and once in a blue moon when Mazz went home they were sure to drag it out. Bobby standing in the middle looking like a frightened rabbit miming hopelessly, the rest of the band looking stiff apart from Charlie, who was caught in a close-up giving this outrageous wink to one of those dancers they used to pay to go among the audience. Only bit of the video Mazz could watch without wincing. That was the only time they did it. Next week the single went up to nine but it needed to go up again for them to get back on the show and instead it dropped down to eleven. Still the momentum carried on for a bit: they did TV in Germany, Sweden, Holland – all of them in and out in a day, pissing off Col and Emyr who'd been pretty keen to check out Amsterdam. And so it went on for another two or three weeks until at last they were dumped back in Cardiff, sick and exhausted, at the end of March.

As for Tyra and the pregnancy and all, Mazz knew the timing was bad. All the stuff they had to do for the record, there'd hardly been any time to talk. Every night there'd been people to meet: record-company people from Germany, journalists from America, distributors from Scotland. Mazz had been pushing himself hard, thanks be to Simon who was always there with a little of the powdered stuff when he really felt he couldn't get up and do it again, but like he kept saying to Tyra, now's the time, got to push now, might not be a second chance – well God knows he was right there. And he did his best to shield Tyra from the worst of it, made sure she got back to the hotel as early as possible each night, held her tight in the mornings when she was feeling queasy. Let her know he was going to be there for her soon. Once they had a little time.

In fact they had two weeks. It would have been less but the studio Jason wanted them to use to record the album was booked up till then, and Charlie, God bless him, had put his foot down when an alternative venue was mooted, told Jason flat out if he wanted this album to have anything going for it at all, he needed to let the band unwind a little. So. Two weeks.

8

THE PLOUGH AND HARROW

1999

The police station was just up the road, so Tyra popped in on her way home. Asked for Jimmy Fairfax on the desk and a minute later there he was, looking like one of the lads this time in jeans and a Tommy Hilfiger sweatshirt.

'Just knocking off now,' he said. 'Anything urgent?'

'Well sort of,' she said.

Jimmy gave her a smile and said, 'Tell you what, let's have a little walk down the road.'

And so next thing she knew she was sat in the White Hart with Jimmy Fairfax buying her a brandy and a pint for himself and she was checking her watch making sure she had time before picking the kids up from school, which she had.

'So what's up?' said Jimmy once they'd sat down at a table, his leg brushing distinctly close to hers.

'My dad's flat,' she said. And then she started sniffling up and he brought out a hanky – clean, believe it or not – and he wiped her face with it which was definitely getting on the intimate side of things and she pulled herself together then sat back and told him about the flat.

Thing was, she sensed as she was telling him all about it that he knew already. He made all the right noises of shock and surprise but there was something off there, she was sure of it.

'It wasn't like that then, when you found him?' she asked finally.

'No,' he said, 'no way. Anything like that, there'd have been an investigation straight off. Nah, he was just lying there on the floor in the front room. Like he'd just keeled over with a heart attack or something. Least that's what the doc reckoned.'

Fair enough, she supposed, but Tyra was still faintly suspicious. 'How about the landlord?' she asked. 'Suppose I should let him know then.'

'Well,' said Jimmy, 'sure, but first thing I'll make sure the scene-of-crime boys get round there and have a proper dig about before the landlord gets stuck into the place. You know who he is then, the landlord?'

'Yeah,' said Tyra, 'Vernon Nichols.'

Jimmy raised his eyebrows like this was news to him, but once again Tyra was not convinced, and it was making her angry. Like, this copper who she was at school with and who this afternoon seemed more interested in staring at her tits than anything she had to say was playing her for a fool.

'All right then,' she said, standing up abruptly, 'let us know if you find anything out. I got to pick my kids up.' Jimmy just smiled at her, gave her a wink and said yeah, sure he'd be in touch. Tyra walked out all angry but on the way to the school suddenly a detailed sexual fantasy involving her and Jimmy brought a flush to her cheeks.

Later that same afternoon Mazz was heading for the seaside, sitting in the passenger seat of the Colonel's VW camper, smoking a joint and trying to find something listenable on the radio.

Mazz was feeling about as mellow as he could remember. Just getting out into the countryside had been like turning a switch. Kind of thing Mazz never realised he missed – fields, peace, fresh air, all that – but right now he felt it restoring him. Even the Colonel was starting to relax, after the blazing bloody row he'd had with his woman, Natalie, when he said he was heading off to the beach with Mazz and wouldn't say when he was coming back.

Turned out, you see, that the Colonel loved to surf. Mazz had schlepped round town, finally finding a place in an arcade with a load of surfing gear where they'd told him a couple of beaches to check out, but he hadn't a clue how he was going to get out to any of them so he called the Colonel on the off-chance and the Colonel had told him to come round and by the time he arrived the colonel was packing wetsuits and boards into the back of the van while conducting a shouting match with Nat.

But that was behind them now and the Colonel was steering the van through country lanes past the go-kart track at Llandow, at which point Mazz picked up the Hollies singing 'Carrie Ann' on Capital Gold and stopped fiddling with the radio momentarily.

'You been surfing before, butt?'

'No,' said Mazz.

'Just a knack. You'll pick it up easy.'

'Hmm,' said Mazz, who couldn't actually swim at all, but didn't feel like mentioning it just now.

Another ten minutes or so and the lane came out on the cliff top at Southerndown, Dunraven Bay spread out below them. The Colonel eased the van down the access road to the car park at the bottom. There were about a dozen other vehicles there – a couple more camper vans, a few rusted-up old hatchbacks – all with surf decals plastered over them. The beach itself was deserted, five o'clock on a coldish Tuesday afternoon in May, but there were figures dotted about in the sea. From the car park the waves didn't look like anything much at all, though.

'Big enough to surf, are they?' asked Mazz as they got out of the van.

The Colonel peered out to sea, his hand shielding his eyes against the sun. 'Yeah,' he shrugged, 'good for learning anyway. Here, put this wetsuit on.'

The Colonel handed Mazz an ancient-looking rubber garment, all black, not like the gaudy efforts he'd seen in the surf shop in town. Mazz looked at it in bemusement for a moment, wondering whether he was really going to encase himself in this thing, then shrugged, pulled his clothes off and started struggling into the suit. Five minutes of wriggling and squirming and the deed was done and Mazz was already sweating profusely from the exertion of it all.

'Right,' said the Colonel, grinning broadly at Mazz's discomfort, 'let's get you a board.' There were two boards in the back of the van: a big heavy-looking one with rounded edges, and a shorter, lighter one with pointed ends and an altogether sportier look. The Colonel handed Mazz the big one.

'Best to start on this one,' he said. 'More stable in the water.'

Mazz nodded and took the big board, feeling obscurely pissed off that he didn't get to have the cool-looking one. Then the Colonel led them down to the sea. They picked their way along a kind of broken concrete causeway, then among the rock pools and finally out on to the sand. The tide was a way out, and seemed to recede even as they approached, but eventually they reached the water and the Colonel stopped. He put his board down flat on the sand and motioned for Mazz to do the same. The Colonel picked up the lead attached to the board and fastened the Velcro strap on the end of it around his ankle. Mazz followed suit and copied the Colonel as he dropped to lie flat next to his board.

'Right,' said the Colonel, 'this is what you got to do when you get on a wave,' and he pushed himself up on to one knee as if about to start a race.

Mazz practised it a couple of times, having no idea really what he was doing, but the Colonel seemed satisfied and led the way into the water.

The second the freezing waves hit his feet Mazz was thanking God for the wetsuit. In fact the thing was fantastic: he was now wading up to his waist in the water and, apart from his feet, not feeling a thing. A little bit of water made its way inside the rubber and started circulating around his body, but that was a good thing apparently; it would be warmed by his body heat, the Colonel said, and almost instantly he could tell it was true – in fact it was a definitely pleasurable feeling. For the first time he had some inkling of why people liked to dress up in rubber at those fetish clubs and that.

Now they were in the water the waves didn't look quite as insubstantial as they had from the car park. Two-or three-foot-high waves were coming at them in nice regular sets, requiring Mazz to jump awkwardly with his surfboard to breast them. The Colonel climbed on to his board and started paddling into the oncoming swell. Mazz swallowed, tried to gauge how deep the water would be up ahead, thought about telling the Colonel he couldn't swim but realised it was too late now – the Colonel couldn't hear him. He either had to head back to the shore and look like a total dick, or paddle after the Colonel and hope to hell that he didn't lose contact with the board which was the only thing likely to stop him sinking.

So Mazz, his pride not for the first time winning out over his sense of self-preservation, started paddling out to where the big boys were. He found if he held the board dead in front of him it was easy enough to ride over the waves on it, and after a couple of minutes he was up to his neck in the water and alongside a good clutch of other surfers. None of them were Emyr, of course, but Mazz figured it would be worth canvassing them once they came out of the water, see if they'd seen the lost boy around. For now, though, the job in hand was to catch a wave. The Colonel came over and told him to get on his board, turn back to face the shore and start paddling, wait for the wave to pick him up, don't bother about trying to stand up this time, just lie on the board and let the wave do the work.

Mazz nodded and did his best. He clambered on to the board, desperately trying, and just about succeeding, not to overbalance it. He'd hardly had time to start paddling, though, when he looked over his shoulder him and saw the biggest wave yet rearing up behind him. Shit, he thought, this one's definitely going to drown me. But it didn't, it picked Mazz and the board up perfectly, breaking just as they came together, and suddenly Mazz was roaring forward on the crest of the wave, riding towards the shore at what felt like an incredible speed. Mazz found himself laughing with delight as he hurtled forwards, his laughter redoubling when he looked left and saw the Colonel next to him standing up on his board and then suddenly losing it, toppling spectacularly into the water.

The wave took Mazz almost all the way to the shore and when he clambered off he found himself in water barely up to his knees. Immediately he turned round and started wading back into the deeper water. He couldn't remember when he'd last had a rush like that without chemical assistance.

He caught another couple of waves, neither quite as good as that first perfect one but pretty good none the less, and was just starting to feel like he knew what he was doing when disaster struck. He was out with the big boys just standing about in the neck-high water waiting for a decent set of waves to come, when he must have walked into some kind of hole. His feet just went down and he was instantly out of his depth. And now he was under, his mouth and nose full of water again. He didn't panic, though, this time, not at once. He was still tethered to the surfboard, and that could float; all he had to do was get back on top of it. Only trouble was he could feel there was a current dragging him and he was still under water and if he didn't come up soon . . . He felt for the bottom of the sea, got his feet on the ground and pushed up. In a moment his head broke the surface and he took a couple of great shuddering breaths. The board, though, was starting to pull out to sea and he couldn't figure out how to pull it back to him. He splashed around frantically trying to keep afloat, but it didn't work. He went back under again and this time he really did start to panic.

He kicked and splashed and opened his mouth to yell while still under water and finally somehow, after what seemed like for ever, came back up to the surface. He yelled for real and flailed some more and a couple of surfers looked across at him and for a moment that Stevie Smith not waving but drowning thing came into his head and then he went down again and felt for sure that this was it until, all of a sudden, he felt someone grabbing him by the shoulder and pulling him up.

Coughing, spluttering and frightened, he came to the surface, his eyes blind from the water in them. He could feel himself being pulled along by whoever was holding him and tried to relax, to go with the flow.

Another small eternity later the movement stopped and a voice said, 'Fucking hell, bra, can't you swim?'

The hands let go of him then and Mazz was about to panic once more when his legs descended and found solid ground beneath them. He stood up, wiped the water out of his eyes and looked at the Colonel.

'No,' he said, once he'd recovered himself, 'no, I can't swim.'

'Jesus,' said the Colonel, looking genuinely alarmed, 'you're crazy. You could have drowned out there.'

Mazz nodded, feeling terribly, terribly tired all of a sudden. He waded into the shallows, bent down and took the Velcro flap off his ankle, untying him from the surfboard, which he carried on to the beach, then doubled over and retched up what felt like a gallon of seawater.

'C'mon,' said the Colonel, putting his hand on Mazz's shoulder, 'let's go back to the van, get you sorted out.'

Tyra had just given the kids their tea and was sitting with her book, the one by an American called Ernest Gaines she'd got on to from the Oprah book club, when the phone rang.

'Hello,' said the voice which she recognised immediately as familiar but couldn't place. 'Is that Tyra?'

'Yeah,' she said guardedly. 'Who's that, then?'

'Jason,' said the voice, 'Jason Flaherty.'

'All right, Jason,' she said, wondering what the hell this was in aid of. First time she'd seen him in years was at her dad's funeral. Which he'd paid for of course. She'd wondered then what the catch was. Oh well, she was probably about to find out now.

'Yeah, good,' he said, then in a sympathetic voice Tyra wouldn't have believed he had, 'So how are you coping? Must have been a terrible shock.'

'Yeah,' she said, 'thanks for paying for the wake and that,' thinking right, here it comes.

'Well,' he said then, 'it was a great shock to me too. Always had a soft spot for your dad, least I could do really. Anyway,' he changed to a businesslike voice, 'I was wondering if we could have a chat. There's a couple of things have come up.'

'Yeah?' she said, now thoroughly mystified.

'Tell you what, why don't we have lunch tomorrow? One o'clock in Woods suit you?'

'Woods?' she said. 'Hang on, is that the one down the docks used to be Scott's?'

'That's it,' he said. 'I'll book a table for one then. OK?'

'OK,' she said, then bye and put the phone down. Hell's that all about she wondered as she got the kids their afters, and then what on earth am I going to wear?

By way of sorting him out the Colonel took Mazz to the van, got him to change into some dry clothes, made him drink a couple of pints of bottled water, then announced it was time to go to the pub. He drove the van back up the side of the cliff then wound through ever smaller lanes for a couple of miles, before arriving outside what looked like just another farmhouse but which turned out, on closer inspection, to be an ancient pub, the Plough and Harrow.

The Colonel led the way inside and into the bar on the right, a dark low-ceilinged room with a bunch of folky-type musical instruments on the walls, and John Martyn playing on the sound system. There was a fire going, which seemed a little unnecessary in May, but fragile as Mazz was feeling it was a comforting thing so he went over and sat by it while the Colonel got in a couple of pints of some dangerously strong real ale straight from the barrel.

'Fuckin' hell, butt, you scared me out there.'

'Yeah,' said Mazz, 'sorry, like.'

'You can't swim then?'

'No,' said Mazz, 'not a stroke.'

'Then what did you think you were doing getting in the water?'

'I dunno. Half of it was, like, showing off or whatever, but the other half was I wanted to do it. I never wanted to swim when I was a kid but today I just thought yeah, I could do that.'

'Yeah, well,' said the Colonel, 'how about tomorrow we just try and get you swimming? Leave the surfing for lesson two, like.'

'Yeah, I dunno. Thing is we're meant to be looking for Emyr, not getting me drowned.'

'Yeah,' said the Colonel, 'but way I see it is you want to find a surfer, you've got to think like a surfer, you've got to know how it feels.'

Now on the one hand Mazz thought this was bullshit – you wanted to catch a surfer you just had to go round all the surfing beaches and hope your boy was on one of them – but on the other hand he had an inkling of what the Colonel meant. Out there in the sea today, riding that one great wave, was some kind of a revelation all right. Wasn't hard to see it as a kind of antidote to the endless night of the rock'n'roll life, wasn't hard to see why Emyr might be following it. Also, one thing about nearly drowning yourself: it didn't half make you feel happy to be alive.

'Nother drink?' he said to the Colonel, picking up the pint glasses they'd both emptied quick time.

'Pope shit in the woods,' said the Colonel and Mazz laughed and walked over to the bar.

Another two or three hours later the landlord was bringing the drinks over to Mazz personally, 'cause Mazz was sat in the corner with an acoustic guitar playing all these songs he hardly even realised he knew, fifties and sixties songs he must have learned when he was a kid. Buddy Holly, Everly Brothers, that kind of thing, even a few Beatles tunes which had the whole place singing along, of course. People were calling out requests now. Just a dozen or so people in the bar now all sitting round listening to Mazz.

Bloke called out for 'Wonderwall' and Mazz told him to twat off. Then a girl asked if he knew any Bob Marley, and Mazz didn't but he had a go anyway, painstakingly picked out the chords to 'No Woman, No Cry'. And all of a sudden in his head he was back in Tyra's bedroom twenty years ago, Bob Marley's picture on the wall, then remembering how it had been the week after Bobby Sands died, the week after the abortion, the last time he'd spoken to Tyra back then, the twelfth of May 1981. It was the third item on the news. Bob Marley had died of cancer aged thirty-something – fuck, younger than Mazz was now – and Tyra he'd never seen her like that, devastated by sadness, and him, Mazz, just sitting there, a ball of confusion, part of him thinking he should be the hurting one – like, you killed our kid – but mostly just feeling this terrible guilt like he hadn't been strong enough to make it all right. And it seemed like he'd been running from that guilt for twenty years now and no woman no cry. Everyone in the pub singing and Mazz not the only one with tears in his eyes.

Probably Mazz was the only person in the house who thought it made sense when he went into 'Lick Her Down' next. In fact most people seemed to think it was an obscure joke when he said here's one of my songs, before launching into it. Still, it transformed the mood in a minute, everyone clapping and hooting along to its relentless rhythm.

And afterwards, once he'd finally been allowed to put the guitar down – inevitably having finished up with the Colonel singing 'Born to Run' with Mazz screwing the chords up manfully – everyone was much impressed to discover that Mazz really had been the main man of the Wurriyas – or that ska band what did 'Lick Her Down', as they were better known.

Weird to realise that some little tune you wrote one day when you were nineteen was now a part of regular thirty-something nostalgia: the record you heard in the youth club, on your first date, on the radio when you worked your first summer in an ice-cream van. Depressing to think that was the only thing you'd ever done that registered on the general radar, meant something to the kind of people who'd never heard of the fat Yank. Didn't half make you feel old. Specially when you looked at this woman was all over you and you're thinking to yourself she looks all right but knocking on a bit and then she tells you she loved your record when she was in school and you realise she's younger than you, and maybe you're just a sad fuck who only likes the kind of little Goth girls who follow the fat Yank around. Or follow Emyr around, come to that.

Follow that train of thought for a little while and Mazz wasn't too upset when drinking-up time came and he had to say goodbye to his new mates.

Later still, crashed out in the camper, drinking from a bottle of single malt the landlord had given them by way of a carry-out once he'd discovered they weren't planning on driving anywhere, Mazz was maundering on to the Colonel about where did all the good times go and shit and the Colonel listened and politely forbore to talk about his own spell in the limelight – his time as Cardiff City's first ever libero, the time that got him his nickname – but just grunted agreement and drank more whisky until finally he said, 'Nat's pregnant, you know.'

'Christ,' said Mazz. 'She . . . is she . . .'

'Gonna keep it? Yeah, she's thirty-eight years old, man, course she's gonna keep it.'

'Great.'

'Yeah,' said the Colonel. 'It is. Last thing I was expecting, mind. Dunno why, really, Nat being the age she is and all. But for me, like, I thought I was past all that. Been there done that.'

'You got a kid already?'

'Two,' said the Colonel, smiling. 'Both grown now. Steve's at college in Swansea, Becca's an artist. That's the funny thing really: it was through Becca I met Nat. She was Becca's tutor at the art college.'

'Oh,' said Mazz, his booze-struck brain becoming ever more addled under this onslaught of new information. 'Great,' he said again.

'Yeah well, great for Nat, really pleased for her, like, but I've got to say I'm worried I'm too old for it. All that getting-up-in-the-night caper. Needs my beauty sleep I do these days. Talking of which, time for a little shut-eye, I think.'

And with that the Colonel pulled the sleeping bag tight around him, put his head down on a cushion and virtually instantaneously started to snore. Mazz meanwhile just lay there in the dark smoking a fag and looking up at the roof of the van, wondering. What it would be like to have had that kid with Tyra, that kid that would have been grown up now. And wondering too what it would be like to have a kid now. Was a thought he seemed to have now and again these last few years. Though one thing about being a bloke, wasn't like you had a deadline or anything. The Colonel was living proof of that, have a kid when you're fifty no trouble. Though there were limits of course; kids didn't want some old geezer for their dad. So, yeah, there it was: he was broody, he guessed. And hearing about the Colonel and Natalie – Natalie, who was his age, Natalie who, assuming he was remembering her right, he'd done it with, that thing that makes babies – well, got to say he felt jealous. How come the Colonel, who did nothing far as Mazz could see except drink and play pool and now surf, how come he had the nice house and the nice girlfriend and the kid on the way? How come Mazz had been working away all these years and he had none of that stuff? Had made a record that all those people in the pub knew and he didn't have shit.

Answer lay in the business he'd got into, of course; rock'n'roll. Pathetic, really, bitching about it not having a pension plan and guaranteed nice little house with a nice little mortgage and nice little wife, but there it was. You might not be able to have your cake and eat it but there was no law saying you couldn't want it, couldn't want it all. Yet it wasn't just the financial insecurity of the life – though that was bad enough – it was also the people you met. The women, he meant. Too fucking young for the most part. Even the ones where it wasn't out and out cradle-snatching – the ones who were like twenty-two or something – they might see you as good for a little walk on the wild side but they didn't want to have your babies. Apart from the stalker anyway.

The stalker had first turned up at a gig in Osaka. Mazz had been flattered at first. This big Japanese girl in a polka-dot mod dress – well, big for a Japanese girl anyway – showed up backstage with all these record sleeves from the Wurriyas on, practically everything Mazz had ever played on. Kind of thing that happened to the fat Yank all the time – fact when you thought about it that was how the fat Yank had met his evil squeeze – but anyway there was this girl giving Mazz the obsessive-fan treatment for once and he couldn't help but be a bit pleased. And she was nice too, far as he could tell, 'cause she didn't speak a lot of English. Not that good-looking though, to be honest; Mazz wasn't exactly aquiver with lust at the sight of her, but yeah she was nice. And so he was happy enough to see her the next three nights of the tour, stretching halfway across Japan, bringing him little presents each time, all wrapped up special and everything – dear God they like their packaging out there – and he'd offer her a drink and stuff though she'd only have a Coke and he'd try and chat to her a bit, and it was fine.

It was only when she turned up a month later in London that he started to worry. In fact not even then – Japs were always coming over to Britain to visit the famous Camden Market and meet all their friends from Tokyo. But when she showed up at Manchester, Liverpool and Newport, Shropshire – a gig at which she was one of only twelve people in the audience – he really started to get uneasy.

And the gifts started getting weirder: packages of very strange-looking sushi, two dolls customised to look like Mazz and the girl, a poem that appeared to be written in blood and, oh God, he still couldn't believe in the midst of all this he'd slept with her. He'd invited her up to his room to tell her, honestly, to tell her to stop, desist and find a more appropriate outlet for her affections and generally leave him alone. But she looked so sad and he'd put his arm round her and let her stay and then they hit the mini-bar . . . OK, look, he knew perfectly well he was crazy, she was crazy, etc. But anyway you can guess where it went from there: the phantom pregnancy, the scenes, the insane, the totally bloody freaky gifts, the awful fucking showdown when he'd told her she wasn't fucking pregnant, she needed fucking help. And then she'd just vanished out of his life. The way women did when Mazz finally managed to hurt them enough. Yeah, well, that was the closest he'd come to having a kid in recent years. Jesus, thought Mazz as he turned over and willed himself to sleep.

Next morning both Mazz and the Colonel were woken by someone banging on the back door. Mazz sat up and peered through the curtain.

Tony, the pub landlord, was standing there looking inordinately cheerful. The Colonel opened the door and shuddered as the sunlight hit him.

'Breakfast, boys,' said Tony.

'Uh,' said the Colonel, and then, after a pause of several seconds in which he appeared to be attempting to remember how to talk, 'OK.'

Tony smiled and shook his head. 'When you're ready, boys,' he said, 'just come in the bar,' and he walked off.

Half an hour later Mazz and the Colonel were sat at the table next to the fire already beginning to feel the hangover-blasting benefits of the full English, black pudding and all.

'Well,' said the Colonel, mopping up the last of his fried bread, 'better get down to work then. You got a picture of our boy Emyr?'

Mazz nodded, dug in his jacket pocket, brought out the picture Jason had given him, a press shot from a couple of years back, and handed it to the Colonel.

'Thanks, butt,' he said, then got up and walked over to the bar where Tony was busy getting things ready for opening time. 'You seen this feller in here at all? Maybe with a bunch of surfers?'

Tony looked at the photo for a while, thought about it.

'He got long hair now, this feller?' he said, tapping the picture.

'Yeah,' said Mazz, 'that's right.'

'Then I'd say yeah, I've seen this feller a few times. Bunch of them come in here, hardcore types you know. Guys who'll come in December and go surfing off the rocks down there.' Tony waved an arm in the direction of the rocky beach a mile or so down the lane. 'Doesn't say much, more of a smoker than a drinker, if you know what I mean. That sound like the guy?'

'Yeah,' said Mazz, 'it most certainly does.'

'So,' said the Colonel, 'any idea where we might find these guys?'

Tony shrugged. 'Usual places, I suppose – 'Gennith, Trecco Bay. Depends on the wind a bit. I were you, I'd head out to Llangennith; that's where you'll find most of the boys sooner or later.'

'Cheers,' said Mazz.

'No worries,' said Tony. 'Why d'you want to find him anyway?'

'Oh,' said Mazz, 'we used to be in a band together, years ago, like.'

'Thinking of a reunion then, is it?'

'Yeah,' said Mazz, 'a reunion.'

'Grand,' said Tony and moved back over to the bar. 'One for the road, lads?'

'Don't mind if I do,' said the Colonel.

9

CONEY BEACH

1999

You came out of Tyra's place, cut through Mount Stuart Square and over James Street, and you were in a different world, and one getting more different every time she walked through it . . . It was funny, the bay development – you'd heard about it for years; since the eighties they'd been knocking stuff down getting ready for it. But for ages that was all it had been, just knocking stuff down and leaving it there. Nice old pubs like the Mount Stuart and the Sea Lock all gone but nothing coming to replace it. Then gradually it started happening. They moved the Norwegian church right on to the bay. Looked nice, to be fair. They built the brand-new Techniquest building and the Harry Ramsden's next to it. Fair enough, kids loved Techniquest. The UCI, of course, suddenly landing like a giant space ship the far side of Bute Street – twelve screens, bowling alley and all. Kids loved that too, and it was packed from the start, all these people never came down the docks in their life piling in, driving there in their cars and driving straight out again. They turned one of the old docks buildings into the Sports Café, which wasn't her cup of tea but her mate Paula had a job behind the bar. And then suddenly there was the new hotel right on the end there and the barrage was meant to be finished soon, and now, looking for this Woods joint, she could see that all of a sudden there was this half-built shopping mall where the Maritime Museum used to be. Pace of it was getting frightening and she could see it was starting to work. Another couple of years and the place would be swarming with tourists and that.

And the old docks, the docks she half remembered herself, and had grown up hearing about in her dad's stories, what about all that? Maybe they'd open a Tiger Bay theme bar to remember it by: cute murals with cute prostitutes and sailors, a little whiff of airbrushed long-ago vice, give the visitors a thrill.

Still, it had to be better than letting it rot, she supposed. It was just a bit unsettling to feel like a stranger in your own patch. Harry Ramsden's, the Sports Café; there were no memories for her there. Only place that looked even vaguely like it used to was the Windsor, all boarded up now but you could still see the big sleazy old pub it used to be and she could still remember the dances there. Her and Tony. Tony and her. All those years – as kids, as grown ups, as grown ups with kids. Tony like a thorn in her heart. A lesson learned: love has its limits. The third time he'd gone to jail, after he'd made all those promises, that had been the limit for her. When he'd come out that last time she'd hardened her heart to him. And now he was gone. Spain they said he'd gone to. Not the only thing they'd said, friends you know, always ready to give you the stuff you really didn't want to know – for your own good, like. Stories about Tony and Mandy. Mandy he'd always said was like a sister to him. Sister!

Yeah, well, like she said there were limits, and Tony was history now, like the Windsor, boarded up and waiting for demolition, redevelopment, she didn't know. Someone had said they were going to open a lap-dancing club there. Hah, chance of a job after all, girl. And right next to the Windsor was Woods, another old building, some shipping office if she remembered right, turned into some posh restaurant. She'd walked past it once or twice, never paid it much mind.

Now, though, walking up to it she felt nervous. Felt shabby, to be honest. It had thrown her into a total panic looking for something to wear. Nothing looked remotely right. Made her realise how long it was since she'd had anything to dress up for. How long it was since she'd been out somewhere nice. She had a couple of dresses she hated and had had for years – things she'd wear for weddings and funerals – and she had the stuff she wore every day: jeans, leggings, T-shirts, sweatshirts – usual mumsy crap. Called up her mate Lisa, who worked in a lawyer's office in town, and was nearly as tall as her, and she brought some things over but it was no good, she just felt like an idiot. Ended up wearing a pair of black jeans that weren't too bad and a velvet blouse she really liked but she'd had for a few years now, and walking in here, seeing all the people all looking if not stylish well rich anyway, she just felt like she should be working in the bloody kitchen. Fact was people like her didn't come to places like this.

Then she glimpsed herself in the big mirror over the bar and thought damn it, girl, don't give into this shit. She looked good, she knew she looked good, she'd always looked good, and she'd never thought she was destined to be bound by her roots, by the docks. She'd proved that when she'd got up and been in the Wurriyas; she could damn well prove it again now.

So she walked straight up to the first waitress she could see, pretty little blonde girl, said she was meeting Mr Flaherty and the girl took her through the bar area into the main bit of the restaurant and there was Jason sitting in the corner looking bigger than life with a bottle of red wine in front of him. He stood up as she approached, nearly tipping the table over, and took her hand then kissed her cheek, and she nearly burst out laughing.

'Jesus, Jason,' she said when they'd sat down, 'you've got a bit smoother over the years.'

Jason laughed, poured her a glass of wine and, not sure how to play or what they were playing come to that, Tyra picked up the menu to give herself something to do. Menu looked nice too – all that stuff you see on the TV food shows and wouldn't dream of cooking yourself. Which always seemed like the point of going to a restaurant to Tyra, getting something you couldn't cook at home. So she ordered a complicated-sounding salad and a confit of duck and Jason smiled and said he'd just have a steak, well done, please, and kept up this solid line of chat. Lot of stuff about the old days, about the Wurriyas, which was nice. It was funny; it was like it was a whole part of her life she'd blocked out 'cause it didn't seem to make a lot of sense alongside the life she was living now, it was like it had happened to someone else really. But there it was and as Jason talked it started coming back.

'You remember that German TV show?' Jason said.

Tyra shook her head then started laughing. 'Yeah, *Club Rock* or something, yeah. The one where the interviewer thought Bobby was a boy?'

'Yeah and Charlie – your dad – pulled the hostess.'

Tyra laughed again. Actually at the time it had been embarrassing as anything, her dad chatting up anything blonde, Teutonic and skirt-wearing, but now she had an aching rush of fondness for how he'd been then, still in the last of his prime. 'Everyone loved Charlie, didn't they?' she said, a choke in her voice.

'Yeah,' said Jason, then paused, 'except for Charlie, I suppose.'

Tyra stopped sniffling and looked at him closely. He was right, of course – you got much sense of self-worth you didn't end up in the gutter – but it wasn't the kind of observation she expected from Jason. Then she hadn't thought about Jason as a person at all really, more a rather scary force of nature you were just glad to have on your side.

'Yeah,' she said, 'I suppose you're right . . .' and tailed off, thankful to see her first course approaching.

As they ate Jason filled her in on what he'd been up to the past eighteen years. He'd stayed in the music business for a few more years, ridden the New Romantic thing for a bit, then saw that the smart money was moving away from bands and into clubs. He'd been a partner in opening a big club in London in the mid-eighties, then spotted that the even smarter money didn't hang around running clubs; it went straight into the property market.

'Late eighties,' he told her, mopping up his steak, 'you had to be a total dickhead not to get rich. Bought any old dump in London, ex-council whatever, converted into flats, flogged them off to yuppies – remember them, funny how people stop using words after a bit, innit – anyway you sold them these shit flats for a fortune then bought up a whole lot more dumps and did it again. Then of course, summer of '88, Chancellor gets it into his thick head to change the tax allowances at the end of July. Any moron can see that it's going to create a feeding frenzy, shoot the prices up and then make them collapse in August.'

Jason paused, picked up the bottle of red wine, drained it off into their glasses then signalled for the waiter to bring another and carried on. 'Least it was obvious to me anyway, so I cleaned my portfolio out that summer then sat around for a year or so waiting for the crash to bottom out, then I started buying again. But this time not so much flats, more office buildings and that. And now construction. Course there isn't that much space for construction in London 'cept for Docklands and the big boys had that all sorted out – no one was going to give Jason Flaherty Canary Wharf to build so I looked around a bit. And you know where I looked?'

'No,' said Tyra automatically, enjoying this, sitting opposite a man who did stuff, didn't just sit about complaining how the world was against him or just doss along in the slow lane for ever. No, she was getting a bit of a buzz off of Jason.

'Course you do,' he said, 'I looked back home. Right here in Cardiff. The docks specially. Loads of land, loads of government incentives to develop the place. Same thing as with the flats in London. You didn't have to be smart to see it, you just had to have a bit of bottle and a friendly bank manager.'

He leaned forward now, giving Tyra a look that was almost soulful if you can imagine a soulful behemoth. 'Difference is of course,' he said, 'difference is that, up in London selling the flats to the yuppies, it didn't matter to me what happened to those places, it was just making money. Situation now it's a little different. First, I've got money now, I don't have to do any of this. Second, I know this place. Not just Cardiff, yeah, but the docks. I've got friends here. Fellers like Kenny. Kenny who I'm not bullshitting is like a brother to me. Ah, bollocks, what I'm trying to say is the developments I'm involved in here all show some respect for the community, bring in jobs, new housing, primary schools, all that good stuff. And what hurts me is when I can see that I'm getting screwed over by some fucker who doesn't care for anything 'cept his own pocket.'

Jason paused finally. Tyra, feeling a little lightheaded now – was that a second bottle of wine they were on? – said, 'Oh yeah, anyone in particular?'

'Yeah,' said Jason. 'Nichols, Vernon Nichols. The bastard who broke into your dad's flat.'

'What?' she said, completely blindsided. 'How d'you know someone broke into Charlie's flat?'

'Like I said, I've got a lot of friends round here. People tell me things.'

'OK, but why d'you say it was Nichols?'

'Well, seems obvious enough.'

'Oh yeah?'

'I heard there was no forced entry and I'm sure the police didn't leave the door open. So must have been someone with a key. And old Vernon's the landlord.'

'Yeah,' said Tyra, 'but why?'

Jason looked at her quizzically. 'You don't know?'

'Course I don't know.'

'Charlie never said anything to you then? 'Bout some information he had, about old Uncle Vern. Evidence, he might have said.'

'No,' said Tyra.

'Well, you know he was having trouble with Vern?'

'No,' said Tyra, 'I don't know anything. He wasn't like that with me. Charlie didn't confide much. Specially not these last few years.'

Jason nodded. 'All right then, let me fill you in a bit. Month or two back Charlie comes to me. It was a bit of a regular event, really. He'd come by, see if I had any little jobs for him or maybe some royalties from the Wurriyas — you know "Lick Her Down" 's out on a compilation? — anyway, be honest with you, he was pretty desperate a lot of the time and I'd see what I could do. But anyway this time he comes and he's in a right state, he's had a letter from Vern saying the council is compulsorily purchasing the property. Well, you can imagine Charlie wasn't too keen on that.

'So I said I'd have a little dig about, 'cause I didn't like the sound of that, sounded to me like old Vern had got the council doing his dirty work for him. But I had to restrain Charlie a bit, he was threatening all sorts about Vern. Said he knew what Vern was up to and he had the evidence to prove it. Wasn't really clear what he was talking about or if he was making the whole thing up. But you can imagine he went round to see Vern and started carrying on like that . . . well . . .'

Tyra sat back in her chair. 'You saying, you saying Vernon Nichols might have killed my dad? Over a bloody flat?'

Jason shook his head. 'I'm not saying anything, I'm just filling you in on some things I thought you most probably already knew. But one thing I should point out: it's not just a flat. If Vernon's got permission to knock that whole block down and build something new there – well, that's lot of money involved.'

He paused, looked at Tyra carefully. 'Look,' he said, leaning forward and putting his hand over hers – a gesture which surprised Tyra – 'tell you what, I'll ask around a bit more, speak to some of my friends in the police force and that, and anything I find out I'll let you know. Meanwhile maybe it'd be a good idea you have a think what Charlie might have done with this evidence – if it exists at all – 'cause it looks like someone believes it's out there. You find anything, you let me know and we'll have a think what to do, how about that?'

Tyra nodded.

Jason sat back, smiled and called over a waiter to ask for the dessert menu.

One for the road turned unsurprisingly into two and a chaser but even so an hour later the VW was rolling out of the car park and along the coast road. They skirted the seaside villages of Southerndown and Ogmore, with their farms and retirement bungalows looking equally grim beneath the day's grey skies and persistent drizzle. Then it was a question of whether to cut inland and take the motorway to the Gower, the prime surfing area in this part of the world, or work their way around to Porthcawl, a faded holiday town that still had a decent surfing beach.

'Worth a try, butt,' said the Colonel and Mazz concurred.

Hardly seemed likely that Emyr would pick a place like Porthcawl, but still he was curious to see how the place had changed from the days when he used to come down with his folks and stay in a caravan there for two weeks every summer. The miners' fortnight. Half the valleys would come down to Porthcawl, whole streets transporting themselves on to a row of caravans. Christ, seemed like another century, another world. The valleys weren't like that any more – you could hold the miners' fortnight in a bloody Portakabin these days – and he didn't suppose Porthcawl was what it was either.

He was right there. Porthcawl on a rainy Wednesday in May was genuinely dismal. The centre of town was the kind of place that would be gentrified if Kwiksave moved in: the beach had a couple of miserable-looking donkeys offering rides to even more miserable-looking kids. The funfair, Coney Beach, which Mazz remembered as the absolute highlight of his childhood, was now tawdry beyond any kind of glamour.

'Tell you what, mate,' said Mazz to the Colonel as they walked past the crooked house and Mazz's eyes scanned the place looking to see what had happened to the boating lake, 'when I was a kid and I used to come here, Coney Island, I used to dream of Coney Island in New York. I figured if Coney Beach here was the best place I'd ever seen and its name was like a rip-off of the one in New York, then the New York one had to be truly fabulous. Anyways. I finally make it over to New York. I'm twenty-two, playing with this fucking eighties haircut band, and first thing I want to do is go to Coney Island. Every New York fucker I meet looks at me like I'm mad, what would I want to go there for? But I'm determined so I get the subway map and spend like bollocking hours taking the Z train all the way through Brooklyn and I finally get there and there's like a giant Ferris wheel, a giant bungee-jump thing and a really, really scary-looking rusted-up old rollercoaster, plus all these Puerto Rican guys fishing off the pier and these old Russian-Jewish guys playing klezmer music on the boardwalk, and basically I had a hot dog and went back again and everyone took the piss out of me for wasting my time.'

'Yeah,' said the Colonel, not really paying attention, watching some sucker trying to lob ping-pong balls into goldfish bowls, 'that's living all right.'

'Uh yeah,' said Mazz, 'but, like, disappointing as it was, yeah, well, compared to this place,' he waved his arm in the general direction of Louis Tussaud's wax museum, 'it was still bloody fucking glamorous.'

The Colonel shrugged and laughed. The further end of the funfair petered out into a kind of half-hearted boot sale, so Mazz and the Colonel turned round and headed back towards the beach. As they passed the water chute a bloke came out of the ticket booth, walked along the side of the big rusty structure, came up to a piece of metal lying adjacent to it and kicked it out of sight under the railings. As he did so he saw Mazz staring at him, gave him a smile and a wink and went back to the ticket booth.

'Fuckin' hell,' said Mazz and the Colonel simultaneously and they headed past the Burger King on to the road winding alongside the beach and up to the caravan park. Mazz was half tempted to follow it and check out the old caravan, see if it was still there, but the Colonel led the way down on to the beach and out towards the rocky headland that separated Sandy Bay from Trecco Bay.

'You see that?' he asked, pointing at the black rocks stretching out from the headland. 'That's the Point.'

'Yeah,' said Mazz vaguely.

'Yeah,' said the Colonel, 'one of the biggest breaks anywhere round Britain, least it used to be.'

'Christ,' said Mazz, looking harder at the rocks. 'People surf by there?'

'Yeah, Well, people who can swim do.'

Coming closer to the sea, Mazz realised once again that he'd been wrong about the waves. From the car park they'd looked like nothing much but up close they were two to three feet and coming in fast sets cracking fiercely against the rocks. But where the previous day's sunshine had brought out the day trippers in relative numbers, today it was just the hardcore few. Or, to be precise, the hardcore one. The only person Mazz could see out in the water was a big bald feller on a board that looked too small for him. Mazz and the Colonel stood there on the headland watching him struggle out through the waves.

'Too choppy,' said the Colonel. 'Miracle if he gets on a wave out there.' Mazz nodded, demonstrating the bloke's inalienable right to become an instant expert on any kind of sporting activity. And for a while the Colonel's verdict seemed to be right; time and again the bloke would try to get on a wave only to be rapidly dumped unceremoniously off it and left with another fierce paddle back out. But then, just as the Colonel was turning to head back, the guy caught one, the biggest smoothest wave they'd seen all afternoon. He got on the wave, got half up on his board, rode it crouching for a while then, with a roar Mazz could hear even above the noise of the sea, stood right up and skimmed along the top of the wave, all the way into the shore.

Once in the guy got off his board, looked back out to sea then shook his head, shouldered his board and headed out of the water, evidently having made his mind up that he'd had the day's one good ride.

Mazz and the Colonel walked slowly along the beach, timing it so they bumped into the surfer just as he was approaching the car park.

'All right, butt,' said the Colonel as the guy came near.

'All right,' said the surfer.

'Nice going,' said the Colonel.

The guy shrugged, his eyes scanning Mazz and the Colonel quickly, assessing them for trouble and then relaxing. 'Been out there a couple of hours and that was the first decent wave I got.'

'What sort of board you got there?'

'Custom,' he said. 'Feller makes them for me.' He turned the board round so the Colonel could see it, an old-school longboard with a logo based around the letters ESP.

'Got your own personal board maker?'

'Yeah,' said the guy. 'I run a surf shop in town here. Point Break Boards.' He carried on past them. 'Come by and have a look. It's just off the high street there.'

Mazz and the Colonel looked at each other and shrugged and half an hour later they were sat in the shop having a cup of tea with the guy whose name turned out to be JT, and who looked even bigger indoors, dressed in baggy surf pants and an oversize fleece, than he had done out in the water.

The Colonel had kicked things off telling JT they were looking for this surfer guy. And brought out the picture of Emyr. This time the guy obviously knew who Emyr was instantly and he immediately narrowed his eyes.

'You taking the piss? This is the rock-star guy went missing innit?'

JT then went from disbelieving to suspicious as the Colonel explained that Emyr was a surfer these days. So Mazz weighed in with the story about wanting to get the band together for a reunion, and the guy looked more sceptical still until Mazz started reeling off names of people JT could call to verify Mazz was who and what he said he was and the guy put his hands up and said, 'OK, fair enough.'

'What's the big deal anyway?' asked the Colonel. 'You seen him or something?'

'Nah,' said JT, 'just don't like people taking the piss.'

'You got any ideas then? Where a bunch of hardcore surfers might hang out?'

JT shrugged. 'Well, the wind keeps on getting up like this there'll be a gang of them out later on, the night surfers.'

'Night surfers?'

'Yeah. Tell you what. You boys meet me in the Hi Tide Amusement Arcade about nine, I'll show you.'

'Appreciate it, man,' said the Colonel, stood up and led the way out of the shop.

The next four hours passed easily enough. Couple of games of table football in the Sportsman's club on the front, then, looking for somewhere to get some food, Mazz spotted a place called the Tribal Coconut attached to some kind of surfer hostel. They went inside, flashed Emyr's picture around to no avail, but decided to stick around anyway and ate a couple of kangaroo steaks and listened to the people on the next table, a bunch of Aussies, lying to each other about how big the waves they used to surf back home were.

After that they walked back round to the funfair which had livened up a little now, acquiring that air of tension and danger which is what distinguishes the old-school carny type funfair from your modern theme park. One option offers you state-of-the-art rides, negative G-force rushes and the finest special effects Hollywood's smartest can throw at you; the other gives you a water chute that offers every prospect of actually dicing with death, a ghost train made of papier mâché, and lots of bad boys with tattoos, G-force hormonal rushes, sex and violence here, there and everywhere. Specially if you were sixteen of course.

At the far end of the amusement park, past the Burger King – the one indication that the last thirty years had impacted on this relic of working-class recreation – they finally came upon the Hi Tide Amusement Arcade.

Inside it was the usual merry hell of strung-out mothers feeding the fruit machines, kids blasting zombies, blokes with prison tats concentrating very, very hard indeed on Tekken 3, and absolutely no sign of JT.

The Colonel wasn't too bothered. He spotted one of those skiing simulators and was on it in a flash, spent the next ten minutes slaloming his way down virtual mountainsides with practised skill. Mazz drifted off, lost a couple of quid on the fruit machines, wandered back and found the Colonel still going, then wandered off again and noticed there was an upstairs, headed up and found JT there finishing off a game of pool.

Mazz lit up a fag, waited for him to finish. Couple of minutes later they'd prised the Colonel off his skis and headed out to the car park between the Hi Tide and the Sandy Bay caravan park. There in the moonlight were half a dozen vehicles; a camper much like the Colonel's, a beat-up Sherpa, a couple of rusty old hatchbacks and, incongruously, a brand-new Suzuki jeep. A couple of teenage boys were standing in the shadows furtively eyeing the jeep.

'Stupid bastards,' said JT and walked over to them. He bent down to say something to the boys, and as he spoke their posture went from hard to defeated, and they slunk off back into the arcade.

'Just told them who the jeep belongs to,' JT said, smiling at Mazz and the Colonel.

'Yeah?' said Mazz.

'Yeah,' said JT, 'Danny Lewis Jones. Father owns half this fucking town. Planning to build a state-of-the-art new theme park here, he can get permission. Danny works for him, runs a couple of clubs for him, looking to expand operations into Cardiff too, from what I hear. Now, got your wetsuits, butts?'

'They're in the camper,' said the Colonel.

'Well, you best go get them. Night surfers aren't going to talk 'less you get in the water with them.'

The Colonel shrugged and said he'd go get the camper and bring it round; JT and Mazz elected to wait. The two of them stood there smoking, looking out towards the black sea below.

'Flaherty says hello,' said JT after a while.

'What?' said Mazz.

'Yeah, you mentioned his name, said he'd vouch for you and the rock-star guy. So I called him.'

'I didn't give you the number, though,' said Mazz, started.

'No need, mate, I knows Jason of old, like.'

'Christ,' said Mazz, 'don't we all? How'd you run into the bastard?'

'Working on doors and that. No, be honest, it was before that. I was going to judo and Flaherty started showing up. Always paired him off with me 'cause we were the two biggest bastards there. Then I found out he had the security business, like, and he started giving me work. Used to do a little bit of business on the doors, like,' he looked at Mazz and winked, 'then when I got a little bit of money together I came here, opened the shop. Anyway Flaherty keeps in touch, called me the other day asking about Danny LJ, as it goes, so, like I say, I called him up and he seemed pretty keen I help you find this guy.' He paused for a moment. 'Fact of the matter is it seems it's more him that's looking for the guy than you, like.'

Mazz shrugged. 'Lot of people looking for Emyr, all right.'

'Uh huh,' said JT, 'Well, probably teaching my grandmother to suck eggs, like, but I were you I'd watch your back on this one. Make sure Flaherty isn't standing right behind you.'

Mazz raised his eyebrows and was about to say something but just then the Colonel pulled up in the camper. Mazz and the Colonel got changed in the back. JT just opened up his kit bag and stripped off right there in the middle of the car park, then led the way down a steep path on to Sandy Bay beach, right in front of the funfair. At first there was no sign of any activity at all, apart from a teenage couple staggering across the sand, mouths locked together, evidently in search of a friendly sand dune. Then, as they got closer to the water, the waves started to come into focus and so too did a black shape riding them.

JT strode out towards the waves, his arm raised in greeting. The Colonel deliberately hung back. 'Be careful out there, butt. Don't go deep, don't try to be clever. You get worried, act like you've pulled a hamstring or something, and get out. You got me?'

Mazz nodded the nod of a man who didn't need to be told twice, and shuffled towards the sea with an ever slowing gait. Once in the water, though, it was different. He paddled out a little way, making sure to stay within his depth, then turned and looked back at the funfair, lit up against the night sky, a quarter moon dangling above it. He glanced over his shoulder, saw a respectable-size wave coming at him, started paddling, lying flat on the board, and caught it nicely, and the wave sent him swooping in out of the darkness and towards the bright lights. And once again the exhilaration hit him. He paddled straight out again and repeated the process two or three times. He didn't attempt to stand up on the board the way he could see the Colonel, JT and the others were doing, just worked within his limitations. The fourth time, though, as he paddled out the board got away from under him and Mazz swam after it and caught it then suddenly realised what he'd done: swum. Some kind of a makeshift breaststroke that he'd managed without thinking about it.

Laughing at himself, he got back on the board and paddled further out towards where the other surfers were basking, waiting for the big wave. Took him a little while to get out there and when he did he looked round, his eyes adjusting to the dark now, trying to spot the Colonel. Couldn't see any sign of him; must have just caught a wave, Mazz figured. He saw JT, though, just a few yards over to the right talking to another surfer, bloke with a very flash-looking board indeed, probably the Danny guy, Mazz figured, then he looked to his left and no more than ten yards away he saw, he was sure, Emyr.

Even in a wetsuit in the dark, the white-blond hair was a giveaway. Their eyes locked for a second and Mazz was about to call out when he saw the other surfer's eyes swivel behind his and widen.

Mazz turned too, saw the biggest wave of the night so far bearing down, and with what was now becoming some sort of instinct prepared to get on it. He failed dismally. Timed it all wrong, came off his board, went under and sucked water, came back up, looked around and saw the surfer he took to be Emyr speeding away from him, standing tall on his board and heading for the shore. Mazz spat and choked and swore and tried to ride the next wave and the wave after that, but when he finally got on one under-powered wave he saw the surfer getting out of the water, on to shore and start jogging across the beach.

Mazz gave up trying to surf, just waded through the water as fast as he could. By the time he made it to the shore, though, he could barely see the dark shape of the surfer ahead of him on the beach. Mazz peeled off the Velcro strip holding his board's leash to his ankle, debated for a second whether to carry the board with him, then thought to hell with it, put it carefully down on the sand and ran across the beach, hoping the other surfer's board would slow him down.

The plan seemed to be working at first, Mazz running across the wet sand, the other surfer struggling across the beach heading, Mazz was sure, for the Hi Tide car park. But then as the beach grew drier it became more treacherous and each footstep was sinking inches in the sand. Mazz felt that awful dream sensation of wading hopelessly forward and never moving. By the time he got through on to harder ground again the other surfer was disappearing into the deeper darker shadows closer to the boardwalk. Mazz ran after him, heading blindly towards the Hi Tide, knowing the guy had at least thirty seconds on him. As he came off the beach on to the steps up to the car park, he cursed as something sharp cut into his foot, but didn't slow down. He took the steps three at a time and came running into the half-lit car park.

Nothing. No sign of the surfer at all. Mazz scanned the parked vehicles, frantically trying to work out if there was one less than earlier. He hadn't a clue. He started towards the Hi Tide, opened the door and peered in. No immediate sight of the surfer but three different blokes turned round and laughed at him standing there in his wetsuit. He went back out into the car park and stood there looking around for any sign of movement. Suddenly he heard something from behind him, coming up from the beach. He whirled round and there was the Colonel, carrying both surfboards, a quizzical expression on his face.

'Whassup, butt?'

'Emyr,' said Mazz. 'He was there in the water. He ran off when he saw me. I followed him up this way, but he vanished.'

'In a car?'

'I dunno. Maybe. It didn't seem like there was time. But I dunno where else he'd be.'

'Well, let's have a little look around, shall we?' The Colonel already had his wetsuit half off and was digging around in the van for some towels. He chucked one to Mazz and after a couple of freezing minutes spent extricating himself from the rubber clutches of his suit Mazz was ready.

'So where d'you reckon?'

'Well, let's say he didn't get away in the car 'cause if he did we're buggered. If he didn't he had two ways to go, either through the funfair or the caravan park. He was wearing a wetsuit, yeah?'

'Yeah.'

'Then we can pretty much rule out the funfair. So let's check out the caravan site.'

The Colonel locked the gear in the van and they crossed the road and headed through the gates of the Sandy Bay caravan park. At once Mazz felt it was hopeless. The site looked huge in the dark, caravans and trailers heading off in all directions. They took the main path, heading for the site office. Eventually they came to it, stuck in a little square cum precinct with a boarded-up news agent's and Glynis's Fish Shop; whole place had the vibe of the most depressed council estate you've ever seen, picked up bodily and plonked down next to the sea. The site office was closed, of course, so no chance to find out if any tall blond surfers had recently checked in. There was no one around at all, in fact, except for the inevitable clusters of early-teenage kids doing their best to look hard. They went into the fish shop, Mazz got some chips and the Colonel asked the woman about Emyr. She shook her head automatically.

Out of the fish shop, they hesitated briefly. The Colonel led them away from the main path deeper into the site. Suddenly they came through a row of trailers and found themselves looking at a great sunken oval field, like an abandoned running track set right in the middle of the site, surrounded by caravans. Mazz felt like there were eyes in every caravan staring at him. Christ, if Emyr had chosen this place to hide from the world in, he could hardly have done better. And he was welcome to it.

'C'mon,' he said to the Colonel, 'this is a fucking waste of time.'

Back in the car park, JT, the guy with the flash board and a couple of others were getting changed.

'Any sign of your mate, then?' said JT.

'Yeah,' said Mazz. 'He was out there. I saw him.'

'Yeah?' said JT, apparently surprised. Mazz wasn't sure whether to believe him or not.

'You didn't see him then, blond guy, late thirties? Shit, you know what he looks like.'

JT shrugged. 'No, didn't see him, like I said. Dark out there, y'know, bra. Tell you what, go down the Apollo, over on the front there; the whole crew will be there sooner or later. See if anyone can help you out.'

With that JT went back to changing out of his wetsuit, the guy with the flash board gave them a bit of a look, not hard exactly but suspicious, and Mazz and the Colonel got into the camper, headed round to the town centre.

The Apollo turned out to be a shoebox of a club, stuck between a curry house and a failed theme pub on the front. The DJ was playing oldies when they got there, seventies disco records, which suited Mazz fine – he'd given up attempting to like modern dance music some time in the techno nineties. Apart from reggae, of course; always had a soft spot for anything out of Jamaica. Not much chance of hearing any of that here, though; he knew it was only a matter of time before the housey-house tunes came out.

They found a table over near the bar, got a couple of bottles of Pils in and sat back to wait for the surfers to show up. Didn't take too long; the DJ was only just into his Abba medley when JT and his three mates arrived, got the beers in and parked themselves around the table.

Mazz was sure they must have had a talk beforehand, 'cause it was like they were all on edge.

JT introduced his mates. The guy with the flash board, who was now kitted out like a model for Quicksilver, was indeed Danny the theme-park heir, then there were Steve and Jacko, who looked like regular enough surf bums. Little bit of joshing about, all still feeling a bit artificial, and JT started in.

'Well,' he said, 'I told my brers here about your little problem. And they think they might know the geezer you mean.'

Course they do, thought Mazz, they've been surfing with him an hour ago, but he managed to bite his tongue.

'Thing is they're a little concerned about your motivation, like.'

'Yeah,' cut in Danny. 'The point is it's Emmo's life. He doesn't want to be found, that's his decision, isn't it?'

'Yeah,' said Mazz, thinking *Emmo*, he'd never heard anyone call Emyr Emmo, 'and I respect that. All I want is to have a little talk with him, 'bout a couple of matters, and if he wants to leave it at that – go surfing, let the world think he's dead – that's fine by me.'

Danny nodded, looked like he was taking Mazz's point, so Mazz carried on then immediately wished he hadn't.

'And don't worry about Jason,' he said, looking at JT, 'Emyr doesn't want me to tell Jason, I won't.'

'Jason,' said Danny, glancing curiously at JT. JT shrugged, acting like he didn't have a clue.

Mazz wondered what was going on there, answered anyway. 'Emyr's old manager. He's looking for Emyr too, of course.'

'Oh yeah?' said Danny and went silent for a moment then leaned forward. 'Tell you what,' he said, 'why don't you and your mate go to Llangennith, the camp site there, Hillend. I'll get the word to Emyr, tell him what you said and if he wants to see you he'll find you there in the next day or two. OK?'

'Yeah,' said Mazz, 'that's great. Thanks a lot, man.'

'No worries,' said Danny as he got up, clasped hands with JT, and headed off.

10

THE SALUTATION

1981

First day off from the Wurriyas, Tyra went back to her mum's and Mazz went back to the flat. Got there about five minutes before the landlord, little Polish bloke, always had an unlit roll–up nestling in the corner of his mouth. He was ready to shout blue murder about the rent and nearly had a heart attack when Mazz dug in his pocket, pulled out a wad of money and counted off four tenners. Actually lit the cigarette as he walked off.

Mazz spent the balance of the day reclaiming his territory. He lay in the bath for an hour, took his clothes over to the launderette, bought a couple of samosas from the Indian shop, had a chat with Mr Johnson in the secondhand shop.

'Fucking brilliant what you done for Charlie,' he kept saying, and Mazz shrugged, couldn't see it himself – what Charlie had done for him looked a lot more considerable from Mazz's point of view. Still, someone wanted to see Mazz as a philanthropist, that was a novel enough experience to let it ride. Made him a little uneasy, though, the implication that Charlie was in a state before the band got going. Mazz didn't want Charlie to have troubles; he wanted Charlie to be his rock.

Around six, Mazz walked over to Tyra's. Got his usual reception – giggling girls in the front room, stone-faced mother in the hall. Mazz wondered if Tyra had told her about the baby. Probably not, he reckoned; she wouldn't just be stone-faced, she'd probably have a shotgun ready for him. Instead she just jerked her head towards the upstairs.

'She's up there.' Not a hello, not a how are you doing, not a well done having a hit record making my girl a star. Nothing. Bitch, Mazz thought. Reminded him of the chapel-going types where he came from, never happier than when pursing their lips about someone's transgressions, never a word of praise, things went right. Bitches the lot of them.

Mazz went up the stairs, and found Tyra lying on her bed sobbing, the six o'clock news on in the background.

'What's the matter, love?' he said, walking over and sitting on the bed next to her, stroking her hair for a moment till she slapped his hand away, didn't like anyone touching her hair.

'Bobby,' she said after a while, 'Bobby Sands. I saw him on the news. Hunger strike's going again. He's dying, Mazz. He looked like a bloody skeleton, something out of Auschwitz. They're murdering him, Mazz. Fucking bastards.' She raised her head then sat up. 'But you know what?'

'What?' said Mazz.

'He's standing as an MP. There's a by-election there and he's standing. Think about that. They're saying he's just a common criminal and if he gets elected to Parliament, then what?'

'Christ,' said Mazz.

'Yeah.'

After that she brightened up a bit, stuck a record on, *Scary Monsters*. Tyra loved 'Ashes to Ashes'; Mazz too, something so desperate about it, seemed to chime with the time. Mazz asked if she wanted to go for a drink and she said maybe later but really she just wanted to take it easy. So they sat around, watched *Coronation Street*, listened to some more music, talking about this and that, nothing serious, news again at nine, Bobby Sands all over it. Real edgy stuff, you could see all the TV reporters suddenly waking up to the reality of the situation. All these years they'd been bollocksing on about how the IRA were just a tiny fringe bunch of nutters with no support. Now they were busily preparing the public for the fact that this terrorist might actually win a democratic election. Sad, of course, that the guy had to be killing himself to get any attention but Christ you had to admire the way he was sticking it to them.

Time the news finished, Mazz was starving.

'Fancy coming down the chip shop?' he said, figuring the chances of Tyra's mum coming through with any food for him were on the slim side.

'No,' said Tyra. 'Still feeling a bit sick, you know. You get some.'

'All right,' said Mazz, standing up. 'You sure you don't want anything? Just a plain portion of chips?'

'No thanks,' said Tyra. 'Actually, Mazz, I think I might just go to sleep now, you don't mind?'

'Oh,' said Mazz, 'right. You want me to stay with you?'

Tyra didn't reply, just rolled her eyes theatrically towards the downstairs, her mother's realm, then shook her head.

Then she stood up and kissed Mazz. 'Thanks, love,' she said. 'I'll see you tomorrow, yeah.'

Walking out of the house, the sitting-room door was open and Mazz noticed a big velvet portrait of Elvis Presley on the wall. He shook his head to dispel the illusion and looked again, but there it still was, a portrait of Elvis in his *Jailhouse Rock* period.

Walking back through town, Mazz bumped into Ozzie, one of the social-worker types who ran Grassroots. Ozzie said he was going for a pint, so Mazz followed him into the Salutation, a little Brains pub by the Monument. Ozzie's mates turned out to be a couple of boring-looking lefties, so Mazz went over to the Space Invaders machine, still the mark one model in here, and he spent half an hour or so blasting away, getting a load of dirty looks from the female lefty making loud comments about how nice and quiet it was in the pub – usually.

Mazz sat down for the second pint then, let Ozzie ask him about the band and that, bloke seeming genuinely enthusiastic. Suppose it made him feel like Grassroots was working, bunch of kids who hung about in there getting on to *Top of the Pops*. So Mazz chatted for a little but, be honest, last couple of weeks he'd just about ODed on talking about the band so he drank up and headed out to pick up some chips on Caroline Street and home to crash.

Middle of the night he half woke and turned over to put his arm round Tyra, woke up then with a shock when she wasn't there. Realised how accustomed he'd got to her.

Still, wasn't like he couldn't bear to be without her for a single night so he turned over, went back to sleep and kept on sleeping on and off till two the next afternoon when the phone rang, Tyra asking if he wanted to go into town.

An hour later they met at the Hayes Island Snack Bar. Mazz had a tuna sandwich and a cup of tea, Tyra nothing, said she was still feeling sick. Mazz said she should be eating more not less at a time like this. Tyra told him he knew so much about it he should have the fucking baby. Then she said sorry. Just feeling a bit weird, you know, and Mazz said sure and put his hand on hers and they went for a walk round town.

Walked through the market, Tyra hurrying Mazz past the fish stall, said her sense of smell was going crazy, went up to Kelly's and had a look through the records. Mazz bought Tyra the Susan Cadogan album with 'Hurt So Good' on it; Tyra laughed, asked if he was trying to tell her something. After that they just wandered, looking idly in the shop windows, not saying much, but happy together, and ended up at the Lexington, Tyra suddenly announcing she was hungry after all and proceeding to wolf down half a burger and chips before pushing it aside and saying she had to go home now.

Mazz walked her back and from then on it was the same deal as the night before. Past the gauntlet of Tyra's mum's disapproval into the bedroom. News on. Government obviously waking up to the possibility that Bobby Sands would win, starting the damage limitation. Record on after that, the Susan Cadogan. How about doing a cover said Tyra after they listened to it the third time. You reckon Bobby would sing a thing like that said Mazz and Tyra laughed.

'You told your mum yet?' asked Mazz later on, lying jammed up on the single bed together, Mazz spooning Tyra, his hand stroking her belly.

'Christ no,' said Tyra. 'She'll bloody kill me.'

'Bloody kill me, more like.'

'Yeah.'

'Seriously, though, you got to tell her.'

Tyra sat up, suddenly angry. 'She's my mother, right. Just leave it to me.'

Mazz put his hands up in surrender but something went out of the evening then and it wasn't long before Tyra said she was tired again, and Mazz said there's no way he could stay was there and Tyra shook her head and said sorry, babe, no way, and see you tomorrow, and kissed him and there he was back on the street again at nine o'clock.

This time he didn't even pretend to head straight home; he went round the Philharmonic and found a handful of student girls he knew, friends of Kate's, who all went ooh Kate's so pissed off with you and pretended to give him a hard time but really he could see two out of the three at least would be seriously interested in taking Kate's place.

So he stayed about and even though he didn't do anything he shouldn't have, just flirted a little bit and stayed there till the late licence expired downstairs some time after midnight, he couldn't help feeling a little disloyal as he walked back over the river to the flat, still feeling the place where one of the girls, Miranda, had put her arm round his neck for a slightly too long moment, making a joke about something or other, letting him know she was interested.

Christ, he thought, must be growing up, turning a sure thing like that down.

Again he woke up in the night expecting Tyra to be there and again soon forgot and went back to sleep. It was only when the same sequence was repeated for a third day and night – the meeting, the cup of coffee in the Sarsparilla Bar, the heading back to Tyra's place, the sitting around, the I'm feeling a bit sick now you'd better go, the walk home that this time somehow took in the Student Union disco – that Mazz started to wonder if things were OK.

'Next day he came out with it point blank.

'Listen,' he said, sitting in the big Astey's café, 'why don't you come over to mine tonight?'

It was like he'd slapped her.

'Look,' she said, 'I don't need this.' And started crying.

'Christ,' said Mazz, 'I'm sorry. I didn't mean to . . .'

'Didn't mean what?' she said, suddenly raising her head up from the table. 'Didn't mean to get me pregnant?' Put her head down again, resumed crying.

'Look,' he said. 'Look, it's great you're pregnant. It's like everything's going right.' And he put his hand on hers and stroked it.

'Mazz,' she said after a while. 'Think about it. How are we going to look after a baby? You're living in a rented room, I'm living with my mum. We're in this band, the last few months we've been on the road. We still haven't got any money . . . It's just not going to work.'

Then Mazz let himself think, and then say, the a-word for the first time. 'You want to have an abortion, that what you're saying?'

'Yes. No. Oh Christ, Mazz, I don't know what to think. I'm sorry, that's why I just have to be by myself at the moment. It's not you. I just feel so confused.'

They left then. Mazz offered to walk Tyra home but she shook her head, kissed him on the lips, said she was sorry again and she'd see him tomorrow. Mazz walked home feeling like shit, went over the Four Ways later on for a couple but didn't even feel much like drinking. Back at the flat he watched the football highlights and was asleep by midnight.

A banging on the door woke him up an hour later. Mazz stumbled downstairs and opened up. There was Tyra standing there on the doorstep, looking half-drowned. She threw her arms round him at once and practically dragged him up the stairs and into his bedroom. Neither of them said a word and in just a few more seconds they were both naked on top of the bed and fucking like, well, like there was no tomorrow, like tomorrow was something that had to be denied. The first time it was hard, fast and tumultuous, neither of them holding back, just sucking, biting, scratching, grinding their way to what felt like an explosion of pent-up emotion. As Tyra came she was hammering Mazz on his back with her fists, screaming obscenities in his ear.

Mazz would probably have called it a night at this point but Tyra barely relaxed for a moment before she was stroking his dick again, getting down and sucking him, getting him hard even though it was almost painful. Soon as he was ready she was on top of him, sitting up riding him and so it went on. Afterwards it seemed dreamlike; how often had they done it? Three or four times? The memory that always came back to him of that night was somewhere lost in the pre-dawn, fucking Tyra from behind, his hand curved around her belly, feeling for signs of life.

II

THE KING'S HEAD

1999

Next morning Mazz woke up early with a crashing headache and an urgent need to take a piss. He staggered out the back of the camper, found himself being stared at by an old man and a dog, smiled feebly, then hopped over the sea wall and clambered down on to the beach looking for a secluded spot. Unable to find one, he just turned his back to the town and pissed on the rocks, looking out to sea as he did so. There was a lone surfer out there. Not much of a swell, a couple of feet maybe, but enough for this die-hard to ride easily. Mazz wondered for a moment if it might be Emyr, but couldn't muster up the enthusiasm at this time of the morning to care very much either way. So he climbed back up over the rocks and the wall, endured the glare of the old man and the dog, who didn't seem to have budged an inch, and got back into the relative warmth of the van.

It had been three or so before they'd crashed the night before. After Danny'd left the club the atmosphere seemed to lighten up and JT and the Colonel, in particular, seemed to get on pretty well. Specially when JT figured out who the Colonel was – bad boy of Welsh football 1973, the first sweeper Cardiff City ever had, and near on the last when the manager sacked him for smoking dope in the changing rooms at half time. Long time ago and a lot of water under the bridge and for the most part the Colonel didn't seem to like to talk about it, even though he'd kept the nickname the fans gave him back then – 'the Colonel', like Beckenbauer was 'the Kaiser' – but last night he'd been up for it. Lot of stories, lot of drinks.

Mazz had got a bit fed up with it, to be honest. Kept trying to get the conversation round to the Wurriyas. Sad, really, like my one top-ten hit's better than your two seasons at the City. Anyway no one seemed much interested in Mazz's on-the-road stories, just wanted to know what Robin Friday'd really been like, and Mazz had ended up spending the last hour or so pumping money into the fruit machine. Then when he'd gone to sleep he'd dreamed of Tyra. Simplest dream he'd ever had: no weird plot, no complicated business with people changing into other people, just Tyra getting into bed with him, him reaching out to her, touching her, holding her, bringing her close to him, kissing her, letting his hands wander over her body. And waking up to find himself thirty-nine years old and stuck in a camper van in Porthcawl with the Colonel snoring across the way.

He lay back on his bunk convinced that he was doomed to stay like that for hours waiting for the Colonel to wake up. Next thing he knew was the Colonel standing over him with a cup of tea saying, 'Rise and shine, mate, time we were moving on.'

Mazz couldn't believe it. He knew he was going to be feeling like shit the whole day after last night's excesses, and yet the Colonel, who was a good ten years older than him, didn't seem to feel the pace at all. Be honest, it was starting to get on Mazz's nerves. Far as he could see, the Colonel had it all. Money, house, woman, kids grown up, kid on the way. And he didn't even get hangovers.

Mazz was still in a foul mood as they drove out of Porthcawl, heading west towards the Gower.

'You think he's going to show, your mate?' asked the Colonel.

'Probably not,' said Mazz. 'Still, may as well go and have a look. I got fuck all else to do.'

'Hey,' said the Colonel, 'what's the problem? We got the weather' – he waved his arm in the direction of the blue sky that had replaced the early-morning mist – 'we got the music' – he stuck a tape in the stereo and turned it on – Southside Johnny doing his soul revue thing – 'and out there we got the waves.' The Colonel gestured towards the sea, just visible beyond the miles of belching gasworks that welcomed you to Port Talbot, the heavy industrial sprawl town that stretched for most of the way from Porthcawl to Swansea Bay.

Mazz just hitched himself back into his seat, didn't say a word. Though to be fair he did restrain himself from telling the Colonel to shut the fucking plastic soul off.

The Colonel looked over at him. 'Fancy a smoke then, butt?' With one hand he pulled a cigarette case out of his pocket and flicked it open, took out a ready-rolled joint and snapped the case shut again. Picked up a lighter from the dashboard and lit up, inhaled deeply then passed it over to Mazz. Mazz raised his hand to refuse the spliff.

'Christ, butt,' said the Colonel, 'got out the wrong side of the bunk this morning, didn't we? Tell you what, though, this'll give you a laugh.' He suddenly braked, pulled over a couple of lanes of motorway traffic and took the next exit, for Port Talbot.

Then, instead of following signs to the middle of the town, he headed straight for the giant gasworks. A couple more turns and they were on a company road almost through the gasworks and out the other side. Finally they came to a wire-frame gate that blocked the road off. There was a sign on the gate warning people to keep out – British Gas property – but it didn't look like anyone had been down here in years. The Colonel parked the van and Mazz sighed theatrically, uncomfortably aware that he was starting to behave like a moody adolescent, and followed the Colonel out.

The Colonel clambered over the gate, then down the track in between a couple of deserted storage areas. The track took a sudden right turn and promptly petered out in the middle of a sand dune. Mazz and the Colonel scrambled over the dune and then there they were, looking out at a completely deserted beach.

'Christ,' said Mazz, unable to stop himself from smiling.

'Yeah,' said the Colonel, 'good, eh?' He surveyed the area carefully. 'Actually, I just had an idea your mate might be here. JT told me about this place last night, said it was a real hardcore spot. Figured it had to be worth a go.'

'Worth it anyway,' said Mazz and led the way back to the van, then sat there in a more companionable silence as the Colonel drove back on to the motorway, through Swansea, up on to the moor that took up the central part of the Gower Peninsula, through the little town of Llanrhidian, and along the winding lanes that ended up in the village of Llangennith, where the Colonel got the van parked in the campsite another half mile down the windiest lane yet. It was a different ballgame from Porthcawl this place, though: nice cars parked up by the trailers, whole place neat and tidy, hippy takeaway place set up in a van down the hill. Big scene all night when the summer gets going said the Colonel.

Wetsuits on then and a short walk through the dunes and out on to one of the longest, finest beaches Mazz had ever seen. Which wasn't saying that much as, not being able to swim and all, he'd never been a great one for the beach. But still, by any standards, a good beach and today with the sun out it looked idyllic. There was a fair bit of wind up and the temperature wasn't really sunbathing-hot yet so there weren't too many people out on the beach, but there was a steady stream of folk with wetsuits and boards heading for the water and Mazz followed the Colonel along the beach away to the right and then into the water near a line-up of older-looking guys with real anticipation.

Somehow, though, he couldn't get into it. The waves were a little bigger than anything he'd dealt with before, and he still hardly felt confident in his ability to swim. Plus he felt intimidated seeing the Colonel with these older surfer guys who he seemed to know from time, though with the Colonel you could never be sure: people seemed to gravitate to him so naturally that for all Mazz knew he'd never met any of them before in his life. Anyway they were all doing the business, riding the waves, standing tall, and Mazz was feeling like more and more of a dickhead as he lay flat on his board doing his best not to get drowned and occasionally picking up a little bit of a ride through the shallows. Then, after an hour or so, he was just paddling out as a surfer picked up a wave and came arrowing towards him. Mazz thought he was going to get his head taken off but then the surfer swerved out of his way at the last moment, and then when the guy came back out he swore at Mazz and Mazz thought fuck this for a game of soldiers, waved to the Colonel indicating he'd had enough and trudged back to the van.

Which was where he found Natalie. She was sitting next to the van in a deckchair reading a book, wearing a fifties-style sundress with a cardie over the top and a pair of Catwoman sunglasses. The baby wasn't showing and she looked, Mazz reckoned, as cool as fuck.

'Hi,' she said, stretching and putting the book down. Mazz glanced at it quickly, just to make sure it wasn't *Captain Corelli's Mandolin*, like every other sorry girlie on the beach was reading waiting for their surfer boys to return. It wasn't, it was some Ted Hughes thing.

'Hi,' he said back, and wondered why she was smiling quite so broadly at him, then became conscious he was standing there wearing an elderly wetsuit. He reached round trying to undo the zip.

'Want a hand?' said Natalie. She stood up, walked round behind him and pulled down the zip with one easy movement.

'Ta,' said Mazz, then went round the far side of the van to get changed in relative privacy.

'Wasn't expecting to see you here,' he shouted as he towelled himself.

'Oh,' she said, 'Ronnie called me this morning and said you were heading this way so I thought I'd surprise you boys. Make sure you're not having too much fun.'

Mazz pulled on his jeans and a new shirt and walked round to where Natalie was sitting. She stood up, stretched.

'Fancy a walk?' she said. 'Ronnie will be in the water for hours yet, I know him.'

''Spect you're right,' said Mazz. 'Let's go.'

Natalie led the way, walking north from the campsite through the dunes parallel to the beach, heading towards somewhere called the Blue Pool – a special place she said. As they walked Mazz filled her in on the doings of the previous few days and Natalie nodded and laughed as appropriate but didn't say much. Then Mazz asked her about her book and she started telling him about how it was these poems Ted Hughes had written about his wife who'd killed herself – 'a wonderful poet called Sylvia Plath,' she said, like Mazz wouldn't have heard of her which pissed him off a bit – and how interesting it was because, like, she'd always thought that Hughes was a right bastard but now, reading his side of the story, you could really relate to him and actually she thought it was kind of noble that he had waited all this time and let people write all this stuff about how evil and macho he was, and didn't it make a change from all these people these days who the minute anything even vaguely interesting happens to them they go and write about it in the papers.

And then they were at the Blue Pool, which is this big rock pool up in the hills above the next bay round the corner from Llangennith, and it was lovely and mysterious and deserted and the sun was shining so of course Natalie stripped off and jumped into the pool and laughed at Mazz when he said he'd had enough wet for one day and he got in anyway 'cause he didn't want to feel like a voyeur sitting there on the side watching Natalie bounce around. So they splashed around a bit and Mazz was trying to keep near the edge 'cause the pool shelved steeply and God knows how deep it was in the middle. He asked Natalie and she said like way, way deep and then, playing around, she dived underwater and pulled his feet from under him, dragging him down like a mermaid. And Mazz kicked out in panic to get her hands off him and she reared away, and came up looking hurt. Then, when she saw Mazz gasping frantically for air, she started laughing and couldn't stop even as he scrambled to the side and got out, and kept laughing as he tried to get dry, and Mazz was sure she was looking at his dick which was about as big as you'd expect it to be when you've just jumped in a freezing rock pool, then been roundly terrified and half drowned.

'Oh God, I'm sorry for laughing,' she said a little later when they'd got their clothes on and were walking back towards the campsite, 'you should have told me you weren't much of a swimmer.'

Mazz laughed too and they kept on walking up dune and down dune and after a while, standing at the top of yet another smooth bracken-covered incline, Natalie said, 'D'you get the feeling we're going round in circles? We don't seem to be getting anywhere at all.'

Mazz just laughed once more and then suddenly tripped Natalie and sent her rolling down the dune and then he dropped down and rolled himself after her, rolling over and over and falling on top of her. And suddenly her arms were round his neck and his around her waist and then they were kissing and then Natalie broke off and looked Mazz in the eye and said, 'You don't remember me at all, do you?'

Mazz took this in in the space of a single blink. She was the same Natalie he'd had the one-nighter with all those years back. It stood to reason really. But the funny thing was that the more time he'd spent with her this time around the less he seemed to remember the art student he'd picked up in 1981. He realised there was only one thing to say that wouldn't get him into trouble. Nothing. He didn't say a word, just smiled and rolled his eyes at her in a way she could interpret how she liked.

'You were a fucking bastard,' she said, 'only time that's ever happened to me. I let someone pick me up, shag me and kick me out the next morning, didn't even give your phone number.' As she spoke she was methodically undoing the buttons of Mazz's shirt and pulling it off. 'I thought about you for months. Waited for you to call, went to your poxy gigs.' She had his zip down now and with his active co-operation was pulling his jeans off.

She pushed him back on to the bracken then, didn't undress, just pulled her dress up. Nothing underneath, climbed on top of Mazz and took him inside her. He almost asked her if she was using anything, you know. Then he remembered, she was pregnant. Then she started moving on top of him and, well, if it was a bloke you'd have called what happened next premature ejaculation. She can't have lasted more than a minute before she was shuddering and biting his neck, her whole body in orgasmic spasm. Mazz was just lying there, bewildered as much as anything.

'Well,' she said after a moment, 'you going to fuck me then?'

'Yeah,' he said, 'not this way, though,' and he pushed her up and off him, then clambered round behind her.

'Mmm,' she grunted, on her hands and knees now, sticking her face in the ground and her bum up in the air. He started fucking her then, fast and hard, only one goal in sight. As he did his hand curved around her to feel her tits under the dress, but ended up resting on her belly instead. And suddenly he was plunged back into memory, fucking Tyra this way when she was pregnant. He came in an instant. And as he pulled out and sank to the ground next to Natalie it was all he could do to stop from crying – how had it all come down to this?

They rearranged their clothing in silence and started heading back to the campsite. Mazz led the way, stomping up dune and down dune, his mind in turmoil. Now and again he'd look back and Natalie would be there calmly following in his wake, a small smile playing on her lips from time to time. Mazz had an urge to hit her to wipe the smile off, or maybe to grab her, throw her down on the ground and do her again, keep on doing her till everything else went out of his mind. He kept on going on his hands and knees now, struggling straight up an almost sheer dune rather than go round it. What the hell had he been thinking of? The Colonel was his mate. As good a mate as he had right at the moment. Was Natalie going to tell him? Was that how it worked, a little power game between the two of them – 'Ooh, guess what, Ronnie, I've just fucked your mate'? Sit there and watch the Colonel beat shit out of Mazz, as he no doubt would? Maybe that was it, all an elaborate plan to get back at Mazz for that one-nighter. Probably no more than he deserved anyway.

'Cause more than that, the thing that was in the front of his mind was how he'd felt with this pregnant woman. What he'd remembered: Tyra, Tyra, Tyra. How she'd had the abortion, then. How he'd thought after that she was probably right and it was all for the good, they were too young, there was plenty of time. Well, he was thirty-nine now and genuinely felt older like they don't say in the personal ads. And he felt empty.

The Colonel was lying on a rug next to the van smoking a fat joint and staring up at the clouds. Mazz walked towards him with a sense of utter dread, sure he had the world's cheesiest smile plastered over his face. But he needn't have worried. Natalie just went towards the Colonel, bent down and putted her arms round him, kissed him, natural as anything. The Colonel patted her belly then sat up and made room for her next to him on the rug. Mazz stood there feeling like an idiot and when the Colonel passed him the joint he accepted it gratefully, Tried to drag the whole thing into his lungs with one great intake of breath.

'I still don't believe it,' laughed Tyra, talking to Bobby that night, the day after her lunch with Jason Flaherty, Bobby there to tell Tyra what she'd found out about the ransacking of Charlie's flat.

'Me either, girl,' said Bobby. 'So what happened next?'

'Well,' said Tyra, 'like I said. 'He ordered up another bottle of wine and talked me into having a dessert, twisted my arm right, and then I saw the time and said I had to go get the kids. But he says can't anyone else pick them up, and I say well I'll call my mum so he passes me his mobile and I get that sorted and we have the dessert and that and it's about half three and he says why don't I come back to the office with him.'

'Oh yeah?' said Bobby.

'Yeah, well I was interested, wasn't I? Not every day I get to spend time with someone actually has an influence on things, like. So anyway I says OK and he calls a cab and we go into town and we're just going round by the city hall when he tells the cab to stop and we get out and he says you been in the Hilton yet? And I nearly say what Hilton but I look over the road and the old Prudential building there it's got a sign on it saying Hilton and they've gone and converted it and I hadn't even noticed, so I says no, and he says oh let's go up to the bar, it's got a marvellous view.'

'C'mon, girl,' said Bobby, 'you must have figured he was chatting you up by now.'

'Yeah, well,' said Tyra, smiling, 'doesn't happen to me that often these days I'm going to walk away from it. So we take the lift up to the top floor and we walk in and the guy there he takes one look at Jason and it's all Mr Flaherty this and can I help madam off with her coat and then we're sat by the window looking out at the city and it's a beautiful day and he's right, the view's marvellous, you can see the stadium being built – really looks like they're getting it finished now and all – you can see the new hotel down there and everything – and he orders up a couple of cocktails and . . .'

Tyra broke off halfway between blushing and laughing. Bobby hooted. 'Yeah!' she said. 'Go on, girl, then what?'

'Then what yourself. Then what d'you think?'

'Wouldn't know, girl, wouldn't know. Probably you just had the drink, went out and got the bus back.'

'Not exactly,' said Tyra. 'Then I lean over and snog him – even as I'm doing it, I can't believe myself. Like, is that all it takes to get me going? Let alone what the waiters and that must have thought. Anyway one thing leads to a bit of the other, like, and then he tells me he's got a suite on permanent standby any time he wants it, like. Did someone a favour sorting out the planning apparently. So . . . Well, I'll spare you the details, like . . .'

'Too right,' said Bobby, making a face. Then she added, 'Just as long as you didn't let him get on top of you, girl!' and started laughing. Tyra joined in and soon the two women were in near hysterics sitting there on the sofa, Robson Green smarming away on the TV in the background.

'You going to see him again then?' asked Bobby once they'd both calmed down.

'Dunno,' said Tyra, suddenly serious. 'It didn't really seem like that. More a spur-of-the-moment sort of thing, you know what I mean. Nice, though,' she said, her eyes lighting up, 'nice.'

In fact it had been great. One thing about getting older, all that stuff you read in the women's magazines about women hitting their sexual prime in their thirties, it was true enough. It was like she could really enjoy it these days for what it was. Thing that pissed you off was thinking about all that sex you had when you were young and men were all over you and most of the time you didn't get much out of it. Now she was well ready for it but hardly anyone seemed to want to give her the chance. And Christ had she needed it. She'd felt so much better after. Got home, picked the kids up from her mum and her mood was just so up. So no, it was hardly love, her and Jason, but he wanted to do it again she wouldn't say no, Nice meal, nice hotel room, no commitments, no bullshit, why not?

'So,' said Bobby, 'get that grin off your face and tell me what he said about Charlie.'

Tyra ran through what Jason had said about Vernon Nichols.

Bobby listened intently then frowned. 'So how did Jason know about the break-in?'

'That's what I was wondering. He said something about friends in the police . . .'

'Yeah,' said Bobby, 'that'll be it. Who was the copper you saw?'

'Fairfax. Jimmy Fairfax.'

Bobby burst out laughing. 'Jimmy Fairfax. Course it would be. City boys together they were. When I first used to go down the City back in the day, seventy-seven, seventy-eight, Jason and Jimmy they were two of the top faces. Any trouble kicked off, you just got in behind one of them you'd be all right. Specially Jason, you remember how big he was even then?'

Tyra nodded.

'Yeah, well, you lined up with Jason nine times out of ten the other lot would just run for it. That'll be the connection all right. Jason and Jimmy. So – you believe him, this stuff about Vernon Nichols?'

'Yeah, I suppose. Why, you heard anything?'

'This and that,' said Bobby. 'No dirt on Nichols in particular. But one of the girls was talking about how she'd heard they were planning to build a casino down the docks.'

'A casino?'

'Yeah, a big casino hotel like in Las Vegas. Probably just pie-in-the-sky stuff, but the girls were getting quite excited by the idea, bound to pull in the punters a place like that. Most of what's happening in the bay so far is all family stuff – not much good for the girls hanging round Techniquest or Harry Ramsden's, is there?' Bobby paused, 'Though we got hopes for the Assembly,' and gave a big dirty laugh.

'Oh yeah, that's the other thing,' said Tyra then, 'Jason was talking about how Nichols has some MP in his pocket, like he was blackmailing the guy or something. You hear anything about any MPs from the girls?'

Bobby shrugged. 'Not off-hand, like – well apart from Ron Davies of course but everyone's talking about him – but I'll check it out. Any MP in particular?'

Tyra's turn to shrug. 'The local guy, I suppose, Derek what's-his-face?'

'Christ,' said Bobby, 'doesn't look like he'd have the bottle to get up to any trouble, but you never can tell, like, so I'll ask about.'

Bobby fell silent for a bit, then spoke up again in a quieter voice. 'Talking of asking about, I've been thinking of trying to trace my dad.'

'Yeah?' said Tyra.

'Yeah, well, be honest with you, it's your dad dying that did it. Look, I know this sounds pathetic but I always had a little idea that maybe he was my real dad. Sorry, it's like I'm trying to muscle in on your . . .'

'No, I understand,' said Tyra, thinking about how urgently Bobby had been looking through Charlie's papers the day they went round to the flat, and a wave of sympathy went through her.

'Yeah, stupid I know, but anyway, I thought it was about time I made an effort to find out . . . Before he dies too.'

Bobby stopped talking and choked back a sob. 'Shit,' she said, 'I'm sorry. Just talking shit.' She stood up. 'I'll see you,' she said and made for the door but before she could get there Tyra was cutting her off and folding her in her arms, holding Bobby the way she'd hold Jermaine. Bobby stiffened then relaxed in the hug, stayed there for a full minute, then pulled apart, whispered the word thanks and headed out the door into her car and round to the Custom House to meet her girlfriend Maria at the end of another hard night's hustling.

Later that night Mazz, the Colonel and Natalie were in the King's Head in Llangennith itself. It was the first really warm evening of what now seemed like summer and the place was rammed. They were sitting at a table in the garden out in front of the pub and all the time more people were piling in, more and more cars and vans were streaming down the lane towards the campsite. Most of them seemed to be Cardiff people who all appeared to know each other, all talking about this club they'd been to or that docco they were making.

Mazz had calmed down now. Calmed down pretty quickly in fact soon as he realised Natalie wasn't going to say anything. Colonel didn't seem to suspect a thing, thought it was nice of Mazz to take Nat walking. Made you feel a bit shit that, but to be honest it wasn't exactly the first time Mazz had been in that sort of situation. Story of his life, really, knocking off his mate's women. Most awkward one had been when he'd done it with the fat Yank's wife the evil Jap – that was before he'd realised how evil she was, mind. Done it a couple of times, on an American tour. It wasn't that Mazz had been worried about the fat Yank finding out – the amount of smack he was taking that tour he was hardly doing his bit in the marital-duties front – but more that if he pissed Kizumi off he could end up getting kicked out of the band, which would not have been cool, the money he was earning already owed. Made him feel like a bit of a dick that, though, Mandingo servicing milady.

So, anyway, there they were sitting in front of the King's Head, Mazz and the Colonel getting drunk, Natalie watching them. They went inside for a bit, had a game of pool. Natalie said she was tired, she'd head back to the campsite; Mazz and the Colonel could come with her now in the car or walk back later. The Colonel said they'd walk. Natalie gave him a bit of a look but then smiled and kissed him and said she'd see him later.

Thought hit Mazz then, where's he going to sleep? In the van with the Colonel and Natalie had to be a bridge too far, even by Mazz's standards.

'No worries,' said the Colonel, 'got a tent in the van. Put it up when we get back. 'Nother drink?'

Another drink it was, and then a couple more. At one point Mazz was coming out of the bar into the garden carrying a couple of pints and he nearly walked into the Asian girl he'd seen in Le Pub. Didn't recognise her at first, which wasn't too surprising, state he'd got into that night, state he was getting into this night. But she remembered him all right, gave him a big smile, said why didn't he come and join her and her mates; she waved at two girls perched on the wall, they'd just got here. Mazz just said yeah sure and walked through the crowd to where the Colonel was sitting slumped over the table showing every sign of being asleep.

Mazz whacked down the pint in front of the Colonel and he raised his head and said, 'Oh God, am I still here?' and promptly put his head back down again.

Later still Mazz and the three girls, with a couple of blokes from Swansea and a partially revived Colonel, were walking down the lane towards the campsite passing round an assortment of bottles.

At the campsite the Colonel pulled himself together remarkably to put up Mazz's tent in no time flat then crawled into the van. Mazz wandered off to where the girls were, sitting round a campfire with the Swansea boys and a bunch of German hippies. Mazz had a bottle of red wine in his hand. He reckoned the girl from Newport, Anita, might be up for something, but he was too drunk and too confused by what had happened with Natalie to reciprocate.

Next morning Mazz had a vague memory of passing a joint back and forth with her and snogging in between puffs. But that was all. There was another memory too. Sometime deep into the night a couple of the surfers from Porthcawl showed up and, somewhere round the bottom of the bottle of red wine or maybe the bottom of another bottle, who knew, one of the guys said to Mazz, 'You won't find your mate here, butt.'

Mazz nodded. Actually he'd all but forgotten that was why he was here at all, looking for Emyr.

'You want to find him, try the Severn Bore. It's a five-star on Tuesday.'

The bloke probably said more than that but that was all Mazz could remember when he woke up the next morning, the tent half collapsed around his lower body, his head full of the unbearable heaviness of living. Severn Bore. Five-star. Tuesday. What did that all mean?

12

THE SEVERN BORE

1999

Next morning Tyra realised there was one person could probably fill her in as to what the story was with Charlie and Vernon Nichols.

'Hiya, Mum,' she said, 'all right if I come round after I drop the kids off to school?'

Her mum, Celeste, sounded a little surprised which made Tyra feel guilty, like she never went round there to see the old lady apart from to drop the kids off or pick them up. Still, just 'cause you were family didn't mean you had to live in each other's pockets. Least that's what she'd always thought, but with her dad dying alone like that maybe she was just being a selfish bitch. Trouble was, she spent too much time with her mum she'd probably end up killing her and all.

Anyway, quarter past nine there she was round at Angelina Street at her mum's place, the house she, Tyra, mostly grew up in. When she'd been little – though she didn't really remember this much, only half remembered it the way you do from looking at old photos and people telling you this is where you used to play – they lived in Sophia Street. That was in the old Butetown – the crumbling overcrowded Victorian terraces they used to call Tiger Bay. Then the sixties redevelopment had come when she was three or so and they'd been moved out to Ely for a year or two – a time her mum used to talk about with great bitterness.

Then they'd moved back to Butetown to the brand-new house in

Angelina Street. And Tyra grew up hearing the mantra that the house was lovely but it wasn't the same. Course people always go on like that . . . When did you last hear anyone say how much better things are these days? But still it was true, though, her mum's mantra. The houses were nicer; even the big blocks of flats in Loudoun Square were a hell of a lot nicer than the – no other word for it – slums that had been there before. No one's nostalgic for TB and outside toilets. But the life thing, that was true too. It wasn't just the redevelopment. Butetown had been declining since the war; coal and steel weren't what they were, the shipping dropped off, the population declined. March-of-history time. But still again she had a powerful nostalgia for the docks life her dad used to tell her about, a nostalgia all the more powerful for being on the very fringes of her memory. Scattered images: her dad standing outside a club on Bute Street – was she there herself, a little girl, or was she remembering a photo? She couldn't say. But she missed all these places she couldn't really remember – the Cairo, the Ghana, the seamen's missions, the opium dens, the whole Tiger Bay business.

And her dad, of course, had missed it more than anyone. It had been his kingdom for a while back in the late fifties when he had his Lonsdale belt, when he was the quickest lightweight in the world according to the best judges. When he'd fight in London or New York and come home to a club full of people all waiting to shake his hand and buy him a drink. Then it had all gone at once. He'd started losing, the way all boxers do when the reflexes slow, and Tiger Bay got knocked down too, right from under him.

When Celeste and Tyra had been moved up to Ely, Charlie had simply refused to follow. He'd hung around Butetown then signed on for a while as part of a band touring the Northern clubs impersonating the Drifters – apparently there were three different sets of Drifters all out there simultaneously. By the time Celeste and Tyra were back in Butetown he was established as the semi-detached daddy she knew and loved.

Drove her mum mad when she was a kid, how she would idealise her dad. All the while she was growing up, her mum never seemed to have a good word to say about the man. Even when she'd had another kid by him, her little sister Corinne, there'd been no let-up, like the baby was just another wrong he'd done her.

Result was over the years Tyra had pretty much stopped talking to her mum about Charlie. Specially as Charlie had gone downhill these last years. She couldn't face her mum going I told you so – her dad nothing more than a shiftless drunk, boring people in the pub about what he used to be. That's what had made her furious at the funeral, seeing her mum giving it the grieving widow. She shivered at the door, not looking forward to broaching the subject now.

Inside, her mum made the tea and looked at her, obviously waiting for Tyra to reveal the reason for her visit, so she jumped straight in.

'Mum,' she said, 'what d'you know about my dad and Vernon Nichols?'

'Vernon Nichols,' said Celeste heavily, 'Vernon Nichols. I just don't know, girl. Long time ago I would have told you Vernon Nichols was a good man. He was Charlie's backer, like a boxing manager, you know. Big Vern they used to call him, which was a joke 'cause he was a sawn-off little man. Well, Big Vern help your father a lot in those early days, that's what he used to tell me. Any time he needed a loan or something, Big Vern was always there. Use to have big parties too, all sorts of people would come, boxers from London and all over, singers, Shirley Bassey, Lorne Lesley, American singers too like the Platters, they all used to come down to Butetown back then. Of course those were different times, dear. Lot of water under the bridge since then.'

'Yes, Mum,' said Tyra. 'But he kept in touch did he, Vernon?'

'Not for a long time, girl, least not as far as I know. Though what your father got up to, who he saw, I can't tell you. Next time I remember hearing that name was in the seventies, I think, when your father told me that Big Vern had offered him a job.'

'A job?'

'Well, not what I would call a job, girl. He said he'd pay your father to be at the new casino he opened up in town, Caligula's. All your father had to do was hang around the bar, greeting people who came in and have a drink with anyone old enough to remember when Charlie was the champion. Like a mascot. You ask me, that's when your father's drinking started to get bad. Every night sitting there telling the same old stories, people buying him drinks. Now I told him he shouldn't do it, he should have more dignity. But he wouldn't have it – nothing but thanks for Vern Nichols for giving him the job. You ask me, girl, I think Vern was enjoying it, watching your father humiliate himself for a few drinks. Like he was getting his own back. He was always jealous of your father, of course.'

'Jealous?' said Tyra. 'Why was that?'

'Oh, the usual thing with men. You know, women.' And then to Tyra's great surprise she saw her mother start to crease with embarrassment.

'Mum,' said Tyra, laughing, 'not jealous over you, was he? Is that it?'

'Was a long time ago now, girl, I don't remember too well,' said Celeste feebly.

'C'mon, Mum,' urged Tyra, delighted to have found some sign that her mother wasn't always the stern disapproving figure she remembered.

'All right, it was nothing really. There I was, just fresh off the boat, living with my neighbour auntie's cousin Pearl and her family in Loudoun Square, and just starting work in the infirmary. So a few of the girls we go out to the Ocean Club every Friday, dance to the rhythm and blues, and there's all sorts down there and one day this little white guy, smart-looking feller in a nice suit, comes up to me, asks if I ever did any singing, said he could put me in a talent show . . .' Celeste broke off, looking more embarrassed than ever.

'Mum,' said Tyra, laughing hard now. 'You fell for that old line?'

'Course I knew it was a line, girl, I wasn't born yesterday, but like I say he was a smart feller and, well, you know things were different to what they were back home, so I went out with him a couple of times, let him think I was swallowing his line about the talent contest and . . .'

'And what?' said Tyra eagerly.

'And nothing. Just round then Pearl's cousin friend Charlie, the famous boxer she was always talking about, came to visit and that was that for me. Bye bye, Vern. And Vern couldn't say nothing of course 'cause Charlie was his great black hope.'

Tyra fell silent. She wanted to know just how far her mum went with Vern, but she couldn't quite bring herself to ask. And at the same time she was assailed by a memory of her and Jason in his hotel suite two days ago. What was she to him? Another notch on the bedpost? She didn't think so. He'd been kind of shy, Jason, when it came down to it, vulnerable with his clothes off. But maybe it was worse than just point-scoring, maybe there was revenge there too, revenge on Mazz. Mazz who'd been the golden boy when Jason was the big fat manager. A cold wind suddenly seemed to blow right through her. Time to get back on track.

'So what then, Mum? He didn't stay at the casino for long, did he?' She had a distant memory of this casino period, must have been when she was nine or ten, Charlie bringing her a toy roulette wheel.

'No, six months, a year maybe, then him and Vernon have a big row. Your father getting a little fresh with this young lady croupier. Probably Vern had his eye on her as well . . .'

'And after that did Dad have much more to do with Vernon?'

'Not that I heard of.'

'You know he was Dad's landlord, the place on James Street?'

'No,' said Celeste, her brow furrowing, 'I never heard that.'

Mazz figured the Colonel would know. The Colonel near enough knew everything. Mazz had seen him in action on Quiz Night in his local in Penarth; they had to handicap him to give the other teams a chance. State capital of Iowa, first man to score a century and double century on test-match debut, number of comets to enter the earth's atmosphere in the past century, number of top-ten hits Bananarama had . . . all well within the Colonel's purlieu. So the significance of Severn Bore and five-star should be no problem. Tuesday Mazz guessed he could work out for himself. He clambered out of his tent and walked towards the van. Even from a little distance he could see it moving, rocking. A couple of involuntary steps closer and he could hear Natalie crying out. Mazz shook his head, walked on past the van over the dunes and on to the beach, saw the water as flat as anything, stripped down to his boxers and taught himself to swim.

Couple of hours later he'd managed to swim twenty yards or so in a kind of makeshift breaststroke, his hangover had dissipated somewhat and he was feeling a whole lot better. Back at the van Natalie and the Colonel were sitting out on deckchairs drinking cups of coffee and looking like an ad for bohemian holiday-making.

'Bloke comes up to me last night,' Mazz said, once he'd sat down, 'says,

"You're looking for Emyr, there's a Severn Bore, five-star, Tuesday" – any of that mean anything to you?'

'You know the bore's a wave, yeah?' the Colonel said.

Mazz nodded. He had some vague memory that there was this, like, tidal wave that went up the River Severn, but he thought it was every seven years or something.

'Yeah,' he said, 'goes every seven years or something.'

'Nah,' said the Colonel, 'there's a few every month, more in spring and autumn.'

'All right,' Mazz said, 'how about five-star?'

'Well, I'm guessing now, butt, but I reckon that's how big the wave is. They have like a timetable and stuff for it. So that's got to be it, yeah, and like, a five-star wave's got to be a big one.'

'OK,' said Mazz, 'and I can work the Tuesday bit out myself. So there's going to be a big Severn Bore on Tuesday. What's that to do with Emyr?'

'S'obvious,' said the Colonel.

'Yeah?' said Mazz.

'Yeah. It's a wave, innit? People surf waves. Your mate's going to be surfing the Severn Bore on Tuesday. Least that's what this bloke thinks.'

The Colonel was right of course. Mazz got a lift back to Cardiff that afternoon with the Anita girl and her mates, all pissed off because of the lack of waves – everybody was a surfer these days, far as Mazz could see. He'd gone with them as being around the Colonel and Natalie was just too weird really, after a while.

Back in Cardiff he went into this surf shop, asked about the bore. Guy there scratched his head, said yeah he'd heard people did that. Fuckin' hardcore thing to do, you asked him. Mazz thought that sounded like Emyr and went round the cyber-café where a little bit of work on the Internet got him the timetable and said that yeah sure enough there would be a five-star wave passing a place called Newnham, ten o'clock Tuesday morning. Tomorrow morning.

He called the Colonel on his mobile. The Colonel was well up for it. Said him and Nat would be back in Penarth that night. He'd pick Mazz up at eight in the morning from outside the castle.

Mazz was there on time, clutching a cup of coffee and an Egg McMuffin. The Colonel rolled up a couple of minutes later and Mazz got in the van, still eating the muffin.

'Breakfast of champions,' he said, expecting a laugh, but the Colonel just grunted. Early-morning ill-temper, thought Mazz, and sat back quietly in his seat, finishing off the food while the Colonel drove out down Newport Road.

Forty-five minutes later they'd turned off the M4 at Chepstow and headed up the A48, the road that follows the Severn up to the bridge at Gloucester, and the Colonel still hadn't said a word. Mazz started to figure that maybe this was down to more than the earliness of the hour. Bastard Natalie must have told him last night. Bastard women can't just do a thing, they've got to talk about it too, make sure everybody gets to hear about it. Bollocks. Nah, that was pathetic. Like fuck it was her fault. What the hell had he thought he was doing? Didn't even fancy her that much or anything; when he'd come he'd been thinking about Tyra. Maybe that'd make it all right. Don't worry, mate, I wasn't really shagging your woman 'cause I was thinking of someone else while I was doing it.

Trouble was till the Colonel said something there wasn't much Mazz could do. Otherwise he'd be starting off saying, 'Colonel, look I'm sorry I shagged Natalie, right, it's just we had a bit of history and I wasn't feeling myself, like,' and then the Colonel could just look at him like what the hell did you just say. So they just sat there in this festering kind of silence till they got to Newnham which is some Heart of England-looking place, an olde worlde rivertown. They carried on through to the end of town then the Colonel pulled over into a little car park on the right. There were a couple of cars parked, and on a small embankment a regulation middle-aged anorak stood there consulting some kind of timetable.

'Christ,' says Mazz, 'a wavespotter,' and the Colonel actually started to grin for an instant.

Mazz climbed up on to the embankment and had a look around. The river was higher at this point, looked a good couple of hundred yards across. As wide, he reckoned, as the Mississippi in Memphis and about as viscous and muddy and generally unappealing to get into.

'Fucking hell,' said the Colonel, the first words he'd uttered all morning.

'Yeah,' said Mazz, grateful for any kind of an opening. 'You see anyone out there?' and he scanned the mudflats and sandbars downriver.

'Yeah,' said the Colonel, 'I think. Over there.' He pointed towards a sandbank over on the far side of the river. There was a small black figure just visible.

'So,' said Mazz. 'What d'you reckon?'

'Well,' said the Colonel, an expression of grim resignation on his face, 'it's what we came to do so let's do it.' He led the way back to the van and they changed into their wetsuits. They clambered back on to the platform and the anorak turned to look at them.

'Have to be quick, lads,' he said, tapping his timetable, 'bore's coming through in five minutes. Best thing you can do is get in just by here,' he pointed to the edge of the raised platform area they were standing on, 'drift downstream and paddle across to the far side, I think you'll find.'

Mazz nodded his thanks but the bloke carried on, 'Course, you ask me it would be better if they banned all you surfers and canoeists from riding the wave. Then maybe we'd have a proper one, 'stead of it getting all broken up.'

Mazz smiled again, this time rather fixedly, and started gingerly lowering himself off the platform and on to the riverbank itself. A moment later the Colonel was there next to him.

'You sure you want to do this?' said the Colonel.

'Yeah,' said Mazz, smiling unconvincingly.

'Your funeral, bra,' said the Colonel and walked into the water, his board held in front of him.

Mazz put a foot in the water, thanking Christ the Colonel had brought along flippers for them both, took another step, then another, then lost his footing completely and bellyflopped in on top of his board. His face plunged into the murky river and he frantically tried to pull it back out without swallowing any of the water. Ahead of him the Colonel was lying prone on his board and paddling across the river while letting the current pull him downstream.

Mazz did his best to do likewise, which turned out not to be too difficult, the current doing most of the work. No, the difficult bit was not being put off by all the shit being carried down the river. The usual plastic detritus was bad enough; worse was the animal refuse. Mazz saw two dead rats, then another one which, Christ, didn't seem to be dead at all. Then, shit, he didn't believe it, a dead dog, a big dog all puffed up. He turned his head away, concentrated on paddling like hell to get away from this nightmare.

As they got closer to the sandbank on the far side, the figure there started to come into focus. It was a surfer, all right, one wearing a natty Billabong suit and carrying a shortish gun of a board, which surprised Mazz as the night before the Colonel had assured him this would be a longboard job. Closer still and Mazz could begin to make out the surfer's features. Emyr, he was sure of it. At the same time he could hear this faint roaring noise, something like a big plane in the distance, but he looked up at the sky and there was no plane. Christ, it had to be the bore, coming their way.

Closer still now, and the waiting surfer was Emyr all right. But just as they approached the sandbank, Emyr started wading into the water then climbing on his board and paddling out into the river.

The Colonel changed direction to follow him and for a moment Mazz wasn't sure what to do; most of him just wanted to get to the sandbank and forget about the whole thing. Really there was no choice but to go after the others, unless he wanted to walk to Gloucester, cross over the bridge there and walk back again along the other side.

The noise was building up now, a great roar coming from downriver. He looked to his left and could see it, a great wave spanning the whole width of the river, still a couple of hundred yards away but moving at a stately pace towards him. There was nothing else for it. He started paddling upstream.

Emyr was twenty yards ahead of him, the Colonel maybe ten yards, both of them paddling hard, going against the current, trying to get up a bit of momentum ready for when the wave picked them up. Mazz had a go but he had no rhythm and the current was dragging him downstream. He hoped to hell the wave would pick him up. If it somehow passed him by, he suddenly realised the current would like as not take him all the way downstream, past the Severn Bridges and out into the Bristol Channel. That happened and he would be, not to put too fine a point on it, dead.

He was just about ready to panic when he looked back over his shoulder, the noise now amazing, near deafening, and he saw the river gone mad, the placid inevitable downstream current replaced by a four-foot-high wall of water coming straight towards him.

And then – woooff – it picked him up and, once again, despite everything, the exhilaration hit him. He was flying down the middle of a river. Well, not flying exactly – there wasn't the pace of a sea wave – gliding was nearer the mark; he was gliding down the middle of this enormous river. The wave picked up the Colonel next and he got on easily and after a moment or two stood up, looking as relaxed and unconcerned as a man on one of those long horizontal conveyer-belt escalators you get at airports.

Next up was Emyr. Emyr's style was completely different. The moment he got on the wave he was up on the board and not content to ride it peacefully forwards like Mazz, lying prone, or the Colonel, standing up, but fighting the wave, gunning himself to left and right across the wave, heading for the edges of the wave nearer the bank where it was bigger and looked, though Mazz couldn't figure how it could be, faster.

They were carried along this way for what seemed like miles but was probably only a few hundred yards, past the platform where they'd got on and into a long straight passage running parallel to the road, when suddenly Mazz noticed that up ahead the wave seemed to break into three. Emyr seemed to be heading for the right-hand part of the wave, the one that looked to be heading dangerously close to the far bank. Mazz was still in the middle and the Colonel had somehow drifted over to the left and his wave was suddenly building in size and destined, as far as Mazz could see, for a spectacular wipeout in a clump of trees dead ahead of him.

Mazz wasn't sure what to do. Try and keep on the wave and follow Emyr or try to get over to the side and help the Colonel out. His instinct was to go after the Colonel; only problem was he wasn't sure how to move sideways along the wave. The one thing he wanted to avoid was losing the wave himself and getting swept downstream. He was just cautiously trying to shift his weight to the left when he looked down and realised that he was not the only creature to have been picked up by the bore. Right next to him was one definitely live rat, surfing like a pro, and there – oh shit – swept in front of him was the dead dog. Mazz had a sudden nightmare vision of the pointed fins underneath his board catching the dog's carcass and ripping its putrid stomach open. He yanked the board over to his left, suddenly gained momentum and started shooting along the wave just as the Colonel was trying to edge his board to the right and away from the clump of trees. Mazz caught the Colonel full amid boards, they both came off, and the wave suddenly building to six foot of foaming water flung them both, boards and all, into the trees.

They came to rest on a mud bank tangled up in brambles and tree roots. Mazz opened his eyes and looked left and saw the Colonel sprawled upside down on the bank. He couldn't help laughing and all at once the Colonel started laughing too.

This was the moment, Mazz thought. Tell him now, get it out in the open and deal with it. But he didn't. He hesitated, thought he'd wait till they were on dry land. And then, once they'd pulled themselves, muddy and stinking, up on to the bank, the Colonel got in there first.

'Sorry, man,' he said, 'I'm a bear with a sore head today and I know it. Just had this total stand-up shouting row with Nat before I came out. I'll swear this baby thing is driving her crazy.'

There it was, the moment gone. No way was Mazz going to launch into his spiel now. 'Yeah?' he said non-committally. 'Best to give her some space then.'

The Colonel nodded. 'Yeah, that's what I reckon, butt. So let's go catch up with your mate.'

'How we going to do that?' said Mazz. 'You got a motor boat? The wave's gone.'

'Yeah,' said the Colonel, 'the wave's gone, all right. It's gone at about ten miles an hour up the river. We get in the car and drive at fifty miles an hour up the river. Find somewhere to park, then we spend half an hour freezing to bastard death waiting for him.'

'D'oh,' said Mazz and he followed the Colonel's lead, clambering back on to the bank then squishing his way along the towpath back to the car park. They got into the van still wearing their muddy soaking wetsuits, the Colonel just discarding his flippers so as to drive in bare feet, and headed back on to the A48, both aware by now that this quest had long since ceased to have any rational purpose, just its own increasingly insane momentum.

The road carried on straight along the riverbank for a half mile or so till it reached the White Hart at Broadoak but the bore had already passed by this section and now the road headed a little way inland. They kept on going for a few more miles and the road resolutely refused to get back to the river; instead they were cresting a rise well above the river. They came to a place called Westbury-on-Severn that nevertheless seemed to be a good mile or two from the water. Finally, in impatience, the Colonel swung the van right into the next lane he saw, signposted to somewhere called Epney.

The road dead-ended with a house and a stile. The Colonel parked the van as close to the verge as possible, then the two of them jumped out and climbed the stile. Ahead was a small field and the river embarkment. The field turned out to be a bog, though and they had to skirt it gingerly. Eventually they came to the riverbank.

'Listen,' said the Colonel, and there was the roar of the bore.

'Shit,' said Mazz, 'cause there it was no more than twenty yards away. No chance of getting through a thicket of brambles and down into the river in time to catch it. And there was Emyr, lying prone now but still riding the bore, as easy as you like.

'Hey,' shouted Mazz, and Emyr turned and waved. Then he climbed up on to his board and slalomed his way out of sight.

Mazz turned to see the Colonel already running round the edge of the field back towards the van. Mazz pelted after him and the two of them, now wet and muddy and stinking, got back in the vehicle. The Colonel pushed it through the lanes, driving like a madman now, and in two or three minutes they burst back on to the A48. The Colonel turned right, shot straight in front of an infuriated artic and floored the accelerator. No more than a couple of miles further on they crested a hill and saw the river coming back towards the road below them. At the bottom of the hill was a pub, imaginatively named the Severn Bore. The Colonel swung the van into the car park, once more paying no heed to the oncoming traffic, and the two of them jumped out once again. There was no easy access to the river from this side of the pub, so they walked around to the far side, climbed over a stile and found themselves on the towpath, along with a half dozen or so spectators: a family group, a couple, and an intent-looking bloke with a beard and serious camera, who was busy fiddling about with his light meter.

There was no obvious way into the water from here, apart from a strange rusted-up piece of machinery in the pub garden itself, looking like it was some kind of loading bay and including a ladder leading directly down on to a mudflat. Mazz and the Colonel looked at each other.

'Try down the footpath,' said Mazz and the Colonel nodded.

They walked on for another fifty yards or so, then found a spot which had evidently been used before and lowered themselves into the water. The Colonel forged ahead as usual; Mazz had to battle with himself before getting back in the river, but eventually he pushed off too.

They paddled over to the far side and just concentrated on keeping their position for a minute or two until the now familiar bore roar started resonating in the distance.

Five freezing minutes later and the bore was upon them. Emyr was still there, still prone on his board. He must have done this dozens of times before, Mazz figured, otherwise it was a miracle he'd managed to negotiate the changing currents without losing the wave. Anyway, he was here and so was the bore. The Colonel was just ahead of Mazz and got on the wave, which was now a pretty ferocious four-footer, with ease. Mazz started paddling hard, half caught the wave then lost it, spun off his board and went under. Came up to find himself in the backwash with the Colonel and Emyr disappearing into the distance.

Mazz flailed about till he reunited himself with his board then paddled hard to the shore. More by luck than judgement, he'd ended up right by the spot where he'd climbed in. So he pulled himself out and walked back along the footpath.

'Hard luck, mate,' said the male half of the couple waiting on the embankment.

'Fuck off,' said Mazz without even looking at the bloke and climbed over the stile while the bloke's girlfriend restrained him.

Mazz walked round to the van. Blessedly, it was open with the key still in the ignition. He pulled off his flippers and sat down on the already soaking seat. He took a couple of minutes to get acquainted with the controls then nearly reversed straight up on to the embankment. Eventually he got the thing going forward and got back on the road.

Three or four miles further on he finally got close to the river again. There was a big junction with the A40 and the first bridge over the river since the Severn Bridges twenty miles back. Mazz pulled the van over into a layby just off the roundabout, right next to a Suzuki jeep, shouldered his surfboard one more time and, ignoring the stares of the passing motorists, followed a path down towards the riverbank. He climbed over a fence with a No Entry sign and made it to the embankment. Looked up and he could see there were not one but two bridges, the other being a railway bridge just downriver of the road bridge. Up on the road bridge Mazz could see another gaggle of spectators, the glint of more cameras. Mazz wondered if they would realise just what a picture they'd be getting. Missing rock star surfs the bore. Nah, course they wouldn't.

Mazz sat there by the river for ten minutes or so, as cold and uncomfortable as he'd ever been. It was actually a relief when he finally heard the bore coming and jumped in. This had to be something close to the end of the line, he was sure. Soon enough the wave came and there were Emyr and the Colonel both rising from prone to greet the watchers on the bridge and moving from left to right as you looked at them, to pick up the dominant wave barrelling along the west side of the river. The Colonel raised his hand to the watchers and Emyr did the same. They raised their hands again as they saw Mazz peel off the back and join them.

This time he too caught the wave fine. And felt the rush as the three of them entered a long fast straight section.

In fact Mazz was so thoroughly wrapped up in it that it was only Emyr yelling in his ear that saved him from disaster.

'Mazz, man,' called Emyr, 'time to bail out.'

Mazz just grinned vacantly and pointed up ahead, determined now he was finally on the wave to enjoy it. But then Emyr peeled off left towards the bank and the Colonel did the same and reluctantly Mazz followed suit, pushing his board left until the wave deposited him none too gently on the side.

'Christ,' said Emyr when Mazz rejoined the others on the towpath, 'I thought you were heading straight for the damn weir.'

'Weir?' said Mazz.

Emyr laughed. 'Yeah. Rips there could cause you some serious trouble, bra. Anyway, man,' he went on, putting his wet rubber arm round Mazz's wet rubber shoulder, 'you've been looking for me, I hear?'

13

TK MAXX

1999

Tuesday morning, Tyra thought she'd go into town, have a little look round, maybe buy a new dress, about time she had something decent and next time she saw Jason – next time, she chided herself, thought you said there wasn't going to be no next time.

She walked over on to Bute Street and was just passing the Custom House when a car pulled up, and Maria and Bobby got out. Tyra nodded at Maria; she'd had the kid for Col and Tyra wasn't going to blank her like a lot of people did just 'cause she was hustling. Maria nodded back, gave her a quick smile then darted into the pub. Bobby came round the car, smiled at Tyra.

'Fancy popping in for a quick one?' she said.

Tyra shook her head. No way was she going to be seen drinking in the Custom House. 'No,' she said, 'just going into town. You fancy a little walk?'

'Yeah,' said Bobby, 'why not? I'll just park the car.'

Tyra watched as Bobby drove the car into a private lot over the road, winked at the attendant and came back over.

'Let's go,' she said, linking arms with Tyra.

In town they had a bit of a laugh finding Tyra a dress. Bobby kept trying to squeeze her into the skimpiest, most figure-hugging thing you could imagine, kind of thing Tyra reckoned you had to be about sixteen to wear. Anyway that's the way it went, Tyra trying to find things looked as much like a chador as possible and Bobby digging out things Scary Spice might have found a bit too revealing.

Eventually, after what seemed like days trawling through the jumble-sale racks of allegedly designer clothes in TK Maxx, Tyra managed to find something she could live with: a grey dress not too sexy but didn't make her look like an off-duty nun either.

Desperate to sit down now, Tyra led the way over to the Queen's Arcade and the café there.

'Well, girl,' said Bobby once they'd sat down with a couple of coffees, 'I been asking around a bit, about what you said, the MP guy Derek whatsit.'

'Yeah?' said Tyra expectantly.

'Not a thing,' said Bobby. 'Well,' she carried on, seeing the look of disappointment on Tyra's face, 'that doesn't mean much. Most of the girls wouldn't notice if Tony bloody Blair showed up, long as he paid. But I put the word out there, like, so . . .'

'Yeah,' said Tyra, 'thanks.'

'Told Maria too,' continued Bobby, 'well, I tells her anyway to keep a look-out for anything strange, anyone wants a bit of strange.' She paused for a moment, her face darkening. 'Lot of strange fellers out there, you know. I worries about her.'

'Yeah,' said Tyra feelingly, her sympathy right out there on the street with Maria. She'd been there once or twice in her life. That terrible couple of weeks in Bristol after the abortion and the band splitting up. She'd been in strange men's cars. She knew worried all right. And she knew not caring what happens to you. She'd felt it again year or so back, when Tony was inside and everything had gone to hell, Kenny coming round asking for his money. She'd tried to but she couldn't go through with it. It was her kids made the difference. You might not care what happens to you, but what happens to them that's something else . . . Course Maria had a kid too. She'd know worried.

'You ever get tired of it all, Bob?' she asked finally.

'Yeah,' said Bobby eventually. 'Seriously tired. You look at me. C'mon, look at me like you've never seen me before.'

Tyra looked at her, saw a short stocky mixed-race girl with short dreads, wearing a pair of Calvin Klein jeans and a brown leather jacket, gold chain round her neck and a couple of gold teeth in her smile. She knew everyone mistook Bobby for a boy, a teenage boy at that, but she couldn't see it any more. All she could see was the woman.

'Right,' says Bobby, 'you knows me, you knows I'm the same age as you. I'm thirty-six years old, I had a hysterectomy last year, you know that?'

Tyra shook her head.

Bobby ground out a half laugh devoid of humour. 'Had a cyst in my womb, size of a bloody orange. Course everyone said it was luck really, what did I need a womb for? Wasn't like I was going to have kids. True enough. But I'm a woman, Tyra, you know what I'm saying?'

Tyra nodded, put her hand on Bobby's.

'And now I'm empty. Thirty-six years old and empty.'

They sat there for a moment, Tyra's hand on Bobby's, not speaking. Then suddenly, and with an obvious effort, Bobby pulled her hand away, drank up her coffee and gave Tyra a smile.

'Tell you what, though,' she said, 'you do have to laugh sometimes. I was out talking to Maria on the beat the other day when this car pulls up. I'm about to fade out, leave Maria to do her business, when the window rolls down and there's a woman in there. And she calls out excuse me and waves at me. At first I think it's a mistake but then she waves to me again and says excuse me, young man, and Maria's cracking up right next to me and then I get up close to the car and you can see it's not a woman at all but a man in drag, and he asks me if I'd like to take a ride with him. Can you believe it?'

'What d'you do?'

'Told him to fuck off of course. I think he realised and all when he got up close I wasn't going to be doing him much good. Nice motor he had and all, one of them Audis.' Bobby shook her head in bewilderment at the ways of people, then sat forward with a start. 'Christ,' she said, 'I knows what I wanted to talk to you about, sister. You give Big Jason my mobile number?'

'No,' said Tyra, looking surprised. 'Haven't got it myself.'

'That's weird then,' said Bobby, ''cause he called me.'

'Yeah?'

'Yeah, yesterday afternoon. Asked if I wanted to come by his office, talk about some Wurriyas business. He say anything about that to you?'

'Not really,' said Tyra, trying to recall anything about that lunch rather than what followed it. 'No, he said something about some people wanting the band to get back together to tour America.'

'Damn,' said Bobby.

'Yeah, mad. He was talking to Charlie about it before . . . First I'd heard of it, though. Apparently "Lick Her Down"'s been reissued on some compilation album too. Maybe that's what it's about, p'raps he's got some money for you.'

'P'raps,' said Bobby. 'Doesn't sound like Jason, though, calling you up 'cause he's got money for you.'

Tyra shrugged. 'You going to see him then?'

'Might as well,' said Bobby. 'Tell you what, girl, seeing as we're in town, why don't we go round there now?'

Mazz, the Colonel, Emyr and Danny Lewis Jones were sat round a table in the White Hart, right on the river. Lewis Jones, who was evidently an old mate of Emyr's, hadn't been in the water; he'd been following Emyr along in his jeep, shooting a bit of film with a top-of-the-range digital camera the Colonel was examining appreciatively in the pub.

All three of them who'd been in the water were still shivering and damp under big jumpers but starting to warm up under the influence of a second round of pints of Guinness. The introductions and the haven't-seen-you-for-years bullshit had been done and it was time to get down to business.

Mazz had been studying Emyr looking for signs of the feller he used to know. The physical changes were obvious – even under a big baggy surfer sweatshirt it was clear that he was thinner, almost gaunt, his face nothing but cheekbones and sharp blue eyes.

The person inside, though, was harder to read. To be honest, when he thought about it Mazz had never been that close to Emyr all those years back in the band. For one thing Emyr had always been stoned; for a second thing he was a drummer. Yeah, yeah, all that what d'you call a bloke who hangs around with musicians stuff, but it was true, you couldn't help stereotyping people. Or maybe people couldn't help stereotyping themselves. Mazz knew he was pretty much of a typical guitarist, but which came first, chicken or egg, he wouldn't like to say. But a musician changing identity the way Emyr had done, going from drummer to singer and piano player, that was frankly weird. So Mazz was studying him hard now trying to fathom what he'd missed all those years back. All he could see, though, was what looked like just another skinny surfer bum, easy and jokey in the company of his old mate Danny. No sign at all of the tortured poet he was on record. Curious.

Mazz was just about to turn the conversation to the business at hand when Emyr pre-empted him.

'So, how's old Jason then?' he said, fixing Mazz with a grin that didn't reach his eyes.

'Jason?' said Mazz, returning the grin.

'Yeah,' said Emyr, 'he sent you, didn't he?' Emyr's eyes were slipping right to look at Danny.

'No,' said Mazz and paused, giving Emyr time to give him a disbelieving look before carrying on. 'He's looking for you, all right. And I dare say he'd appreciate it if I got you to give him a call. But Jason's not why I'm looking for you. It's for Charlie.'

'Charlie,' said Emyr, his face breaking into a genuine smile this time. 'He been on to you about re-forming the Wurriyas, has he?'

'No,' said Mazz, puzzled for a moment. Then he caught on. 'You know he's dead?'

'What?' said Emyr, the little colour there was in his face draining away. 'Charlie's dead?'

'Yeah.'

'How?' said Emyr, an urgency in his voice now.

'Natural causes, they say.' Mazz shrugged. 'Heart attack maybe, though God knows how they can tell. He'd been lying in his flat for a week before they found him.'

'A week,' said Emyr, 'I only saw the old bastard a couple of weeks ago.'

'Yeah, well,' said Mazz, 'sound of it, you may have been the last person to see him. You and Charlie went to see Jason, yeah?'

'Yeah. Jason tell you why?'

'Like you said, Charlie wanted to get the Wurriyas back together again.

And he pulled you out of the hat. Never mentioned it to me, mind. So was that right? Were you really going to do it?'

Emyr looked awkward then, stared down at his hands. 'I dunno really. Thought I might get something out of Jason for him anyway.' He smiled up at Mazz then. 'Actually I thought it might be a laugh, you know. Make a change from the old doom and gloom.'

Mazz grinned back. 'Yeah, I can imagine. But how'd Charlie get hold of you? Thought half the world was looking for you.'

'It was the other way round really. We were on a little run into town to pick up some windsurfing gear. And I just saw him. We're at the lights and I'm looking at this old alky stood outside the bookie's drinking a can of Special and suddenly I realise who it is. So we ended up going for a drink with him and he told me about Jason looking to get the Wurriyas back together again, go to the States. Well I wasn't up for that, of course, but a one-off sounded OK. Well, it did in the pub, you know what I mean. Anyway I gave him Danny's number and really the state he was in I wasn't expecting to hear any more about it. But a few days later he calls me, tells me he wants a meet with Jason, and I thought what the hell.

'But this time Charlie was a bit different. Seemed to think people were out to get him. I thought he was being paranoid really, didn't really take it too seriously. In fact it put me off the whole thing. That and seeing Jason. Me and my brers been on a little surfing trip and Charlie never called, so I was kind of thinking that was the end of it.'

'So did he say anything in particular to you?' asked Mazz. 'Anything in particular he was worried about?'

'I dunno,' said Emyr. 'Just ranting and raving about how they couldn't take his home away. And then he kept going on about this treasure he had stashed away. Just raving, man.'

Mazz shrugged, couldn't think what else to say.

'So where've you been hiding out, bra?' asked the Colonel, filling the lull in the conversation.

Emyr laughed. 'This trailer out in Porthcawl. Danny's people own a whole bunch of them. Got a few specially done-up ones for his mates. And no one stays there would have a clue who I was.'

The Colonel got up then to get some more drinks in and Emyr leaned over to Mazz. 'Bad news about Charlie, man. They have a funeral and everything?'

'Yeah,' said Mazz, 'big do down the docks, Jason and Kenny Ibadulla all over it.'

'Kenny,' said Emyr. 'Christ, is he still around? Thought someone would have shot him years ago.'

'Hey,' said Danny then, chipping in for the first time, 'Emmo, I just remembered something else your mate Charlie told us, you know that last time we saw him. Kept going on about how people were out to get him. Said it was a bloke called Vernon Nichols. You remember?'

'I dunno,' said Emyr, puzzled. 'Vernon Nichols? I don't remember.'

'Vernon Nichols?' said the Colonel. 'What's Big Vern got to do with anything?'

'You know who that is?' asked Mazz.

'Yeah,' said the Colonel. 'Big Vern, construction business, used to be a boxing manager. Big interests down the bay.'

Tyra was sat in the corner of Jason's office drinking a cup of coffee and watching Jason and Bobby play pool. Bobby and Jason were obviously locked in competition but Tyra wasn't really paying attention. Instead she was locked in a deeply sad little fantasy involving her being Jason's secretary and him making her do all these sexual things for him so she could keep her job. Sad, you see. God knows where you had these ideas stashed away in your brain; she wasn't careful she'd be dressing up in French maids' outfits next. That was the thing about fantasies, she supposed: they were clichés 'cause they worked. Kept Ann Summers in business anyway. That was another thing she couldn't believe about the way things were today: Ann Summers shop right in the middle of town you'd see mums and daughters walking in there together, couples, teenagers. Didn't anyone have any modesty any more? Not that she could talk just at the moment. She uncrossed her thighs then and made a conscious effort to follow Jason and Bobby's game.

Bobby wound the game up a couple of shots later, doubling the black the full length of the table, and both players turned to face Tyra.

'What d'you think then?' said Bobby.

Tyra shrugged; she didn't know what to think really. Jason had told them he'd been contacted by an American promoter wanted the Wurriyas to play a thirty-date tour across America. The money was not great but OK – oh and by the way here are some royalties from the reissue of 'Lick Her Down'. Three hundred pounds each which had them both buzzing. Wasn't every day three hundred quid came to you out of thin air.

Touring America, though, that was something else. She could see it appealed to Bobby – big smile came over her face when Jason said the word America – but for her with the kids and all she couldn't really see it.

'How about the others?' she said. 'You asked them yet?'

'Mentioned it to Mazz and Col,' said Jason. 'Emyr, as I expect you know, has gone walkabout and your father of course is sadly out of the picture. But, to be honest with you, as long as one or two of the originals are there – specially you, Bob, you don't want to do it then we do have a problem – we can always bring in a couple of new guys.'

'I dunno,' said Bobby, 'dunno if it would feel right with new people. Bad enough without Charlie.'

Jason's turn to shrug now. 'Up to you, Bob. No skin off my nose you do it or not. I'm just passing on the information really and I'll help out with it if you want me to. Normal fees apply of course.' He winked at Tyra then and Tyra couldn't help blushing, was relieved when Jason's phone buzzed and he walked over to his desk to answer it.

Put the phone down then and came back over to Bobby and Tyra. 'Well,' he said, 'guess what? Looks like we're having a little reunion . . .'

'Yeah?' said Bobby.

'Yeah. Mazz is downstairs. And not just him, the man of mystery and all.'

'Emyr?'

'That's the feller.'

'Christ,' said Bobby and all three of them lapsed into silence for a moment until there was a knock on the door and Jason's secretary ushered in four blokes. Two of them were Mazz and Emyr, who neither Bobby nor Tyra would have recognised if they hadn't known he had to be one of the four fellers walking into the room. The other two were a tall grey-haired hippy, who Bobby recognised as the Colonel, and a sharp-looking bloke who was a stranger to them all.

The sharp feller introduced himself to Jason straight off. 'Danny Lewis Jones,' he said, sticking his hand out.

Jason paused, his eyes narrowing, then he stuck his hand out too. 'Porthcawl?' he said.

'Yeah,' said Danny, 'that's right.'

Jason stared at Lewis Jones for a moment longer then turned to Emyr. 'No surfboard today, then?'

'Nah,' said Emyr, deadpan. 'It's in the van.'

Jason smiled and shook his head, but Emyr ignored him, walked over to Tyra and hugged her. 'Just heard about Charlie,' he said. 'Really, really sorry to hear it.'

'Thanks,' said Tyra, pulling back from him, confused. Then she caught Mazz's eye looking at her over Emyr's shoulders and the confusion suddenly turned into something deeper and she felt her legs start to go and next thing she knew she was in a chair with Bobby bending over her handing her a glass of water.

Whoa, thought Tyra, I must have fainted. Suddenly she just felt like she had to get away from these people. She looked at her watch, not even registering the time, stood up and said, 'Look, I've got to go, pick my kids up from school,' and before anyone could say anything she was out of the room and down the stairs.

Tyra was fifty yards down the road and just going into Queen Street when Mazz caught up with her.

'You all right?' he asked.

'Yeah,' she said, not even turning her head, crossing the road towards Burger King. 'Fine.'

Mazz didn't say anything more for a bit, just walked alongside Tyra as she went left by Marks & Spencer's into the quieter surrounds of Charles Street. He was just wondering what if anything to say next, when he realised they were walking past Grassroots, the coffee bar for unemployed teenage punk rockers where the whole Wurriyas thing had started, the place Mazz had first met Tyra when Charlie brought her down to rehearsal, said here's your new bass player. Scared-looking tall girl with a bad-tempered boyfriend. Wonder whatever happened to him.

'Hey,' he said, 'Grassroots still going, is it?'

Tyra stopped for a moment and looked at him. Mazz thought she might be going to faint again but she didn't, she just said, 'I've got no idea,' then turned on her heel and walked on.

'Hey,' he said again, 'c'mon, let's have a look,' and he walked up the four steps to the front door of Grassroots. Tyra didn't follow him, but he opened the door anyway, went in and saw nothing but a brightly lit, leaflet-strewn government-initiative zone. He backed out of the door, saw Tyra still stood where she was, grimaced extravagantly and detected this time, he was sure of it, the glimmer of a smile.

He looked to his right, then saw that the building next door was some kind of coffee house. 'C'mon,' he said, 'have a coffee with me.'

Tyra shook her head. 'Got to pick the kids up.' She looked at her watch. 'They'll be out in twenty minutes.'

'Mind if I walk up with you then?'

She raised her eyebrows. 'If you want.'

Mazz fell in beside her and they walked on round the corner, past the library and Toys 'R' Us, still in silence but a more companionable silence this time. They crossed the road by the Golden Cross and headed down under the railway bridge.

'So where d'you find him then?' said Tyra suddenly, shocking Mazz out of a reverie in which he was picturing himself riding the Severn Bore effortlessly for mile upon mile.

'Emyr?' he said. 'Oh, surfing.'

'Surfing?' said Tyra, smiling broadly now. 'I thought Jason was joking about that.'

'Nah. Deadly serious. That's all he's been doing, all this time he's been missing. Living in some trailer in Porthcawl and surfing all the time.'

'Yeah? Thought he was meant to be some sort of sensitive poet type these days.'

'Yeah, well, be honest, I think that's why he disappeared. He's got this image, like, of being this doomy, dressed-in-black Goth type, but basically he's just a bit of a lad, as far as I can see. Wants to hang out with his old mates, have a bit of a laugh.'

'It's funny really, I hardly recognised him. All that time we spent together stuck in the back of vans and that, and I'd probably have walked past him in the street. Only 'cause he was with you I knew who he was.'

'Lot skinnier than he used to be, that's for sure.'

'True, but I think maybe it's me. All that stuff – the Wurriyas – seems like it was another lifetime it happened in, someone else's lifetime.'

Mazz paused. He knew what she meant of course. Playing in bands the way he'd done for twenty-odd years was like continually being reincarnated: the punk Mazz, the ska Mazz – must have fucked up badly there 'cause next time he came back it was as the New Romantic Mazz – then the indie Mazz, the baggy Mazz, last few years it had been the junkie's sidekick Mazz. What was next, he wondered, the industrial Mazz, the lounge Mazz? But still, something in what Tyra said stung. He turned to face her and blurted it out. 'Does the same go for us?' he asked. 'That happen in another life too?'

'Come on,' she said, her voice flat, picking up her pace and walking down Bute Street now, 'you know it did.'

Mazz didn't say anything. What was there to say? It was true. Leastways, you'd asked him a couple of weeks back about Tyra he'd have said it was true. A memory buried away as much painful as sweet, a part of what happened to ska Mazz, nowt to do with fat Yank cohort Mazz. Now, though, just standing near her was giving him an ache. Not a heartache so much as a physical ache that seemed to encompass his entire body, a yearning. A yearning for the child they didn't have, the love that went wasted, the things he'd never settled down for long enough to enjoy. Things? Kids, he supposed. Suddenly he wanted to see Tyra's kids, see how she was with them. Pretend they were his? Well, maybe. He quickened his step, accelerating towards the school.

And was taken from his line of thought again when Tyra changed the subject on him.

'And what about my dad, then, you dig out anything there?'

'Nothing really. Emyr said he saw him all right,' he said. 'They were talking about getting the band together again. Sounds like Emyr was just humouring Charlie really.'

'That's all?'

'Well, he said your dad was going on about some treasure.'

'Treasure?' Tyra frowned. 'You think that's why his flat got turned over?'

'Maybe, but I wouldn't get too excited. Doesn't sound like Charlie was making a whole lot of sense, going on about how people were out to get him.'

'Anyone in particular?'

'Someone called Vernon Nichols, apparently, he kept going on about.'

'Vernon Nichols,' said Tyra. 'Fucking hell.'

Mazz stood silent, wasn't like Tyra to swear, but he still couldn't see what the fuss was about.

'Vernon Nichols? You're sure?'

'Yeah, construction game, isn't he?'

'Not just that, he was Charlie's landlord,' said Tyra, then paused. Mazz could see she was deliberating as to whether to tell him more. He stayed silent and eventually she carried on.

'It was just here, he was living.' They were turning into James Street now and Tyra gestured towards the flats above the newsagent on the other side of the road. 'He was trying to move Charlie too. Apparently he wants to build a casino or something down the docks and he needs to knock down these houses to do it.'

'Jesus, you think he killed Charlie because of that?'

Tyra shook her head. 'Seems a bit extreme, doesn't it? But I thought it might be something to do with this so-called treasure. Someone had searched Charlie's flat after he died looking for something.'

Mazz whistled. 'Maybe you should have a word with Emyr, see if there's anything else he remembers.'

'Yeah,' said Tyra. They were approaching the school now. And Tyra stopped. 'Look, thanks for walking me down, but, you don't mind, I'll pick the kids up by myself. Give me a call about Emyr, though, yeah?'

'Yeah,' said Mazz, 'I'll call you tomorrow.' Then he hurried on, 'And I dunno, p'raps I could bring him over and then we could go and have a drink or something. Or a film. You seen *Human Traffic* yet?'

'No,' said Tyra, frowning slightly.

'Well, come on then, let's do it. Friday night, I'll give you a bell.'

'I dunno,' said Tyra but Mazz had already turned and walked off, left her with it. She didn't want to really, but she couldn't help smiling a little. Got another date.

Tyra hadn't been back home more than an hour, just got the kids' tea and halfway through the washing up when the doorbell rang. Not much good ever came through the front door; mostly anyone she knew would come round the back. She took her gloves off and went to answer it scowling, half expecting to see Mazz there, which would be pushing his luck. She was just planning how she was going to tell him to leave her alone when she opened the door and found herself looking at a skinny old white bloke in an expensive suit.

'Vernon Nichols,' he said, sticking his hand out, 'and you're Tyra Unger, and you know what, you haven't half grown since I saw you last.' He chuckled. 'Bet it's a while since someone used that line, eh?'

Tyra just stood there motionless.

'You mind if I come in then?' Nichols said, still smiling.

Dazed, Tyra nodded and led the way into the front room.

'Nice room,' he said, looking appreciatively round at the freshly painted walls, the books and the African ornaments, the big picture of Robert Nesta in the centre. Then he sat on the nice rust-coloured sofa Tyra had picked up in this place over Grangetown, sold off stuff that got returned to catalogues and that, Habitat-style they said, well near enough for the money anyway.

Tyra couldn't help smiling back; she was pleased with the room. The bit of money she'd come into when Tony had left town, the first thing she'd done was redecorate, make it her place, good and proper, every sign of Tony and his taste dumped in a mini-skip.

'Yes,' said Nichols. 'Celi told me you kept a nice place.'

Tyra's smile turned to surprise. Celi? No one but family called her mum Celi.

'You knows my mum?' She winced. Dead giveaway she was nervous; her accent started getting all Cardiff on her.

'Of course I do. Old friends, Celi and me. Right back from before you were born, dear,' he sighed, 'back when the world was simple and all this was Tiger Bay,' he waved his arm towards the window.

He coughed. 'No time for nostalgia now, though. I expect you know who I am and what I do?'

Tyra nodded. 'I've heard a few things.'

'Yes, I bet you have. Little Jason Flaherty been running round telling tales, has he?'

Tyra almost burst out laughing; first time she'd ever heard anyone call Jason little. But she held it back, just sat there and waited.

'Well, no matter. He's a businessman, I'm a businessman. One thing I should say, though, is that no matter what anyone else tells you, your father was a good friend of mine and I did what little I could to help him. To put it bluntly, it wasn't Jason Flaherty gave your father a flat to live in when he didn't have a bean to pay for it with, was it?'

Tyra felt like chipping in with 'And it wasn't Jason tried to evict him the second he realised the place was worth money', but she didn't, she held her counsel, waited for this Vernon Nichols to reveal himself.

'Now,' he went on, 'if you're anything like Celi, you'd prefer it if I didn't beat around the bush any more and told you why I'm here.' He paused and looked at her carefully. 'Has anyone mentioned allegations Charlie was making before he died?'

Tyra nodded.

'Allegations about me?'

Tyra nodded again.

'Specific allegations?'

'No,' said Tyra.

Nichols sighed. 'This is embarrassing. You see, in his last days your dad took a bit of a grudge against me. The thing is I wanted to move him out of the flat he was living in, that frankly rather squalid place over in James Street, and he wasn't having it. Set in his ways, Charlie was.'

'Not surprising,' cut in Tyra, 'you turf a man out in the street when he's in Charlie's state.'

'Hold on, young lady,' said Nichols. 'No question of that happening, no question at all. I offered Charlie his choice of flats in a new development of mine over on Atlantic Wharf. He just wouldn't listen.'

'Girls upstairs didn't say nothing about being offered an alternative.'

'The girls upstairs are, if you'll pardon my language, a pair of common whores who can quite frankly fend for themselves. Charlie was different. I put Charlie in the flat and I wasn't going to dump him on the street, what d'you take me for? Anyway sadly that's all water under the bridge now. The point is Charlie was making allegations that could do quite a lot of damage.'

'Yeah, well,' said Tyra, 'like you said, all that's water under the bridge now, isn't it?'

'Hmm,' said Nichols, 'let's hope so.' Then he paused. 'Charlie never mentioned any treasure to you, did he?'

Tyra forced out a laugh. 'Treasure? Hardly.'

'Or evidence,' said Nichols, 'he might have used the word evidence.'

Tyra shook her head.

'Ah well then,' said Nichols, 'that's grand. Anything shows up, though. Any of Charlie's property. Maybe papers or something – photos even – who knows, perhaps you could let me know before you go showing it to the world.'

Before Tyra could respond to this curious request, Nichols was standing up again and thanking her for her hospitality, of which there hadn't been any really, and saying he'd be in touch and how nice it was to have had this chat – the first bit of which sounded ominous and the second pure bollocks. Tyra was still frowning as he showed himself out the door.

14

ATLANTIC WHARF

1999

Mazz woke up early the next morning, partly because it was damn uncomfortable on Lawrence's sofa, and partly because he had things to think about. Afternoon before, after he'd left Tyra by the school, he'd drifted back into town and tried two or three bars before he found the Colonel, Emyr and Danny sat in some half-hearted designer joint converted from one of the brownstone offices up the road from Jason's HQ. Apparently Jason had been all over Emyr for information on Charlie's last days, but Emyr had blanked him completely. Danny said he figured a bit of background research would be in order before they filled him in on Vernon Nichols.

Sounded like sense to Mazz, though he was wondering why Emyr seemed to be letting Danny do his thinking for him. Well, apart from the fact that Emyr seemed to be as stoned as ever, popping out back into the deserted yard area, trying to pass itself off as a beer garden, to share a fat one with the Colonel. Little while after that Danny and Emyr had split for Porthcawl, but Danny had given Mazz his mobile number and Emyr promised to come by in a day or two, talk to Tyra – 'Not that I've got much to say, bra. Be honest, I'd never have remembered this Nichols guy's name if Danny hadn't been there.'

Anyway, Emyr and Danny had gone off about seven or so and the Colonel suggested they find somewhere a bit less poncy to drink so they'd walked over the Old Arcade which had been all right for the first three pints but then the karaoke got going and Mazz suddenly couldn't face watching the Colonel do 'Born to Run' one more time and then going back to Penarth and staying there under the same roof as Natalie. So he'd begged off and, unable to think of anywhere else to go, ended up round at Lawrence's which was just as depressing as he'd expected.

And now here he was taking stock. Charlie was dead. He'd been in fear of his life before he died. He'd talked to Emyr about a man called Vernon Nichols who was Charlie's landlord and, by the sound of it, had searched Charlie's flat. You didn't have to be Jim Rockford to figure out that Nichols might just hold the key.

OK then, Mazz resolved to spend the next couple of days finding out what he could about Nichols, have something to surprise Tyra with when they went out. And that was the other thing he needed to take stock of. What was he thinking of there? Let's twist again like we did last summer, rock me tonight for old times' sake, or something more? Did he want to be a stepdad to a couple of kids down the docks? How plausible was that? Best thing he kept himself in line. This was one woman didn't deserve to experience the full Mazz more than once in her life.

On the other hand, when, around nine, he was doing his best to brush his teeth in Lawrence's sink, he noticed he was whistling 'Que Sera Sera'.

Friday evening Tyra was lying in the bath. She'd taken the kids round her mum's, she had a glass of wine next to her, little bit of Grover Washington playing on the radio-cassette. Tacky, she knew, but why fight it? It wasn't about Mazz, she was pretty sure; it was just nice to be going out. Last few years she felt like she'd been cutting off her nose to spite her face. So caught up in her anger with Tony and – to be honest – her love for him, that she'd been staying in acting like a nun, just showing him what a good strong woman she was. Well, he was gone now, Tony, once and for all, and it was time she enjoyed herself. So there she was chilling nicely, letting the warmth of the bath soak into her, when the doorbell rang.

She ignored it, put her head under the water and kept it there for half a minute or so. Sat back up and the bell rang again. She put her head back under again, brought it back up and – fuck – there went the bell again. She checked her watch lying next to the bath. Six o'clock. Mazz wasn't due till half past, so who the hell was it? The doorbell rang once more. She swore, her mood switching instantly to black, got out of the bath, put on her dressing gown and went down to the door.

She opened it, ready to give whoever was there a piece of her mind, and there was Mazz. She was minded to slam the door straight in his face, but before she could do anything he was up to her, pecking her on the cheek, and walking into her front room. She could smell the pub on him as he went past her and hear the clank of bottles in the carrier bag he was plonking down on her table.

'You're early,' she said, cold as you like, tone she'd practised on Tony for, oh, too long.

'Yeah, sorry,' he said, then opened up the carrier, pulled out a bottle of wine and said, 'Bought you some wine,' a big grin on his face like the fact he'd brought a bottle of wine – purely so he could get even drunker than he already was – was meant to make her go into spasms of gratitude. Men. She didn't like to generalise; far as she was concerned people were people and God knew women could treat you badly enough. But this was pure male foolishness, what she was witnessing here. And she'd had enough of it for a lifetime.

'I said you're early. And where's Emyr? I thought you were bringing him.'

'Yeah,' said Mazz, finally seeming to take in the coldness of her tone, 'yeah, look, I'm sorry Emyr can't make it today but, listen, I've found some stuff out you've got to hear.'

Tyra sighed. It was probably nonsense but perhaps she should hear him out before she kicked him out. 'Look,' she said, 'I'm going to go up and get changed. And why don't you make a cup of tea?' she chucked in, pointedly giving the bottle of wine an evil look. Sure enough, like a shamefaced schoolboy, Mazz moved over to the sink, filled up the kettle. Men.

She took her time upstairs, drying her hair, changing her outfit a couple of times, trying to find something she felt nice in but didn't give the wrong signals out to Mazz. A good half hour, spot on half past six, when she finally came back downstairs wearing a cotton skirt and her velvet blouse, a blue denim jacket over the top, to show she wasn't trying to impress him.

Mazz was sat in front of the TV, cup of tea in his lap, snoring. She laughed, she couldn't help it. Then she was suddenly attacked by a pang of tenderness, remembering Charlie there when he'd come to visit those afternoons he'd already lost his stake down the bookie's. And always he'd fall asleep.

'Hey,' she said, standing behind him and shaking him quickly by the shoulders. Mazz came to in a fog of bewilderment closely followed by guilt.

'Christ,' he said, 'was I asleep?'

Tyra nodded and Mazz quickly gulped down his tea and shook his head in an effort to restore some clarity.

'So,' said Tyra, 'what's this you've found out?'

Mazz dug in his bag, pulled out a bunch of photocopied sheets. 'Spent the day in the library going through the old newspapers. Found out this Vernon Nichols is planning to build a casino hotel. And guess where?'

Tyra looked at Mazz smiling up at her and for a moment was tempted to pretend she didn't know the answer, but the moment passed. 'Right on top of Charlie's flat,' she said.

'Oh,' said Mazz, sounding like Jermaine when Tyra failed to be sufficiently impressed by one of his paintings in school, 'you know already.'

'Yeah,' she said. 'But thanks.'

'Oh well,' said Mazz, 'so much for my career as a private detective.' He checked his watch. 'Better get going to the film, yeah?'

Walking to the UCI, down James Street, both averting their eyes from the flat Charlie had died in and hurrying on through the wasteland of building sites that separated the old Butetown from the UCI, Mazz agreed to try and find out some more about Nichols and the planning application before they took Charlie's allegations to the police. To be honest, Mazz would have agreed to anything, he thought it would keep him close to Tyra. When she opened the door to him wrapped in her dressing gown wet from the bath, he damn nearly fainted with desire.

She was so lovely and still had that thing he remembered from back when, she didn't seem to know it. Didn't give herself the airs and graces most pretty girls did. And now she was getting older it was still working for her. Lot of girls, women, Mazz's age, late thirties and that, they started trying a bit hard;

you could see a desperation in them, a disbelief that a prime asset, your looks, could go like that.

Queuing up for the tickets, Mazz realised it wasn't just women worried about getting old. There they were surrounded by hundreds of spotty student types, half of them with long hair and scruffy hippy gear, just like students were when he was growing up. It was like the whole world had come full circle, and the unmistakable fact was he'd moved up a generation. He leaned over to Tyra, whispered in her ear, 'I feel like their bloody parents,' and she gave him the nearest thing she'd offered to a smile all evening. Her frown came back full force, though, when he insisted on going up to the bar beforehand and she stood there pointedly drinking nothing while he choked down a Bud, that great Satan of beers.

Inside the cinema Tyra sat as far away from Mazz as it's possible to sit when you are in adjoining seats, and as the nasty techno music and spotty young cast, who looked unnervingly like the spotty young cinema audience, showed up on screen Mazz started to wish he was anywhere else but there. He didn't much like going to the cinema anyway any more, got out of the habit, hardly seen a film in years, apart from the odd video on the tour bus any time he was in a band doing well enough to afford a tour bus with a video, and nine times out of ten that meant watching *Spinal Tap* all over again. Strange thing was, the more the band resembled Spinal Tap the funnier they found the film. Weird really, like nurses all sitting round watching *Carry On Matron* or priests watching *Father Ted* or Woody Allen watching Woody Allen films. Yeah, yeah, calm down, Mazz, maybe that little line of coke in the toilets to perk yourself up wasn't such a good idea.

Anyway, here he was sat in a cinema in Cardiff watching a film about people young enough to be his kids sitting next to the woman who might have been the mother of one of those kids but who was now making it evident that she too would sooner be any place other than here and he wondered who he was kidding. No way he was hanging around here for long. Chasing old memories. Time to make a few calls, get back on the road.

There it was; he'd said it. Every time it was the same: you came off the road, particularly after a nightmare like the last trip with the fat Yank, and you swore never again. You'd play sessions, you'd play weddings and restaurants, you'd build your own studio. And then a month later you'd wake up one morning, no money left and a sudden hankering to see the Days Inn in Milwaukee, or the Ibis in Lyon, one more time.

His attention drifted back to the screen. Wasn't like it was too hard to keep up with the plot. Bunch of kids with crap McJobs getting ready for the big night out. Main bloke's got a problem getting it up 'cause he's taking so many Es. He's best mates with this blonde girl who's fed up about something or other. You can see it a mile off they'll get together by the end of the movie. In spite of himself, though, he starts getting into it, stops noticing the soundtrack for starters, and laughs out loud at this one guy, this teenage dope dealer who's doing the best impression of someone completely out of their gourd that Mazz has ever seen on film. Reminds him of someone. Emyr, that's who it reminds him of, the way he used to be, back in the day. In fact the whole story, the whole big night out in Cardiff, takes him back to the Wurriyas, the great months when it first clicked and before it turned into a business.

The Wurriyas. Christ, he'd almost forgotten: Jason and the American tour. He'd do it, why the hell not? Got to be better than the fat Yank. Would the others do it? Emyr, he doubted it. Col would, he'd have thought. Bobby might: God knows whether the pimping game was something you could take a sabbatical from. And Tyra. Wouldn't be easy with the kids. He looked sideways at her and saw her leaning forward, obviously wrapped up in the film, and he dragged his attention back to the screen, getting a buzz off it now.

Course the main bloke and the girl do get it together towards the end, and the erstwhile Mr Floppy did the business and Mazz smiled and then almost jumped in amazement as Tyra's hand reached over and clasped his.

Neither of them said anything, just sat there holding hands watching the last scene till they came to the finale with the bloke and the girl walking through the deserted city centre, all young and in love, and just then Tyra pulled him to her, put her lips on his and he didn't know about her but he was nineteen again in an instant.

A little bit of maturity came back with the house lights, however, and Mazz remembered to nip into the Gents before they left and get a packet of condoms.

'You coming back then?' said Tyra when he rejoined her in the foyer, her tone almost aggressive.

Mazz didn't say anything, just gave her his best smile, took her arm in his and they headed out into the night.

'Let's walk this way,' Tyra said, turning to the right as they reached the car park, 'take a little walk round the bay.'

'OK,' said Mazz and let her lead him past the projected site of the Assembly and through to the sea wall by the Norwegian church where they stopped and gazed out at the water. The barrage that would shortly turn the muddy estuary into an elegant marina – at least it would do if you believed what you read in the brochure – was over to the left blocking off the mouth of the bay between the Cardiff Docks and the Penarth headland. Straight in front of them was the new St David's Hotel and above them the stars.

'So what did you think?' asked Mazz after a while.

'About the film?'

'Nah, the football.'

'It was good.' She laughed. 'God, I sound stupid. Made me sad a bit too.'

'Yeah?'

'The old man, the black guy's dad. Reminded me . . .'

'Your dad.'

'Yeah.'

They fell silent for a moment, both thinking of Charlie, then Mazz decided to lighten things up a bit.

'Did we take that many drugs when we were that age?'

Tyra laughed again. 'I certainly didn't. Dunno 'bout you though.' Then she paused again. 'Did I tell you Charlie had taken a load of cocaine before he died?'

'No.'

'Weird, isn't it? Christ knows where he'd have got the money for that from. Wasn't really his thing anyway.'

'No,' said Mazz, 'you're right. Wonder what that was all about.'

He frowned out to sea, puzzling it over, then turned to see Tyra smiling at him. He smiled back, pulled her to him, banished all thoughts of Charlie from his mind as Charlie's daughter put her tongue in his mouth, pulled his hand to her breast with one hand while the other moved down to his crotch. Mazz groaned as she found his dick and squeezed it through the fabric of his jeans. He slid his right hand under her blouse, pulled her bra down till the nipple sprang free then squeezed it, bringing an answering groan from deep in Tyra's throat. She let go of his dick then, guided his free hand under her skirt. He pushed his hand inside her knickers, could feel the heat and moisture from outside, and one, then two fingers slid inside her easily. They stayed like that for how long he couldn't say – maybe five minutes, maybe ten – up against the sea wall, then he breathed into her ear, 'Let's go to yours.'

'No,' she said, 'let's do it here.'

'Here?' He looked around. They were in full view of any passers by but he hardly cared. He was about to lower her to the ground when she said, 'No, follow me,' and pulling herself away, his fingers sliding out of her with an audible squelch, she led him past the Norwegian church and the ice-cream stand to the old lighthouse ship moored in the dock.

By day it served teas but now it was deserted. A couple of chains barred the way to the gangplank but Tyra and Mazz easily climbed over them. Once on deck, Tyra led the way to the far side and then, standing there in the light of the moon, the dark water of the dock behind her, she pulled off her jacket, then her skirt, her blouse, her knickers and finally her bra while Mazz stood there pole-axed by beauty and desire.

'Come on,' she said then, 'what are you waiting for?' and he was out of his clothes as quickly as he'd ever been and no sooner was he naked than she was on him and he was tearing the wrapping off the condom packet with his teeth, and then he was in her and they were fucking so hard Mazz would swear he could feel the big boat rocking in time with them. It didn't last long, couldn't last long before Mazz felt himself losing it, shouted out 'No' into the night, and then Tyra was digging her nails hard into his back, pushing up and grinding herself against him as he came, and then she was coming too and all too soon consciousness rushed back and they were suddenly aware of lying there naked and freezing on the side of a boat that hadn't left harbour in years.

They dressed then in silence, suddenly awkward and unsure. Once they reached dry land again, Mazz moved to kiss Tyra but she turned her cheek away, and he thought he saw her brush away a tear and was taken back twenty years to the first time they'd done it when she'd cried and cried afterwards for what he never knew.

'Shall I come back?' he said nervously.

'No,' she said, 'the kids,' and he nodded and walked along with her in silence to the corner of Bute Street and James Street where she stopped and kissed him quickly and said she'd be fine by herself the rest of the way back and why didn't he call tomorrow and it was only as he was walking away he remembered that the kids hadn't been there when he called.

15

XANADU

1981

Next day was a Friday. Charlie had called a band meeting for that evening. Told everyone to turn up at the Royal Oak at six and bring their sports gear. Mazz was knackered before he even got there. Managed a couple of hours' sleep after Tyra left but it had barely made a difference. His limbs were tired and his head was spinning.

Still he got to the pub early and had a quick pint of SA which perked him up a bit and he was just about to have another when Charlie showed up, told him drinking was for after you did your work, not before, and led the way upstairs. Bobby was there already, looking more like a boy than ever in singlet and shorts, jumping around the heavy bag and jabbing it with much enthusiasm and practically no discernible effect. Col and Emyr turned up pretty soon after, and Charlie had them all well lathered with sweat when Tyra arrived around half past.

Mazz shot her a look like you sure you should be doing this but she just blanked him, found a skipping rope like she'd been here often enough to know where everything was and started working away.

Bobby evidently loved it in the gym. She was buzzing around Charlie asking questions, most of which boiled down to when can I start fighting? Charlie started out laughing her off but Bobby kept on pushing and eventually he caved in and said no reason she couldn't do a bit of sparring.

'Great,' said Bobby, 'ace.'

'Course,' said Charlie, 'you'll have to find someone your own weight.'

Bobby's face fell. 'I don't want to fight some little kid. She whirled round at Col who was openly snickering behind her. 'Shut up, I'd fucking have you. No fucking trouble.'

Col laughed, patted her on the head and Mazz thought Bobby was going to smack him one right then but Charlie was in there in a flash.

'Hey,' he said, 'children, cool it. You want to show someone what you got, show Charlie.' And with that he put on a pair of the big training gloves, climbed into the ring and invited Bobby up there after him.

He held the big gloves out in front of him and looked at Bobby. 'C'mon then, sister, give it what you've got.'

Be honest, it was hard not to laugh. Bobby gave it her best shot, all right; you could see her winding up her frame to put all of her weight behind a series of roundhouse punches. But Charlie just absorbed them on the pads like they were nothing, just smiled and told Bobby to move more, try and jab a bit, not just swing like a fucking farmer, and all the while Bobby was getting madder and madder till she was almost crying with rage by the time Charlie called a halt.

Col was next and, be honest, he wasn't that much better. Used to chops on a lot about how he did karate but when it came to boxing he was just like a stronger version of Bobby, all wild swings and nothing that caused Charlie the slightest discomfort. Emyr and Mazz were no better either. At least Mazz wasn't; be honest, he hardly felt like he had the energy to lift the gloves, let alone swing at Charlie, so he concentrated on trying to get a bit of rhythm going, started moving to the beat in his head till Charlie started laughing at him, told him he should be on fucking *Come Dancing* not in a boxing ring. Emyr was different; he was like a whirlwind. Didn't even aspire to any technique, just flailed around, arms and legs and elbows everywhere, and he actually had Charlie down on the floor, not through a punch but 'cause he tripped over Emyr's legs. Charlie hooted with laughter then and put his hands up in surrender.

'Never fight a drummer, man,' he said, 'they're all crazy.'

Then it was Tyra's turn. She stepped up into the ring and Mazz couldn't help it, he just called out to her.

'You sure this is a good idea?'

Charlie caught it, glanced at Tyra then Mazz, then shook his head and looked away. Tyra came forward then, but you could see she was just going through the feeblest of motions and after a minute or two Charlie put his arm round her and called a halt. 'Don't want to hurt your old man, eh, good girl?' he said, and as they climbed out of the ring his eyes sought out Mazz again.

Down in the bar after, the band for the most part were in good spirits, Bobby taking the piss out of Emyr and Col for their lack of boxing skills, happily oblivious to her own shortcomings. In her head Bobby was the toughest girl on the block and that was all that counted. The other end of the table, the Mazz, Tyra and Charlie end, things were a little more strained. From a distance Charlie was the same as ever – getting the SAs in, joking with his mates at the bar about his new career as a pop star, the landlady threatening to take his picture off the wall, the one with the Lonsdale belt, replace it with the one from the *NME* – but close up you could spot the sidelong looks he kept giving his daughter. Mazz was edgy too, tried to get the whole table engaged in a serious conversation about where the band was going, what they were going to put on the album etc., but that soon dissolved in a barrage of stupid jokes from Emyr and Bobby, and Mazz just slumped back in his seat concentrating hard on his pint.

Little while later he went to the toilet, stood outside for a moment in the cool night air listening to the trains roll by in the distance and wondering why life was going so fast all of a sudden. Back in the pub Tyra and Charlie were on their feet.

'Little girl's decided to come and stay round her old dad's tonight, that's OK with you, boss,' said Charlie. Mazz nodded like he had some say over where Tyra spent the night, and Tyra smiled, kissed Mazz quickly on the cheek and followed her father out on to the street.

Mazz sat down wondering what the hell was going on and fully intending to leave himself soon as he'd finished his pint. Instead he ended up piling into the back room with the rest of the band to see some pop punk group with three girl singers, who were crap but quite a laugh, and Emyr knew one of the girls and she said they were all going to a new club in town, some place called Xanadu near the station, and so they all ended up there in the midst of a bunch of hairdressers listening to David Bowie's 'Fashion' every third record which was OK with Mazz. There was something about that drum sound you couldn't resist; he wondered if they could get anything similar in the studio.

By now he'd really got the taste for drinking and then, digging into his wallet to pay for another round, he noticed a little paper wrap which felt like it still had something in it. A quick tasting session in the toilet revealed the contents to be Simon's best-quality record-company coke, and Mazz not being one to bogart his drugs he passed the wrap round to a couple of acquaintances and so one thing led to another and at four a.m. that morning he was in the Patrice Grill on Clifton Street with two girls from the art college and a bloke called Dave who was Kate's ex and they had one plate of spaghetti between the four of them and a pint of bitter each for Mazz and Dave plus a couple of glasses of liebfrau for the girls.

Later still he was snogging one of the girls – Nicky he thought her name was – all the way through town as he walked back home, got as far as the castle and they'd just pulled into the beginning of the arcade to give it some serious action, when suddenly – it was like in a dream when you're happily flying along and then you remember you can't fly after all and you plunge down to earth – the reality hit him like a sledgehammer – my girlfriend's pregnant, what the fuck am I doing? So he disengaged himself from Nicky, if that's what her name was, and at first she thought he was joking and then when she realised he was seriously going to walk off home and leave her there, lipstick all over her face, her left tit already out of her bra under her sweater, her motor revved up and running, she cursed him out in language that genuinely surprised him.

Tyra came round at seven the next morning, Mazz having had an hour and a half's sleep maximum and not so much hungover as still drunk. Which was lucky really as Tyra just threw herself on him again. At first part of him resisted, like he was being used as some kind of life-size sex toy, but then his libido kicked in and his heart followed, melted by the real need he could feel beneath the hunger.

After the second time Mazz was about ready to cry uncle if she wanted to carry on – in fact every particle of him was screaming the message 'Sleep now' – but instead she turned to him and said, 'I've told my dad.'

'Yeah?' said Mazz. 'What did he say?'

'Nothing really. I thought he was going to go mad, but he didn't, he just said yeah, thought so. Said he just wanted to know if I was all right.'

'What did you say?'

'Said I dunno. I think so. Said I needed any help I knew where to go. Which is a joke, really, never gave my mum much help. Oh God, Mazz, he looked old, you know.'

'He's not old. Never be old, not in his head, Charlie.'

Tyra didn't say anything, just put her clothes on, said she'd call him later, better go back before her mum started worrying.

Mazz was asleep before the door closed behind her.

It went on like that for the next week. Tyra remote and distracted one minute, worried obviously about the baby; the showing up all hours of day and night, acting like she'd just been told this was the last time she'd ever get to have sex. For his part Mazz was doing his best to reassure her. Course he could understand her worries and that about being a mum, but it wasn't like they would be the first twenty-year-olds to have a kid, far as he could see. Christ, his cousin Bethan had had one when she was fifteen, though that was a bit different, like, but his brother Bryn had two already and he was only twenty-four now. Course Bryn was in the army so it wasn't like he did too much of the childcare or anything, but Donna seemed to be fine. In fact Bryn was on leave at the moment, whole lot of them should be in Newbridge.

So Mazz thought it might be an idea to take Tyra back, let her meet the family, and it might reassure her a bit at the same time, see how Donna managed.

The idea came to Mazz on the Saturday afternoon, the weekend before they were due in the studio. He called his mam, said he might bring his girlfriend over for Sunday lunch, like, and when his mam had picked herself off the floor she said that'll be lovely and you know our Bryn's home and Mazz said yeah and his mam said tomorrow then, and Mazz said yeah and put the phone down, and realised he'd done it now, his mother would go spare if he didn't turn up. So he decided to tell Tyra the plan in person.

Walking towards town, he realised how wrapped up in himself he'd been lately. The roars coming out of the Arms Park were hitting him in waves as he headed towards the river. Crossing the Taff there was one almighty bellow which could only mean that Wales had won and Mazz couldn't believe he didn't even know who they were playing.

Didn't take long to find out, of course. The crowd started pouring out of the ground as Mazz got to Westgate Street and as he spotted the England hats and scarves he felt a little burst of exultation. Things were surely going the right way.

Mazz fell in with a bunch of lads from Pontypool as he was walking up St Mary Street and started to get a contact high from their elation. Lads asked if he was coming for a drink. Mazz nodded and said, 'Fuck, aye,' and that's how they ended up in – where else – the Custom House. Wall-to-wall hookers and valleys boys, carousing for the first couple of hours then a steady stream of boys heading for the car park, show that they could score and all in Cardiff on a spring Saturday.

Mazz escaped around half seven – five quick cans of Breaker to the wind – and headed for Tyra's place.

Probably would have been OK if Tyra had opened the door herself, but instead it was her mum as per usual. As Mazz approached her she sniffed theatrically.

'You been drinking?' she said.

'Yeah,' said Mazz, 'there a law against it, is there? Round here?'

Was the most he'd ever said to Tyra's mum and though there wasn't much in the words he supposed the tone made them sound ruder. Either way, Tyra's mum – Celeste, her name was, not that Mazz ever called her that – just went right into one.

Out of my house, leave my daughter alone, you drunken hooligan – all of that. Mazz thought she was going to swing at him for a moment, and he wasn't sure what the appropriate action would be in those circs, seeing as Celeste wasn't maybe quite as tall as Tyra but had serious hard-work forearms looked like she could deck the average bullock with a single punch. Anyway, things were going from bad to ugly when Tyra came down to see what the aggro was all about.

Absurdly, both Mazz and Celeste turned to Tyra to justify themselves.

'Your boyfriend' – she said it like she was saying leper or something – 'comes in here drunk, girl. You know we don't have no drinking in this household.'

'Christ,' said Mazz. 'Had a couple of drinks after the rugby. We won, you know. I've not got any drink with me.'

'And back-talking me, girl, in my own house. You get him out of here.'

'Fine,' said Mazz, 'I'm gone,' and walked out of the house. He got to the end of the street when he remembered he was supposed to be asking Tyra to come to Newbridge with him the next day. He stood still for a moment, decided there was no way he was going back, he'd phone instead, when Tyra came bursting out of the house and ran up the road towards him.

'You bastard,' she said. 'Why d'you have to be like that?'

'Christ,' said Mazz, 'she just went for me. All I did was stand there. She hates me, your mum.' He paused. 'Have you told her or something?'

'No,' said Tyra, and started crying, no preamble just tears coming straight out of her eyes. Mazz pulled her to him then and a couple of kids standing over the road wolf-whistled. Mazz flicked a V-sign at them from behind Tyra's back and they scarpered laughing.

'You want to see my folks?' he said once the tears began to subside.

'What?'

'Meet my family. Come up to Newbridge with me?'

'Yeah . . . I dunno . . . When?'

'Thought we might go up tomorrow, have Sunday lunch, like.'

'Jesus, Mazz, you haven't told them, have you?'

'No. Not yet.'

Tyra didn't say anything for a moment, just kept her head buried in Mazz's neck. Mazz was uncomfortably aware that there were several curtains twitching and passers-by clocking them. Then Tyra raised her head and smiled.

'Yeah,' she said, 'OK. Just don't say anything, OK?'

Mazz shrugged and nodded.

16

CAROLINE STREET

1999

Tyra felt better the second she was on her own. She didn't know what it was with sex: she always felt so guilty after it, specially if it was good sex the way that had been. Good and dirty was what she really meant. 'Cause it hadn't been like that with Tony, least not once they were married and everything – she'd been all right with it. Then again it wasn't that dirty was it, doing it with your husband? Funny thing, though, she hadn't felt that guilty with Jason either and she certainly wasn't married to him. Her thoughts drifted away as, overcome by tiredness, she unlocked her front door, then climbed into bed secure in the blissful knowledge that she was going to be asleep the moment her head hit the pillow.

Six hours later she woke up screaming, fighting her way out of a nightmare where her mother was a man and Charlie was in drag and some kind of a zombie and she put her hand up to his face to touch him and there'd been nothing but worms there and aaaagghhhh she'd woken up. Woken wide awake too, no chance of going back to sleep, nothing to do but think about the night before and ponder what the hell had happened there.

So much for not fancying Mazz any more, eh? Amazing how you can lie more effectively to yourself than to anyone else. She'd told Bobby she didn't fancy Mazz no more, Bob'd probably have laughed in her face. As it was, she'd taken herself in completely. And hadn't prepared herself. And now?

What was the thing they said about buses – they don't come for hours then three come along at once. Well, looked like the same thing was happening to her. No sex for what seemed like decades then two men in a week. And one of them Mazz. Mazz who had caused her more pain than anyone, even Tony. Mazz had broken her heart; all Tony had done was to just about break her spirit. It was Mazz who'd taken her down the first time.

And why'd she done it? 'Cause she was lonely, 'cause her daddy was dead, 'cause she wished she was nineteen again. 'Cause she still fancied him, goddamnit. Maybe you always fancied the first one to catch your heart. Who knew? Maybe if he'd been fat and bald and worked in a bank she'd have felt nothing for him. But he wasn't, he didn't, he was the same old Mazz. Still the guitar player with the cheekbones and those eyes. Battered and lined by the years, maybe, but that only made him better looking, really. Still remembered how she'd felt about him back then, skinny white boy from the valleys burning with ambition; his skin had always felt hot back then, like he was running a permanent temperature. He'd seemed like he was from another planet. And she'd loved him. Which was her big mistake. Didn't do to love a being from another planet.

And the same went double for now. What could Mazz offer her now? Would he be a daddy for her kids? She couldn't see that. Would he live with her and support her? She couldn't begin to imagine it. Would he come and go without warning, leave her lonelier than before? She could see that all right. Bastard couldn't offer her anything but love.

Love? Her mind didn't want to even entertain the idea. You think he loves you, girl? You're nothing but a nostalgia ride for him. Her body said different; her body remembered last night in every pore, and it ached for him.

She sighed from deep down inside and got up, got dressed, got the kids back from her mum's, got herself some coffee and there was Bobby knocking at her back door, well early for a Saturday morning.

'Hey, girl,' she said, flopping down on Tyra's sofa, 'give us a cup of coffee. I'm bloody dying I am.'

Looking at the state of her, Tyra thought she was barely exaggerating. Red eyes practically out on stalks, shaking visibly and her face more grey than brown, it looked like she hadn't slept since Tyra saw her last the day before yesterday in Jason's office. Of course that had to be it: the money Jason had given each of them. Tyra's had gone straight in the Abbey National; Bobby's was evidently circulating around her bloodstream. She made Bobby's coffee then sat down on the sofa next to her.

'So what d'you reckon, girl?' asked Bobby.

''Bout what?'

''Bout what. 'Bout this tour of America, that's what.'

Tyra shrugged; she'd hardly given it a moment's thought. Seemed about as real as those envelopes come through the door telling you you've just won a hundred thousand pounds or a new car. Just some bullshit people dangled in front of you and you learned to ignore. 'I dunno,' she said. 'Just talk, isn't it?' Then she instantly regretted her words as she saw the look of disappointment come over Bobby's face.

'You reckon?' she said, frowning. 'Didn't seem to me like Jason was joking. Never seemed like the joking kind really. Course you'll know him a lot better than me, like.' Bobby was rallying now, giving Tyra a wicked grin.

'No,' said Tyra, 's'pose you're right. Thing is it just doesn't seem real. The Wurriyas − all of that − it seems like another lifetime.'

'Yeah,' said Bobby, 'seems like that all right. Different life anyway.'

Tyra took another sip of her coffee and waited for Bobby to carry on.

'America,' she said then, in some kind of reverie. 'Sounds all right to me, like. So you up for it or not?'

'I dunno,' said Tyra, forcing herself to take it seriously. 'The kids and that . . . Thing is you don't really need me anyway. Who cares who the bass player is? Only person anyone'll remember is you.'

'Yeah?' said Bobby, her face lighting up. 'You reckon?'

'Yeah,' said Tyra, 'course. You're the singer, aren't you?'

'Yeah,' said Bobby, 'that's me,' her gold teeth glinting in the middle of her gap-toothed grin.

Mazz had ended up back at the Colonel's. He'd gone into town after leaving Tyra, still pretty much walking on air. He couldn't believe what it was like once he got there. Friday nights in town he remembered there was hardly a place open, just a couple of night clubs and the casino, and the streets were deserted by midnight. Now it looked like a Hieronymus Bosch made over by Tommy Hilfiger. There were gangs of pissed-up boys and girls all over the place: gangs queuing up to get in and out of the dozen or so theme pubs and clubs in St Mary's Street, gangs roaming Caroline Street in search of dangerous-looking food – that much hadn't changed at least – and gangs just throwing up in every alley and doorway. The benefits of the two bottles of Hooch for the price of one before eleven p.m., no doubt. And from every doorway the sounds of house music. Sometimes, it had to be said, you wondered why you bothered making music. All people wanted in life was to hear a four-square bass drum and Casio tune on the top – the perfect soundtrack to a dozen Red Bull and vodkas.

Time to get out of there before his elation turned to bitterness. A classic foursome were right in front of him flagging down a taxi, two blokes in Helly Hansen jackets, two girls in next to nothing; one of the girls turned to one side and threw up right there on the pavement. The cabbie looked disgusted, wound his window back up and was just about to accelerate forward when Mazz jumped in the front seat next to him.

'Constellation Street, mate,' he said and the cabbie shrugged and put his foot down.

There was no sign of life at all, though, round at Lawrence's place. Mazz banged on the door for a good five minutes then gave up, got back in the cab and told him to drive to Penarth. It was nearly two by the time they got to the karaoke club but thankfully the Colonel was still there, stood by the bar talking to a feller in a big leather jacket looked like an ex-football player. Which turned out to be just what he was.

Couple more drinks then and a nightcap back at the Colonel's and Mazz had woken up on the Colonel's very comfortable spare bed feeling better than he had done in far too long. The memories of what he'd done with Tyra ran through his mind and he could hardly stop smiling. Sure, she'd gone a bit funny afterwards but she'd always been like that. Best thing to do, far as he could see, was give her some space, do some checking up on this Nichols guy then give her a call later on.

So ten o'clock Mazz was sat in the kitchen with a cup of tea all ready to go out and sleuth when the Colonel came in looking as uncannily chipper as ever and started making a cup of tea to take up to Natalie. Mazz told the Colonel what he was planning and the Colonel pointed out that Saturday wasn't likely to be too good a day for checking up on anyone. Plus it was a lovely day out there.

'So why don't we go surfing, butt? Llangennith'll be perfect today.'

'Well, count me out,' said a voice from the doorway. Natalie was standing there in a pair of oversize men's pyjamas, looking pissed off.

'No worries,' said the Colonel, affecting not to notice. 'You stay here and work, that's what you want.' He turned to Mazz. 'So you up for it, butt?'

Mazz was about to say no when he had an idea. 'All right if I make a call?' he said. 'Friend of mine might like to come along.'

'Go ahead,' said the Colonel while behind him Natalie rolled her eyes and gave Mazz a nasty little knowing smile.

Mazz dug in his wallet, found the piece of paper he'd written Tyra's number on, called her.

'You busy today?' he said.

'Mazz,' she said, exasperated, 'I got kids, you know.'

'Yeah, that's why I'm calling. You fancy going to the beach?'

'Beach?'

'Yeah, we can go to the Gower, go surfing.'

'Surfing, Mazz? What the hell are you talking about?' Then a pause at the end of the line. 'You serious?'

'Yeah, my mate's got a camper van. We can all go.'

Another pause. 'OK then,' she said finally. 'That'd be nice.'

And it was nice. Ended up taking for ever to get everyone ready to go, so they had to stop to feed the kids – eight-year-old Jermaine and four-year-old Emily – on the way and the Colonel was getting visibly antsy about missing valuable surfing time, but once they were finally there, walking through the dunes carrying a motley assortment of surfboards and body-boards the Colonel had dug out for the kids, and then looking out on the great expanse of beach, a clear blue sky and nice inviting two- or three-footers rolling steadily in, everyone's spirits soared.

The Colonel spent the whole afternoon out in the deep water with his long-time surfer mates, while Mazz and Tyra just messed around with the kids in the shallows, Tyra trying to stop the fearless Emily from venturing in too deep, and Mazz trying to persuade the fearful Jermaine that lying down on a board in the water and letting the waves whoosh him into the shore might be fun.

Only problem Mazz had all afternoon was keeping his hands off Tyra. She took to body-boarding easily – always had been a sporty girl, he remembered, and having her right next to him in a swimsuit, well it wasn't easy. But she made it clear from the get go that there should be no fooling around in front of the kids and Mazz respected that.

Later on, though, when they were dropping Tyra and her exhausted but happy kids off back at her place, she leaned over to Mazz and whispered in his ear for him to come over after eleven.

So he did and what followed was like an indoor re-run of the night before. Again the sex was almost ferocious in its intensity and again Tyra went moody afterwards, wouldn't countenance him staying the night. So again he ended up on the Colonel's spare bed.

Tyra couldn't stop laughing. She was sat in her front room, a bass guitar perched in her lap. First time she'd played it in at least ten years, been half surprised to find it was still there stuck under the stairs. Col was sat on the edge of the sofa, playing an electric keyboard, and Bobby was prancing up and down in the middle of the room singing through some little karaoke set-up Tyra had borrowed off Linz next door. It was Bobby who was cracking her up. They were trying to run through some of the old Wurriyas songs and Bobby had forgotten most of the words outside the choruses and she was singing the first thing that came into her head instead and it was just so funny, all these lines she was coming out with. Even Col, who never laughed much at anything, too cool for that, was cracked up, had to start rolling an extra large one to get himself back under control.

The more she thought about it, the more Tyra realised she was up for getting the Wurriyas back together. It's a weird thing growing up, it's like an attitude of mind really, she reckoned. Of course you have kids and stuff and you have to get more responsible, get up in the morning, feed them and clothe them and beg, steal or borrow the money to keep a roof over their head – all that was grown up, fair enough. But lot of people – specially women, she had to say – acted like that wasn't enough just doing the grown-up business. No, you had to get all mature. And being mature, what was that all about? Mostly it seemed to be about not going out any more, not listening to music, not going to films unless you were taking the kids – not doing anything much apart from sitting around and moaning about what losers your men were. Well, she knew she'd done plenty of all that herself. But just this now, sitting down and playing with Col and Bobby, made her feel like she was connected to the world. So, yeah, why not give it a go and see what happened?

'What d'you reckon, Bob?' she said as they came to the end of an utterly dissonant run-through of 'Lick Her Down'.

'Sounds like shit,' said Bobby, laughing.

'Nah, about doing it again. Out on tour.'

'Like I tells you, sister, sounds good to me. How 'bout you, brer?' She turned to Col.

Col shrugged and said, 'Dunno, man, depends how the little money things work out, y'know what I mean,' sounding bored but really pretty excited Tyra could tell; he just wasn't going to show it to Bobby. Lot of history there.

'Mazz up for it?' Bobby turned to Tyra.

Tyra shrugged. 'Don't know why you're asking me, girl,' she said, fighting the urge to smile. She didn't want people knowing about her and Mazz yet. Not till she'd thought about it long and hard, what she was getting into there.

'And old Emyr?'

Tyra shrugged again. 'Don't sound too likely but I suppose we can find another drummer easy enough.'

'Yeah,' said Col, 'couple of brers I can think of could play this shit easy enough.'

'All right,' said Bobby, all but clapping her hands together with enthusiasm. 'So how about you and me go see Jason tell him we'll do it?'

Tyra frowned for a moment. Was she really going to go for it then? She couldn't help herself; she burst out in a big smile. 'Yeah,' she said. 'I'll call him in the morning.'

'Bet you will, sister, bet you will,' said Bobby, making little kissing movements with her lips.

Col looked at her in puzzlement then looked at Tyra, who blushed furiously.

'You didn't,' said Col, 'you didn't,' and then, for the second time that evening – possibly a record – Col cracked up laughing.

Monday morning Mazz was just getting a late breakfast together at the Colonel's place when the phone rang. Mazz picked up, said, 'Yeah?' in a neutral tone then was startled as the voice on the other end of the line said, 'Is Mazz there?'

'Yeah, speaking,' said Mazz.

'Mazz, man,' said the voice, sounding so high-pitched and anxious it took Mazz a moment to recognise it.

'Emyr. What the hell happened to you, man?'

'Long story,' said Emyr. 'Listen, man, I'm in Cardiff now. We've got to meet, something I've got to tell you.'

'Where?'

'David Morgan's. Roof-garden café. An hour's time – that long enough for you?'

'Sure,' said Mazz.

'Good,' said Emyr, then he paused. 'Could you get Tyra to come?' he said eventually. 'She ought to hear this as well . . .'

'Do my best,' said Mazz.

'Great,' said Emyr, sounding more anxious than ever. 'I'll see you,' and the line went dead.

17

PENARTH PIER

1999

Tyra led the way into David Morgan's. She liked David Morgan's, old-school department store, reminded her of being a kid watching her mum choose fabric. Mazz followed her through haberdashery and glassware, curtains and gifts till they reached the top floor, then through the toy department and into the café. Tyra ordered them a couple of coffees and Mazz opened the door, walked on to the little roof terrace itself. And there was Emyr in the corner, trying to look inconspicuous, wearing a big sweater and a Quiksilver cap jammed down low over his eyes.

When Tyra got close to him she could see he was shaking, wearing a sweater on a summer's day and shaking. Not too hard to jump to conclusions there. Second he started talking, though, she could tell she'd jumped to the wrong one.

'I'm sorry,' he said, clasping her hand as she sat down, his voice shaking as much as the rest of him.

'Sorry?' she said. 'What for?'

'Charlie. Your dad.'

Tyra's brow furrowed. 'What d'you mean?'

'It's my fault. Me and Danny. You know after I met up with Charlie and Jason talking about getting the Wurriyas together, little benefit for Charlie? Well, I'm walking back with Charlie down towards the Oak. Got the van parked there, and you know how he was, he asks if I've got a few quid to help him out. Course I would have given him some but I literally don't have a penny on me, so I turn to Danny, ask him if he's got anything and he doesn't either and Charlie's cool about it, starts going back on about how his landlord was persecuting him and how he'd got the evidence all stashed away, whatever that meant, and we just stand there for a bit, listening to all this, humouring him, I suppose. And then we were just heading back to the van when Danny says to hang on, he's got an idea, maybe Charlie would appreciate a gram of this coke he had, this super-pure gear. So I said nice one Dan and I ran back after Charlie and gave him it, thought he could probably sell it on to someone, didn't think he'd take it himself. Christ.'

Tyra sat back in her chair. So there was the big mystery solved, it looked like. Pure bloody stupidity all round. Wasn't really Emyr's fault; way she saw it, no one made Charlie stick it up his nose. His age and health, he should have figured his heart wouldn't stand for it.

'Not your fault,' she said coolly, 'just pure stupidness all round.'

'Thanks,' said Emyr quietly, seeming to calm down almost immediately, like she'd said the magic words – 'not your fault'. Tyra shook her head. Christ, weren't men all little kids waiting for Mummy to tell them off. Then she thought of something.

'So you still up for a Wurriyas reunion?'

Emyr frowned. 'Well I'd like to be involved, you know, but strange thing is, Charlie dying and that, well I've started writing some new songs and I've been figuring it's time I got back on the horse, got back to my line. You want to hear the song I've written for Charlie?' He pulled a mini-disc recorder out of his pocket.

'No,' said Tyra, 'I don't,' and she turned and walked back off the terrace into the store, not looking back, but sensing Mazz a few paces behind her.

'Christ,' she said, suddenly coming to a stop in the carpet department, 'the total creep.'

Then she started crying and Mazz held her and when she stopped crying he still held her and they walked back to her place and had sex and afterwards she cried and he held her some more and she cried some more, just because she could, just because there was someone holding her.

★   ★   ★

Later, Mazz met the Colonel in the Oak. The mystery of Charlie's death apparently resolved, Mazz relaxed and he and the Colonel, not for the first time in their lives, had a few drinks.

Mazz woke up on the Colonel's spare bed not feeling any better than he expected to and lurched out into the kitchen to find the Colonel studying the *Western Mail*.

There it was on page three. Casino corruption probe.

'Christ,' said Mazz, peering over his shoulder to read the accompanying story.

Apparently a tip-off had alerted the newspaper to questionable links between Nichols and the council's chief planning officer, one Trefor Howells. Hospitality had been accepted, blah blah blah. And to make the story look rather more sensational Charlie's death had been thrown into the mix. Well-loved Cardiff boxer Charlie Unger had been found dead in a flat belonging to Nichols, a flat the planning officer had just agreed to recommend for demolition. Wheel in a couple of churchmen to vehemently oppose the building of a casino and there you had it, a nice little scandal. Both Nichols and Howells were described as unavailable for comment, though Vernon's office had put out a bland little statement describing the casino plan as a prestige development that would help build tourism in the bay.

'Doesn't look good for Big Vern,' said the Colonel.

'Hmm,' Mazz grunted. 'Thing I don't understand, though, is who gave them the info.'

The Colonel shrugged. 'Your man Jason,' he said, 'Jason Flaherty.'

'Yeah?'

'Makes sense,' said the Colonel. 'Screws Vernon Nichols over good and proper, then Jason moves on in.'

'Yeah?' said Mazz. 'What d'you think he'll do?'

'Vernon? Not much he can do, is there?'

'It'll be Tyra he blames, though, all this stuff about Charlie getting out.'

The Colonel thought for a moment. 'Maybe,' he said, 'maybe not. You could always give him a call, tell him you reckon it was Jason. But if you're worried about it, why don't you borrow the van, take your girl Tyra and her kids off on a little camping trip for a week or two, wait till the fuss dies down?

School holidays must be starting now. Go down to Cornwall, get ready for the eclipse. No fucker'll find you there.'

Tyra was just getting the kids ready for school, trying to get them to stop watching *Nickelodeon* and get their trainers on, when there was a banging on the door. She peered out the window to find out who it was and saw Mazz, standing there holding a newspaper.

She opened the door to him and he unfolded the paper, showed her the story.

'Who's behind that then?' she asked.

'Jason,' said Mazz, 'far as we can tell.'

'Jason!' Tyra was outraged, angry, hurt that Flaherty would use her dad's death like that, just as a weapon to screw over a business rival. Using him just like he always had. 'You sure?'

Mazz shrugged. 'Like I say, just seems the most likely person. The only one had much to gain from this. But anyway I'm thinking we should get away from here for a bit, in case Vernon freaks out, blames you for all this. The Colonel said we could borrow his camper, go off on a bit of a trip.'

Tyra felt dizzy, walked back into the kitchen and sat down. She felt betrayed. Jason, she'd thought he was all right. For Christ's sake, she'd slept with him, and now this. She wasn't sure why she cared but she did; somehow it seemed like one more betrayal of her dad. If Charlie had wanted Jason to get involved he'd have asked him.

'All right,' she said to Mazz finally. 'Let's go.'

They were gone a week. A strange week spent in Devon, in a broken-down old mill belonged to a producer Mazz had worked with a few times. Place had no hot water and a stream ran through the living-room, but it was set in some nice countryside and the sun shone and the kids actually seemed to enjoy themselves which surprised Tyra a bit.

The strange thing, the difficult thing, was how to handle Mazz. The kids weren't a problem – they liked him from the start, already liked him from the day they'd spent at the beach, and he was good with them, she was happy to admit that. Trouble was it was pushing things too fast. They were just back in

Cardiff, she could have been taking things at her own pace. Seeing him every few days or whatever. Give it time to sort out the nostalgia and the sheer bloody randiness, and see what lay underneath. Something real or not. And she would have kept him away from the kids as much as possible, didn't want them thinking here was Mum's new boyfriend till she knew what she wanted.

But now, thanks to Jason Flaherty, they were stuck together all week and the kids couldn't help but know he was Mum's new boyfriend. Well, she'd thought about having him sleep out in the van or something but then the first night one thing had led to another and before they'd made any proper plans they were waking up together in the morning, the kids looking at them, and it was too late. And the thing that broke her heart was just how pleased the kids were, specially Jermaine. She'd thought he might be jealous, and maybe that would come, but for the moment he just seemed to be thrilled to have a man around the place.

Thing was, though, the more the kids liked Mazz and the more they went out and did stuff – went to the beach, went walking on Dartmoor – the more they did family stuff, the more uncomfortable she felt. By the end of the week she felt like she was withdrawing from the whole lot of them, Mazz especially. Except in the night times, of course, in the night times. In the night times she felt like she was nineteen again, so full of need beforehand, so inconsolable afterwards. What had she lost? How much had she lost, all those years since then? Since she lost him. Since he lost her.

In the night times, in the aftermath, after she'd cried and he'd held her and finally he'd gone to sleep, she would get up and go to the room her kids were sleeping in, just stand there and look at them. Wondering how you could love people so much and yet they could sometimes seem so strange to you.

Mazz and the kids would probably have been happy to stay for another week, to wait for the eclipse. Tyra wasn't having it; she said it was because of all the traffic, all the millions of people they were saying were coming down for the eclipse, which sounded like rubbish really – what you heard in the shops was everyone was staying away – but still she said she was worried about the overcrowding and she wanted to get back. Really what it was was she couldn't stand it any more. She had to get back to her life, try and get some distance between her and Mazz before the kids elected him their de facto daddy.

They went to the Colonel's place first on their return to South Wales, to find out how the land lay. Turned out the land looked OK. Vernon Nichols had clearly come to the same conclusion as Mazz and Tyra as to who had the most to gain from giving the story to the press. An arson attack had been launched on Jason's office building the night after they'd left town. The next day there was another story in the press, this time linking the arson attack to Vernon and once again mentioning Charlie's death – which was now described as 'suspicious'. Suddenly Vernon Nichols looked dirtier than dirty.

The following day, in a fit of apparent piety, the council had decided to reject Vernon Nichols's planning application. No wrongdoing had been seen to be done, a pompous statement said, but the council could not afford for even the appearance of wrongdoing to occur. An inquiry would be launched into the full history of Vernon Nichols's dealings with the council. However, they were going to go ahead with the compulsory purchase of the houses on James Street and they were inviting new planning applications for the site. Vernon Nichols had been unavailable for comment, doubtless busy consulting his learned friends and/or hired leg-breakers to plan his next move.

'Looks like that's the end of it,' said the Colonel, and the others agreed. Wasn't exactly satisfying to learn that Charlie had most probably died of a cocaine-inspired heart attack, while all the rest of it was basically no more than sharp-end business as usual.

That night Mazz and Tyra went out. It was his idea. He'd said, 'Why don't you get your mum to look after the kids?' She'd said, 'All right, you want to go over the UCI again?' and he'd said, 'No, it'd be good to go out in the neighbourhood, like,' and she'd given him a bit of a funny look but then shrugged and said all right and now there they were sat downstairs in the Baltimore and suddenly there was that married-couple thing going on, where you've spent, like, all week with someone doing the family stuff, and then when you're out together and you're meant to be having a good time, you haven't got a thing to say and you're looking round desperately for someone else to talk to.

In fact Mazz was about to suggest they went over to the UCI after all when this feller walked in, little guy their age with a flat-top growing out into short locks, and his eye positively twinkled when he saw Tyra.

'How's it going, sweetheart?' he said and came over and kissed her and stuck his hand out at Mazz.

'Mikey,' he said. And Mazz clocked the name, a friend of Col's he was sure.

'Mazz,' he said and then, glad of the company, 'get you a drink?'

'Yeah,' said Mikey. 'Diamond White would be sweet.'

So Mazz went up to the bar and got them in. When he got back Mikey had drawn up a stool a little closer to Tyra, to be honest, than Mazz really appreciated but then they were all sat down and this Mikey it had to be said was a good laugh and after a bit he asked Mazz what he did and Mazz explained about the band and Mikey remembered and told a couple of good stories about Charlie in the old days and Mazz was a bit apprehensive but Tyra laughed harder than any of them and Mikey said well seeing as you're a musician let's go up the karaoke and Mazz groaned and said all right but was really not too disappointed at all when it turned out to be the wrong night.

So then Mikey said, 'Let's go round to Kenny's place. You knows Kenny, Mazz? Course you does, used to be your manager, didn't he?'

'I dunno,' said Tyra, and this Mikey gave her a bit of a funny look but Mazz fancied a drink now so he stood up and said, 'Sounds good to me,' and they headed round the corner to Black Caesar's, smoking Mikey's spliff as they walked.

Going up the stairs that led up to the club a feller passed them on his way down wearing a sharp suit and a frown. Mazz didn't figure out who he was till he'd gone. 'Hey,' he said to Tyra then, 'that was Emyr's mate, Danny Lewis-thing, wonder what he was doing here?'

'Free country,' said Tyra, uncharacteristically short, and Mazz shrugged in return and they headed inside.

Through the door, Mazz got a couple more bottles for him and Mikey, a glass of water for Tyra who hissed in his ear that she was tired and didn't want to stay long. Mazz said sure and leaned back against the bar, took the place in. When he'd been here before for Charlie's wake it had been rammed; now the place was a quarter full at best but dark enough that it didn't feel empty. One thing Mazz did like about it, for once in a club he didn't feel old; most of the punters looked to be locals around his own age and the music was reggae and old-school funk, comfortably familiar tunes in an atmosphere that otherwise bordered on the heavy.

Mazz walked over to the DJ, one of the few other white guys in the room, to compliment him on the music, when he realised he knew the guy. Old hippy called Ozzie, used to work at Grassroots.

Ozzie was well pleased to see him, passed over the spliff and they had a bit of a chat, then Mazz headed back to check Tyra was OK and found her talking to Col.

'How's it going, man?' said Mazz, putting out his hand to shake.

'All right,' said Col, and maybe hesitated a second before shaking Mazz's hand.

'So you two got it back together then?' said Col after a pause.

'Yeah,' said Mazz, leaning over to kiss Tyra on the cheek.

'Yeah, well,' said Col, 'you try and treat her better than last time, man,' and walked off.

Mazz turned to Tyra. 'What's got into him?'

She shrugged and said, 'He looks out for me, you know.'

'Oh,' said Mazz and fell silent, suddenly worrying that people – black guys – were staring at him, like he was coming down there and stealing their women, that kind of vibe. Then, all at once, the biggest, meanest-looking guy in the place was walking towards him and Mazz tensed, felt his hand instinctively tighten around the neck of his bottle, ready to do what he had to do if attacked. Then, as the guy got closer, he looked hard at him and relaxed.

'Kenny,' he said then. 'Long time no see, man.'

'Yeah,' said Kenny, 'long time. You bring that guy down here?'

'What guy?' said Mazz, confused.

'Guy was just here, Danny Lewis Jones. Feller asking if I wanted to sell him my club. Talking about how the area's changing and he could do a real job on this place, redevelop it for the tourist crowd. Pay me top dollar. All that kind of shit. Friend of yours, is he?'

'No,' said Mazz and turned round to look at Tyra, see if this meant anything to her, but she had her back to him already, was talking to a couple of mates Mazz had never seen before. Suddenly he started to feel a long way out of his element.

'No,' he repeated, 'I've seen the guy around. He's a friend of Emyr's – you remember him? – but I don't know anything about him.'

'I'll tell you what he is,' said Kenny, 'that feller he's got it written all over him. He's bad fucking news is what he is.'

With that Kenny walked off and Mazz stood there for a while in a little bubble of his own, next to the bar, wondering if this was somewhere he could ever belong.

Tyra spent the next few days getting the kids back into their usual holiday routines, going round her sister's and her mum's. 'Where's Mazz?' Jermaine kept asking and Tyra was able to tell the truth and say he was up in London, sorting some business out. Plus his ex was threatening to dump his stuff on the street, he didn't come and move it. Tyra hadn't offered to let him bring it round to hers, though he'd hinted pretty hard, so he'd huffed and puffed a bit and finally decided to take it round his mum's, up in Newbridge, get a mate of his to drive it down.

Mazz got back to Cardiff the morning of the eclipse. His mate Mac was driving and they were talking about getting a band together. Didn't mean much; they must have had half a dozen conversations like that over the years. Mac had been around even longer than Mazz, been the singer in one of the real hardcore early punk bands, bunch of Manchester headcases who'd have done a lot better if one or other of then hadn't been in jail most of the time. Anyway Mac had had his difficulties over the years, usual rock'n'roll problems, but he was pretty much clean these days, spent most of his time road-managing for other bands. That was how Mazz met him and mutual loathing of the fat Yank had turned into something more positive.

'So where are we going to watch this thing?' asked Mac as they came down the A470 into Cardiff.

Mazz looked up at the sky. It had been so completely clouded over when he woke up that morning he'd more or less given up on seeing anything, but now the clouds were clearing fast and Mazz couldn't help seeing an omen there.

'Give us your phone,' he said and Mac passed him the mobile. Two calls later he had it set up. They'd pick up Tyra and the kids then meet the Colonel on the pier in Penarth at quarter to eleven.

'Your girlfriend?' said Mac when Mazz got off the phone.

'Yeah,' said Mazz. 'I hope so.'

By the time Mazz had finished giving Mac a little background on him and Tyra, they were pulling up outside her house. Tyra and the kids piled in the back, the kids putting their special eclipse glasses on and then laughing when they couldn't see anything through them.

The Colonel and Natalie were already waiting at the pier when they arrived. The sky was now miraculously blue and a steady stream of people were making for the seafront. Mac endeared himself immediately to the kids by getting them cones of Thayers ice-cream and the party wandered on to the Edwardian pier.

'How was London, butt?' asked the Colonel and Mazz told him while watching Mac play with the kids and Natalie walk over to Tyra and start talking to her with what looked to Mazz like a too-friendly smile on her face.

'Hey,' said Mac then, staring up at the sun, a pair of eclipse wraparounds over his eyes. 'It's starting.'

And so it was. Everyone took turns with the four pairs of glasses Tyra and the Colonel had brought along between them and watched the moon inch its way across the face of the sun. The sky, though, stayed resolutely light. All that seemed to be changing was the temperature; there was a noticeable chill in the air and Tyra had the kids put on their coats.

'Ninety-seven degrees,' said Mazz. 'You'd think it would get darker than this.'

'Makes you think, though,' said Natalie, coming up close to him. 'Three per cent of the sun can still light up the world. Wonder how much good three per cent of a person would be for anything.'

Mazz didn't say a word, just smiled blankly back at her.

Natalie moved closer still, put her arm through Mazz's, smiling at Tyra then at the Colonel to show she didn't mean anything by it. 'I was telling Tyra here how I remembered her from your band.'

'Oh,' said Mazz, suddenly gripped by dread at the thought of what Natalie might say next.

'Hmm,' she said, 'I only saw you all once of course. At the Casablanca. It was a party or something . . .'

Mazz was struggling to stop from shaking; the temperature seemed to be icy all of a sudden.

'Yeah. I was just saying how sexy you used to be. Back then.' She gave a little no-offence giggle.

Mazz swivelled his eyes to look at Tyra then, hoping she wasn't paying attention, but she was. The Casablanca gig, the last gig.

18

NEWBRIDGE

1981

Sitting on the bus winding its way through Risca, at the start of the valley, Mazz was wondering whether this was a good idea. Him and Tyra were sat at the back, but they were getting some looks from the old dears on their way back from chapel. He hadn't really thought about what his mam and dad might think. About Tyra. Didn't think about it much himself – that was why, he supposed. Wasn't like there was any big difference between Tyra and any of the other girls he knew: listened to the same records, watched the same TV shows, wore the same kinds of clothes. Actually there was a bit of difference; he could see it in Bobby too. Thing about black girls, Mazz reckoned, least black girls his age, they weren't quite so fucking up themselves as most of the girls you met. Most girls, pretty ones anyway, nineteen, twenty, you could just tell they thought they were the best thing ever, never had any idea the world was there to do anything except kiss your arse. Girls like Tyra, or Bobby come to that, you could see they knew it wasn't like that; world was waiting there with a baseball bat behind its back ready to lick you down any time it felt like it.

He could tell Tyra was edgy too. She stopped talking as they got to Cross Keys, just looked out the window at the closed-up Sunday streets, the pubs and schools looking greyer than ever in the spring sunshine. She was so wrapped up in whatever she was thinking that it took Mazz two goes to attract her attention when they finally got to Newbridge.

Mazz put his hand in hers as they walked up the hill to his home. A kid on a brand-new BMX made a lewd noise as he passed them and Mazz thought it was pretty much the same deal as him going down to Butetown to her place. Holding Tyra's hand, though, he could feel just how tensed up she was.

Worst moment was when they walked round to the back door and ran straight into Bryn standing in the back garden having a fag while the two little kids mucked about with a plastic ride-on tractor used to be Mazz's when he was little. You could see Bryn was a squaddie from a mile off. Tyra stiffened even more as she saw him and Mazz caught the flicker of sheer surprise that crossed his face when he clocked Tyra and for a moment Mazz thought oh fuck. But then Bryn beamed and stuck his hand out.

'Bryn,' he said, 'and who are you?'

'Tyra,' said Tyra and stuck her hand out in return.

'Christ,' said Bryn, 'and what possessed a lovely girl like you to go out with this little toerag?'

Same kind of thing went on with Mazz's mum; you could see the surprise but what followed it was pure hospitality. As for Mazz's dad, he was at the stage of his drinking by this time of day that the whole world had a rose-tinted glow for a bit. Be different later on, but three or four drinks into the day Mazz's dad loved everybody. Mazz practically had to pull him off Tyra before he could make a complete fool of himself trying to kiss her hand.

Only person who was a bit reserved was Bryn's missus, Donna, but then when she wasn't chasing around after the two little kids she was just sitting there, knocking back the cider, looking completely out of it. Actually after a little while she wasn't the only one who was knocking back the drinks, just the only one who wasn't saying much.

Mazz was enjoying being back, bullshitting around with Bryn who was telling him improbable stories of life in Germany with the Welsh Guards, their dad chipping in with even more unlikely tales about what he got up to in Cyprus during his National Service. Meanwhile Tyra and Mazz's mum seemed to be hitting it off like anything. Tyra went into the kitchen after a bit to help Lena, Mazz's mum, get the roast together and there were peals of laughter coming from that direction. Later on, while the blokes were doing the washing up, Lena took Tyra upstairs to show her the bedrooms and that.

Mazz didn't think anything of it till they were on the bus back about half five, both stuffed to the gills and half pissed and, far as Mazz was concerned, having had a good time. A family time.

'I told her, you know,' said Tyra.

'Who, your mum?' said Mazz in alarm.

'No, your mum.'

'Shit,' said Mazz.

'Well, she guessed really. She asked me if I was and what could I say . . .?'

'Oh,' said Mazz, 'great.'

'Yeah,' said Tyra vaguely, like she hadn't been listening, didn't know what she was agreeing with.

Monday morning Jason rounded the band up in his blue transit, drove them to the studio, a converted chapel in Pontypridd. Smartest studio Mazz had been in yet: twenty-four tracks, separate drum and vocal booths, games room for the band to hang out in with a pool table and drinks and chocolate dispensers.

The producer was there already. Fella called John the record company had decided on. Mazz knew the name; he'd done some power-pop stuff, kind of thing you heard on the radio without noticing much. Anyway seemed like a nice enough bloke.

First day was unutterably tedious once the initial excitement of being there had worn off. John the producer had Emyr in the drum booth all day long just getting the sounds right. Said the drums were the key to the whole thing, you wanted your record to come over on the radio. Mazz took his word for it, though he couldn't help thinking that they recorded 'Lick Her Down', the whole thing, in the time it took this guy to get a snare sound he was happy with, and that had sounded all right on the radio.

Anyway the rest of them just goofed around the games room all day. Bobby ran through the entire supply of Toffee Crisps in the vending machine and won the pool tournament they had so easily that they had to have another one where she had a three-ball handicap. She won that too and the three blokes, Mazz, Col and Charlie, all sulked like mad.

Tyra just sat in the corner most of the time, reading her book. When the rest of them nipped out to the chippy, around lunchtime, she stayed put, said she didn't feel hungry. When they got back she was talking on the payphone.

Next day they finally got down to doing some recording. First the drums, which took up all the morning and was starting to thoroughly piss Emyr off. Why don't we just record it all live? he kept asking and John the producer kept saying something about how that would never work on American radio. Mazz worried a little that maybe they should be thinking about British radio at this stage of the game but he kept his mouth shut. And after lunch John was finally happy with Emyr's drums and started on Charlie's percussion. This time John seemed happy with the sound right away and Charlie got his part down first take.

Tyra was up next. She was nervous, you could see, or at least Mazz could see. John didn't seem too notice, though, just gave her a hard time when she had trouble tuning up. Brought out an electronic tuner, first time Mazz had seen one of them, and did it himself in the end.

After that Mazz was expecting the worst. These days he'd have just told the cunt to fuck off and leave her alone but back then he was impressed, he supposed, and left him to it. As it happened, though, Tyra played perfectly, got a take that John was happy with fifth time through and, be fair to him, he was nice enough to her then.

Mazz was playing pool with Bobby at the time, just lining up a tricky red, so he didn't say anything immediately to Tyra as she came out of the studio. She just looked at him for a second then walked over to the payphone. Started talking quietly into it.

Two more days and they had three tracks more or less down: covers of '007' and 'Skinhead Moonstomp' plus an instrumental of Col's, a kind of speeded-up Augustus Pablo thing called 'East of the River Taff'. Simon from the record company had been down on the Thursday afternoon, said he reckoned '007' should be the next single. Mazz thought that was a bit obvious, better to go with one of their own tunes – he had hopes for a tune he and Bobby had written called 'Night Time', a moody thing sounded a bit heavier than the rest of the stuff. Anyway, point was Simon was happy and took them all out on the town after. Pub, Taurus steakhouse, Monty's, the full works. Bloke was even up for a trip down Kenny's blues at the end of the night. Paid for everything and a constant supply of coke on tap any time anyone fancied nipping to the bogs for a livener. A couple of years later, of course, they'd find out that Simon had done everything, right down to the coke (billed as flowers and champagne), on expenses, the band's expenses, taken straight out of royalties, but that's by the by.

Mazz fell into bed about five and it took Jason practically breaking his door down to get him up the next morning.

First thing Jason said, when Mazz finally lurched out of the front door, 'Tyra there too?'

Mazz shook his head. 'Course not, she went home after the meal, didn't she?'

'Well she's not there now. Nobody there at all.'

The rest of the band were slumped around the back of the van, looking like Mazz felt. Mazz looked at Charlie questioningly. Charlie just shrugged.

'You get in, Mazz,' said Jason. 'Let's go. She'll turn up sooner or later.'

Driving to the studio, Jason had the radio on. Mazz wasn't paying attention, wondering what the hell had happened to Tyra – maybe she'd had to go to the doctor, been feeling pretty sick lately – when suddenly the news came on. Bobby Sands had been elected MP for Fermanagh and South Tyrone, with 30,492 votes. Christ. A government spokesman was quickly wheeled on to explain that this meant nothing at all but Mazz couldn't believe it. Maybe it was the hangover but he found himself actually shaking from excitement at the news. Like all at once a hole had been ripped in the fabric of the lies the establishment told you. The IRA have no popular support, all that shit. Just lies.

Mazz was buzzing by the time they got to the studio.

'Let's do "Night Time" next,' he said.

John the producer pointed feebly at the schedule he'd drawn up that said they were meant to be doing 'Downtown' next, but he looked to have the worst hangover of the lot of them and was no match for Mazz's enthusiasm.

'What about Tyra?' said Charlie as Emyr got behind his drums.

'S'all right,' said Mazz, 'I'll play the bass on this one.' It was easy enough as Mazz had written most of the bass lines himself then taught them to Tyra. In fact Mazz's energy level was such that he managed to override John's protests and get him to record bass and drums together.

'Groove's got to be right on this one.'

In fact the groove was terrific. Mazz and Emyr laid down this dark, sinister back-beat, Charlie added some slow menacing percussion, Col put on a ghost-train keyboard line and when Bobby put down the vocal, as far as everyone in the room was concerned it was there, the track that proved the Wurriyas weren't just one more novelty ska band but serious contenders.

It was late afternoon by the time John had a vocal take he was completely happy with and he was just fiddling about with different reverb sounds when the studio doorbell rang. Charlie went to get it and came back a minute or so later with Tyra plus her friend Maggie.

The second Mazz saw her he knew something was wrong. He walked over to her and was just about to say 'Where the fuck have you been?', pretend to give her a hard time about her no-show, when something in her face stopped him.

'Mazz,' she said quietly, 'you want to come for a walk?'

'Now?' he said, looking round at the band.

'Yeah,' she said, 'now.'

'Shit,' said Mazz. 'OK.'

Mazz turned to Charlie and Col, raised his palms towards them in a gesture of helplessness, said, 'Back in five, yeah,' and followed Tyra towards the door. Maggie started to follow them, but Tyra put her arm out and said, 'D'you mind waiting for me here, Mags.'

Maggie looked at her. 'You sure?'

'Yeah,' said Tyra, 'I'm sure,' so Maggie dropped back, not before giving Mazz a distinctly evil look.

Outside they walked along in silence for a while till they came to a little municipal park, deserted in the drizzle. Tyra led the way to a bench and sat down. Mazz sat down too, and Tyra clung to him. Not saying anything, just holding on to him for a while, then crying. Just crying and crying and crying like she wasn't going to stop.

'I'm sorry,' she said at last, 'I'm sorry, I'm sorry, I'm sorry,' over and over again. For a single moment Mazz had been about to ask what she was sorry for but then he knew, knew where she'd been, knew what she'd done, knew she hadn't believed it could work, and then he was crying too. The two of them sat on the bench together in the rain crying and holding each other, Tyra mouthing 'I'm sorry' over and over in his ear, a mantra of loss and disillusion, on the ninth of April 1981.

Later on Mazz would think maybe he read it wrong, maybe things could have worked out. At the time he figured it was all simple enough; Tyra had made a choice. She'd rejected his baby, she'd rejected him. The next few days in the studio Tyra insisted on coming down, said there was nothing wrong with her physically. Mags was there all the time. Mazz couldn't help it, felt like she was cutting his balls off and laughing at him. Except he could see she wasn't laughing. Her pain was obvious but any time he came near her she just retreated more and more into herself, got to the point where Maggie seemed to be doing all the talking for her, and time and again Mazz's sympathy would turn to anger at being frozen out. God knows how they came out of this time with a record, but they did. 'Night Time' was the standout but there were a couple of other tracks didn't come out too bad at all and Simon was over the moon.

Took another couple of weeks to muck around with the mixing and then they were done. The night after they finished they decided to celebrate with an impromptu gig down the Casablanca. Kenny organised the runnings and it seemed like half Cardiff turned up – docks boys, art students, looked like the Royal Oak had sent a coach party.

On stage it was great, one of their best. Afterwards everyone was elated, all headed straight round to the front of house after the show, all except Mazz and Tyra who sat there backstage looking at each other.

'You OK?' said Mazz, nervous now, the first time he'd been alone with her since she told him.

'Yeah,' she said, 'fine . . .' and then paused. Looked like she was about to say something else when Mags came in. She gave Mazz a baleful look then turned to Tyra. 'Christ,' she said, 'it's a zoo out there. You want me to take you home? I've got the car, we can go straight out the back.'

Tyra nodded wearily, then stood and picked up her bass.

'Right,' she said to Mazz, 'see you,' and followed Mags out the back door.

Mazz just stood there for a moment watching the door shut behind them. Then he shook his head, walked into the club, straight to the bar and ordered himself a pint with a whisky chaser.

A couple of hours later, he was steaming drunk and climbing into a cab with an equally drunk art student called Natasha or something. They ended up back at his place and managed to have brief but surprisingly enjoyable sex before both of them took turns to throw up in the bathroom.

Mazz had woken up dying of thirst with a whisky headache around five in the morning and was lying there trying to summon the willpower to get up and fetch a glass of water when the doorbell rang.

Tyra.

He hadn't realised how angry he was with her till he saw her then. Or maybe he was still whisky-drunk, maybe that would be a kinder explanation. Either way, he lost it as she stood there at his door.

'What the fuck d'you want now?' he roared at her. 'You already killed my fucking baby,' loud enough to wake the dead or at least the couple downstairs – which didn't bother him too much, the number of times they'd rowed, the bloke had stormed out and the woman had played bloody Janis Joplin's 'Piece of My Heart' over and over, four in the morning.

He said other things too, ugly things, and Tyra just stood there in the early-morning cold, her head bowed, till Mazz finished and slammed the door in her face.

Less than a month later Bobby Sands was dead and so was the Wurriyas' career. Things had come to a head when they took the tapes up to London, played them to Simon's boss, Ric. You could see the last drop of Mazz's optimism leak out of him the moment Ric listened to 'Night Time' and pronounced it total fucking crap. The record company, in their wisdom, put out the Prince Buster cover, '007', instead. It flopped, Mazz didn't show for a TV appearance – *Tiswas*, Saturday morning – end of story.

The Wurriyas returned to Cardiff to lick their wounds, to meet up in odd combinations and discuss what should happen next. Emyr was headed for London; he had a new girlfriend up there and was getting bored of banging out the same old beat he said. Meanwhile if Emyr was thinking big, Charlie was thinking small, had a bunch of pub and club gigs lined up if anyone wanted to do them. Col went along with him, as did Bobby, neither of them finally able to countenance the move up to London. Mazz hung between the two camps for a while, not wanting to let Charlie down but knowing in his heart he'd rather be off with Emyr, get another taste of the bright lights. Tyra? No one saw Tyra for a while. Then Bobby Sands died, starved, skeletal and insane, and there was a march on the day of his funeral and Mazz was there on his own in a big black Crombie, and Tyra and Maggie were there too, and maybe they crossed eyes once or twice but they didn't speak.

Mazz spent a lot of the next week drinking, plucking up the courage to tell Charlie he was off, and then on a Tuesday morning, May the twelfth, just as he was packing up his records and his clothes, getting ready to move, the bell rang and he went down and there was Tyra.

He didn't shout at her this time, didn't say a word, just walked upstairs and let her follow. They sat at a table in the empty front room, surrounded by boxes, looking out on the grimness of Neville Street, and neither of them spoke for a while.

'You heard he died?' said Tyra eventually.

'Yeah,' said Mazz. 'I saw you at the funeral.'

'No,' she said, 'not Bobby Sands. Bob Marley, he died yesterday.'

Mazz just looked at her, hardly able to compute what she'd just said.

At the time all he could say was, 'Shit, it's all turned to shit, hasn't it?'

Later he would realise it was one of those pivotal moments, the end of innocence if you like. It was the moment he saw the world wasn't going to change, and with that knowledge came a kind of release. All of a sudden Mazz had the strength to do what he knew he had to do.

'I'm going to London,' he said to Tyra.

'Good luck,' she said.

'You want to come?' he asked.

She shook her head then and reached for him and pulled him down so his head was in her lap, nestled against her empty belly, and they stayed there in silence for a long time, waiting for the dark to let them leave.

19

THE MILLENNIUM STADIUM

1999

Nearly three months after the eclipse, on a Thursday afternoon in late October, Tyra's walking through town, caught up in the atmosphere generated by the Rugby World Cup, forgetting her troubles.

Wales are about to play Western Samoa in the Millennium Stadium which has somehow opened on time and forever changed the way Tyra saw the city she'd spent her life in.

The old stadium, the Arms Park, was almost invisible from the centre of town. You were only really aware of it when you looked at it from over the river in Riverside. The new stadium dominated the centre and you could see it from almost anywhere in Cardiff. And, like pretty much everyone else, Tyra found it surprisingly inspiring. It suddenly made you aware that Cardiff was changing, that all the bollocks you heard people spit on the TV about being a European capital for the new century was really true. Even made you believe that all the bay development could come to something.

And this Rugby World Cup too – another thing you'd been hearing about for years but never seemed to materialise. Well, it was here now and you never saw so many people out on the streets having a good time. So each of the match days Tyra's made a point of being there for a while. Just wandering around soaking up the atmosphere, taking her mind off things.

'Cause things were bothering her. Her and Mazz. Mazz, who was in the Royal Oak now with the Colonel and his mates, born-again rugby fans one and all. Mazz, who she'd been living with more or less since the eclipse.

The eclipse. It was funny that girl, Natalie, trying to upset her then – had the opposite effect really. Course it brought up all that old shit. The abortion, and what happened after. But it wasn't like she'd forgotten any of that. More the opposite, really; it was the memory of it all that was making her keep Mazz at bay. Natalie chucking it in her face like that made her think about it properly. Made her realise maybe she hadn't been that perfect either, you think about it. Freezing him out of the whole thing the way she'd done. Hardly surprising he'd gone off on one. Not like she forgave him or anything, not like she'd put up with anyone screwing around on her now. But you got older you understood stuff, you weren't so self-righteous about life. Couldn't afford to be.

And the sad thing was he still had it, Mazz, that thing he'd had back then which made you dread going out in public with him, knowing half the girls there would have him if they got the chance. Only reason Natalie had behaved the way she had – jealousy, Tyra figured. Yeah, Mazz could still do it to her, still made her feel stuff no one else made her feel.

Trouble wasn't that. Trouble was the things he didn't make her feel. Like safe. Or supported.

'Cause that he hadn't changed was what made him still sexy but it was also what made him impossible. He hadn't changed – he was still a guitar player. Couldn't do anything else, could barely feed himself. And far as she could see, the only way he could make any money doing it was to tour all the time, which she didn't want, but the alternative was to have him there all the time doing nothing, which she didn't want either. She could see him wilting in Cardiff, playing gigs for beer money down the Oak – first time was a laugh, second time was a wake – auditioning for fucking hotel cabaret bands which in the end she wouldn't let him do, couldn't bear to see him humiliate himself that much. Reminded her too much of her dad greeting people at the casino.

So he was just there. Well, except when he'd spend a few days at his brother's up in the valleys when it all got a bit much. But basically he was just there and he was doing his best. He was good with the kids and all but really he was going mad and she was going mad and after a bit all that passion stuff just feels a bit pointless and what was she going to do?

She was just heading up Bute Street, passing the Custom House, leaving the noise of town behind for the quiet of Butetown, when she heard a car pulling up behind her. Her first thought was a kerb crawler, some salesman thinking she was a Custom House girl, and she spun round ready to give the bastard what for when through the car window she could see it was a bastard all right but a bastard she knew.

Jason Flaherty.

'What d'you want?' Just the sight of him enraged her. 'Coming to see where you're going to build your casino?' It had been in the papers, a few weeks back. Council were planning to give the go-ahead for a consortium headed by Cardiff property developer Jason Flaherty to build a casino hotel in the bay. Surprise, surprise.

'No,' said Jason, his big head sweating in the autumn sun.

'Not going to see it?'

'Not my casino, for starters,' said Jason, 'and that's not why I'm here anyway. I wanted to see you.'

'Me?' said Tyra. 'What d'you want to see me for? So you can stick my story all over the newspaper like you did Vernon?'

'What?' said Jason. 'Listen, why don't you get in the car and I'll explain.'

Tyra looked up and down the road. She didn't want her business becoming public property, she'd better get in the car. She opened the passenger door and sat there on the nice leather seat as far from Jason as she could manage.

'Where d'you want to go?'

'Just take me down to James Street, that'll do.'

They drove on in silence for a hundred yards or so, then Jason, who seemed unusually nervous, coughed and said, 'Vernon tell you I gave that picture to the paper, did he?'

'No,' said Tyra, 'Didn't have to. It was obvious.'

Jason didn't say anything for a bit, just drove on round the one-way system and into James Street, then pulled up on the left by Charlie's old flat, now all boarded up and waiting for demolition.

'Wasn't me,' he said flatly.

Tyra laughed sarcastically.

Jason took no notice, carried on talking. 'People in glass houses and all that. I'm hardly going to start bleating to the papers about planning corruption. And I'd have thought you'd have figured out by now who really did give them the info.'

'Who?' said Tyra, curious despite herself.

'Same feller who's going to make a killing out of this casino,' said Jason, waving towards the buildings waiting to be demolished.

'Thought that was you,' said Tyra. 'What it said in the paper.'

Jason's turn to laugh sarcastically. 'Aye, and they never get anything wrong in the *Western Mail*. But you're right, I was in there quick as soon as old Vernon got shafted. Only then I got shafted myself. Same little bastard did Vernon over went and told the council that, as a convicted felon, I was hardly suitable to be running a casino. And next thing I knew the little bastard had blindsided the lot of us, got the contract for himself.'

'Who?' said Tyra again.

'Your mate, the Porthcawl golden boy,' said Jason heavily. 'Danny Lewis fucking Jones.'

'Danny Lewis Jones,' said Tyra, now really confused.

'Yeah,' said Jason, 'Danny. Listen, you got time for a drink before you pick your kids up?'

Tyra frowned, then checked her watch, nodded.

'Good,' said Jason and he started the car up again and took the next left, left again past Techniquest and into the car park for the St David's Hotel, there right on the bay.

Jason led the way into the bar which was deserted thanks to its lack of a TV.

'How come you're not watching the rugby then?' asked Tyra, unbending a little.

'Can't stand the game,' said Jason, pulling back a seat for Tyra.

'No?' said Tyra, eyeing his bulk. 'Thought you'd have been a natural for it.'

'Yeah,' said Jason, bleakly. 'That's what everybody thought. But I never had any skill, I was just big. And after a bit that's not enough.'

Jason sat down opposite Tyra, picked up a drinks list and then, so quickly she wasn't sure if she'd imagined it, brushed away a tear from his eye.

'Look,' she said then, 'this the truth what you're telling me? Danny Lewis Jones got the contract for the casino?'

'Yeah,' said Jason, 'it's the truth all right. Phone the council and ask, you don't believe me.'

'OK,' said Tyra slowly. 'And you say it was Danny gave the picture to the paper.'

'Had to be,' said Jason. 'Only people stood to gain anything from screwing Vernon were fellow developers. Developers who knew about Charlie's death. And I must admit that seemed to narrow the field down to me. That's definitely what Big Vern thought, 'cause he went and attacked my office. But I was forgetting about young Danny. He's making a play to impress his dad, show he's not just the little waster everyone's taken him for up to now. His dad's had plans for years to knock down Coney Beach completely, redevelop the site as a state-of-the-art theme park. That's run into planning problems, though, so old man Lewis Jones has been looking for something else to put his money into, and young Danny's come along saying here you go, Pop, I've got just the project for you. All we've got to do is play old Jason Flaherty for an idiot.

'Which he did very nicely, to be fair, blindsided me completely. In fact it was even me who actually asked him to come in one the deal. He made a few subtle hints when we had that meeting and I bought his line. Didn't see what was coming till he stabbed me in the back.'

Tyra stayed quiet for a moment thinking on that, then something struck her forcefully. 'Christ,' she said, 'he bloody killed him.'

'Who?' said Jason. 'Who killed who?'

'Danny,' said Tyra. 'He killed Charlie.'

'What?'

'Emyr said he gave Charlie a gram of Danny's cocaine. Extra pure or something. Might have been what caused Charlie's heart attack. Emyr said it was an accident. He hadn't thought Charlie would take it himself. But now I'm wondering . . .'

Jason's turn to ponder. 'Yeah,' he said finally. 'That must have been the start of it when they bumped into Charlie – Danny and Emyr – and Charlie started ranting on about Vernon. Danny must have figured it out straight away. Say he did kill Charlie. Deliberately overdosed him. He probably thought that might have been enough to do Vernon by itself. Having Charlie die there just when Vernon was trying to evict him. But it didn't matter when nothing happened 'cause he knew he could just give the newspaper a little tip-off. And being a smart lad he waited till I blundered into the frame. Made everyone think it was me getting even with Vernon and him and his dad stroll through the middle and pick up the prize. Leave me and Vernon standing round scratching our balls looking like prize twats.'

'And my dad dead.'

'Yeah, and your dad dead.'

'Think we can prove it?'

'Prove what?'

'He killed my dad.'

Jason shrugged. 'Like to say yes but I can't see it. He's been cremated, yeah?'

'Yeah,' said Tyra despondently.

'Well,' said Jason carefully, 'in that case I definitely can't see it.'

'So what do I do?' said Tyra. 'Just let him get away with it, that what you're saying?'

'No,' said Jason, 'I'm not saying that. What I'm saying is it doesn't sound to me like you're going to get the police to charge him with anything. Not unless he left some bloody great piece of evidence round Charlie's flat that no one's noticed so far, which doesn't sound too likely. But what I can say is if that's what he did – and it's still not much more than a guess – well, I don't know if it helps but there's something I read I think is true, goes something like this: people pay for what they do, and they pay for it simply, by the lives they lead.'

'James Baldwin,' said Tyra, and they looked at each other, surprised.

Mazz couldn't concentrate on the game. He wasn't the only one, he reckoned; it didn't look like the Welsh team were concentrating on it any too well either. Game they ought to be running away with and they were making stupid mistake after stupid mistake. They didn't pull themselves together, he could see them losing it.

But that wasn't why he couldn't concentrate. Emyr had called up just before kick off. Rang the Colonel on his mobile trying to get hold of Mazz, and the Colonel had just passed the phone over. Emyr said he had a tour lined up. Australia followed by the States. Did Mazz want to play guitar? His regular guy was too fucked up to do it. Well, Emyr didn't say that exactly but Mazz knew the guy in question and he could put two and two together. Be away for two months, decent money – not fantastic but decent – make his mind up by tomorrow.

So was he going to do it? He knew Tyra wouldn't want him to. Made it plain she'd had enough of absentee men. But still, surely being on tour was a bit different to being in prison. Colonel said he should do it. 'Never do anything just to please a woman,' he'd said, 'never works out.'

Mazz had laughed but the Colonel said no, he was serious. 'Thing you've got to learn about women – thought you'd have known it by now – they never want what they think they want.'

Mazz hadn't laughed at that because he knew it was true, and not just of women. Him too. He looked around the Oak – the pictures of the boxers on the walls, Charlie over there behind the bar – and felt an awful sense of kinship. Fellers like him and Charlie, they thought they wanted a family and that, thought they wanted to do the right thing. But, it came down to it, it just took one phone call to remind him where his heart truly was. Always out to sea and looking for the next port of call.

Just then the Colonel's phone went off. He listened for a moment then passed it to Mazz.

'Tyra for you, butt. Says there's something you've got to see.'

Jason had said he'd drive Tyra to the school.

'Only two hundred yards,' she said, 'not worth it,' but then they came back to the car and he unlocked the door for her and she got in, inhaled the rich-man smell of it.

As Jason sat down she turned to him and said, 'You know when you stopped the car by me this afternoon? I asked what you were doing, you said you were looking for me. You never said what you wanted.'

Jason blushed. His whole face went bright red. 'I missed you. I had hoped . . .'

'Hoped what?' said Tyra, suddenly breathless.

'Hoped we'd see each other again. I'd hoped maybe you and me?'

'You serious?' said Tyra, and watched Jason's face fall like he'd had a lifetime of girls laughing at his big self. And remembered how he'd been in that hotel room, how nervous. And she leaned over without thinking what she was doing and kissed him quickly, not knowing herself what if anything it meant, then pulled back before he could react.

'Jason,' she said, 'better get moving. Kids are coming out now.'

Jason looked dazed but still managed to put the car into drive and head for the school. Less than a minute, they were there and Tyra jumped out, 'You mind giving me and the kids a lift back? Be a treat for them,' and shut the door before he had time to say anything.

She went in through the school gates and had both kids out of there in record time, barely exchanging a word with the other mums. Jermaine had hardly time to cry out in delighted surprise before she had him and his little sister bundled into the back of the car. Two more minutes and they were outside Tyra's house.

'You want to come in, have a cup of tea?' she said to Jason, who, still looking like a disorientated bear, nodded and followed her and the kids in. Where they walked slap into the arms of a reception committee.

Tyra's mum and Vernon Nichols were stood together in the middle of Tyra's front room.

Vernon smiled and walked towards Tyra with his hand stretched out to shake, then literally jumped backwards when he saw Jason Flaherty follow her into the room.

'What's going on, Mum?' said Tyra, trying to take control of the situation.

'Vern here, Mr Nichols,' said Celeste, 'was looking for you. He's got something he wants to show you. So I brought him round here to wait for you to bring the kids back.'

Tyra turned her attention to Nichols, who, keeping a wary eye on Jason, started to speak.

'I was just cleaning out the house in James Street, before the demolition boys get to it,' he said, 'when I opened the storeroom at the ground-floor back. Far as I knew, no one had used it in years, bookies had no use for it. Nor did anyone else. Least that's what I thought. Turns out your dad had a use for it.'

'Yeah?' said Tyra. 'What did he keep there?'

'Well,' said Nichols, an odd smile on his face, 'I think maybe it's best if you see for yourself.'

'OK,' said Tyra, 'just give me a minute.' She walked upstairs and into the bedroom, her head spinning, wondering what she was going to find. Evidence of what Danny Lewis Jones had done, perhaps? She couldn't imagine what, but still. Or maybe this was the so-called treasure, the treasure Charlie used to talk about. Though what kind of treasure Charlie might have accumulated she still found it hard to imagine. Or what was the other word Nichols had used? Evidence he said Charlie had called it. What could that mean? Was some new light going to be shone on Charlie's death? And if so why would Vernon Nichols be leading them to it?

Whatever it was waiting for them in James Street, she figured Mazz should see it too. She picked up the phone and called the Colonel's mobile. Mazz sounded pissed off at first, a woman interrupting his rugby bonding session, but when she told him what was going on he sounded eager enough, said he'd be there in five. Just to make sure he'd have time to get there, Tyra spent a couple of minutes freshening up then rejoined the awkward-looking posse downstairs.

And so a motley procession comprising Tyra, Celeste, Emily, Jermaine, Vernon Nichols and Jason Flaherty made their way from Tyra's house to the boarded-up property on James Street. As they reached the doorway a taxi pulled up and out got Mazz and the Colonel.

Vernon Nichols unlocked the front door and led the way down the dark corridor till they reached a locked door at the back of the building. He found another key and opened the door, reached inside to switch on a light then stepped aside.

Tyra walked in and for a moment she thought there was nothing there. Then she looked more carefully and gasped in surprise. There, nailed to the walls, were maybe fifty, maybe a hundred, signs: street signs, a couple of pub signs, a few shop signs. Some of the street names she knew well: Maria Street, Angelina Street, West Bute Street, Sophia Street. Others, though, barely tugged at the edges of her memory: Nelson Street, Gladstone Street, Canal Parade. The pub names too – the Freemasons Arms, the Marchioness of Bute – were just memories. She knew what they all were, though. Her birthright. Her treasure. And evidence too. Evidence of what had once been here and was now gone, past, lost.

'Tiger Bay,' said a voice next to her, her mother. 'These are the old street signs.'

'Yeah,' she said, then she turned and buried herself in her mum's chest, started bawling her heart out, crying for Charlie, crying for herself, crying for Tiger Bay, crying for all the places and people who were lost and gone. Crying for Mazz and her who could never work out, and crying for the baby they never had, crying for her kids standing next to her looking at her with worried eyes, kids growing up in a world she didn't know if she understood any more.

Mazz didn't know where to look, where to put himself. Tyra there bawling her eyes out, him there with leaving on his mind. All these other people – Jason, Celeste, the old guy – just confusing him. He looked at the kids, saw them clinging on to Tyra, could see when it came down to it he was just a nice uncle. Stayed around longer, maybe that would change but for now that's all he was – their mum's new friend.

Unable to look anywhere else, he looked at the signs. Charlie's signs. Charlie's relics of a long-gone life. He looked at one of the pub signs, the Freemasons Arms. He remembered a picture – Charlie standing in front of the Freemasons, wearing a cashmere coat and the coolest hat Mazz had ever seen, smoking. Charlie at twenty-two – king of the world.

And then Jason was standing next to him starting to take the signs off the walls, and Mazz began to help and that's what they did the next half hour or so, carefully removed the signs, piled them up, and took them round to

Tyra's house. And gradually then they all left, Jason first, Jason looking on the verge of tears too, which Mazz could scarcely credit, then the old guy and Tyra's mum, and then the kids went to bed and finally it was just the two of them left, sitting on the sofa, *Friends* on the TV, and they looked at each other and both of them knew without saying that that was it, and neither of them wanting to say it, not just yet, not in the night time.

So they went upstairs and held each other for a while and then holding turned to something else and after a while they were fucking, not love-making, nothing deep or sad, but straight-ahead friendly fucking, the kind that made Mazz at least think that maybe this wasn't over for ever, that maybe there'd be a somewhere down the line, and at least it gave him the strength to say when they'd finished, 'You know I've got to go?' and Tyra just nodded and put her finger to her lips and looked about to cry for a moment but then suddenly smiled and they both knew, he was sure, that in this end there was a new beginning.

And in the morning Mazz was riding the ghost train, Cardiff to London Paddington.

A NOTE ON THE AUTHOR

John Williams lives and works in his hometown of Cardiff. The author of four previous books, most recently *Five Pubs, Two Bars and a Nightclub*, he also writes screenplays and journalism. He has no plans to surf the Severn Bore.

A NOTE ON THE TYPE

The text of this book is set in Bembo. The original types for which were cut by Francesco Griffo for the Venetian printer Aldus Manutius, and were first used in 1495 for knowing Cardinal Bembo's *De Aetna*. Claude Garamond (1480–1561) used Bembo as a model and so it became the forerunner of standard European type for the following two centuries. Its modern form was designed, following the original, for Monotype in 1929 and is widely in use today.